RHYTHM
AND
CLUES

T0018718

ST. MARTIN'S PAPERBACKS TITLES BY OLIVIA BLACKE

Vinyl Resting Place
A Fatal Groove
Rhythm and Clues

RHYTHM AND CLUES

OLIVIA BLACKE

St. Martin's Paperbacks

NOTE: If you purchased this book without a cover you should be aware that this book is stolen property. It was reported as "unsold and destroyed" to the publisher, and neither the author nor the publisher has received any payment for this "stripped book."

This is a work of fiction. All of the characters, organizations, and events portrayed in this novel are either products of the author's imagination or are used fictitiously.

First published in the United States by St. Martin's Paperbacks, an imprint of St. Martin's Publishing Group.

RHYTHM AND CLUES

Copyright © 2024 by Olivia Blacke.

All rights reserved.

For information, address St. Martin's Publishing Group, 120 Broadway, New York, NY 10271.

www.stmartins.com

ISBN: 978-1-250-86012-5

Our books may be purchased in bulk for promotional, educational, or business use. Please contact your local bookseller or the Macmillan Corporate and Premium Sales Department at 1-800-221-7945, ext. 5442, or by email at MacmillanSpecialMarkets@macmillan.com.

Printed in the United States of America

St. Martin's Paperbacks edition / April 2024

10 9 8 7 6 5 4 3 2 1

I've Got Brew, Babe

CHAPTER 1

I've never witnessed a murder before.

I've seen more dead bodies than any humble vinyl record shop owner/barista should ever stumble across, which for the record—no pun intended—is two. I've lost count of how many delicious, caffeinated beverages I've served and how many fantastic records I've sold since my older sisters and I opened Sip & Spin Records in our hometown of Cedar River, Texas, six months ago. But the body count is not something I'll soon forget, especially since I found both of them.

Trying to block out those memories, I focused my attention on the ice rink below me where two hockey players were, as far as I could tell, trying to kill each other. I sat on the edge of my seat, hoping I wasn't about to witness a murder in real time.

"Knock his block off!" the man seated beside me yelled at the players. Beauregard Russell was tall, white, and frankly, unfairly handsome with rich brown eyes and the scruffy beginnings of a beard. Our relationship could best be described as complicated.

On the ice, the man in the white Yetis jersey threw another punch at the man in the Austin hockey jersey. Even from all the way up here in our suite-level seats, I could hear the blow connect. I shuddered.

"Cold, Juni?" Beau asked.

That's me, Juniper Jessup, Juni to most everyone. I was born and raised in Texas. Most of my childhood was spent in my grandparents' record shop, until MP3s and streaming music services drove them out of business. Now that vinyl was coming back in a big way, my older sisters, Tansy and Maggie, and I decided to re-open the family business as Sip & Spin Records.

Speaking of another go at things I'd once thought dead and buried, sitting next to Beau Russell was somehow both comfortable and awkward at the same time. It might be cliché, but he was my high school sweetheart. Until he wasn't. We broke up right as I was graduating from college and moving to Oregon to take my dream job. Six years later, unemployed and firmly over Beau—that's my story, and I was sticking to it—I moved back home. And now, we were on a date, kinda.

Beau removed his scarf and wound it around my neck. "This ought to help," he said, arranging the ends so they laid flat. The blue and orange scarf featured the Austin Thunderbirds logo. Beau had bought the overpriced souvenir in the team store before the game. At the time, I'd teased him that it rarely got cold enough in Texas to need a scarf, but that was before we'd spent a few hours in a hockey arena. "Having fun?" he asked. He had to yell to be heard over the cacophony around us.

While I was genuinely concerned about the well-being of the two combatants on the ice, everyone else in the stadium seemed to be enjoying themselves. And by "enjoying themselves" I mean they were yelling and cheering at the top of their lungs. When the two huge skaters went down in a heap, the referees and their teammates finally decided it was time to step in and put an end to the fight. Both men had started off covered in protective gear—helmets, gloves, pads, mouthguards—which now laid strewn out on the ice around them.

"It's a regular yard sale out there, isn't it?" Zackary Fjord, the man on the other side of me, screamed in my ear.

One of the combatants was dragged away by two men in black-and-white-striped shirts. I'd never seen someone wearing ice skates dig his heels in, but somehow, he managed. The other fighter, surrounded by a huddle of players in Austin Thunderbirds jerseys, wasn't moving.

"He's not hurt, is he?" I leaned forward with my arms on the ledge in front of me.

Zack and his business partner, Savannah Goodwin, had treated us to seats in a private box. I'd never been to a hockey game before, and they assured me that these were the best seats in the house. We were sitting in a row of padded chairs overlooking the center of the rink. Behind us was a tall counter with more chairs, a table laden with snacks, and a small refrigerator stocked with beer, water, and soda.

"Beckel? He'll be fine. He's tougher than he looks. I should know, I used to date his ex-wife, and that woman is absolutely feral. Though he did just go three rounds with Miller 'The Killer.'" Zack shrugged. "Seriously, Miller is a menace. He's been suspended more times than I can count. He should be in jail, not on the ice."

"You dated Beckel's ex?" Beau asked.

"Well, she wasn't his ex at the time, if you know what I mean," Zack replied with a snarky grin.

"Classy," Beau muttered before I could say anything.

Beckel, in his Austin Thunderbirds jersey, was helped to his feet. He waved at the crowd, which went ballistic. The other players started beating the ends of their sticks against the nearest surface, making a racket as he gingerly skated off the ice.

"See? He's fine," Zack said.

The guy who'd started the fight, Miller, was escorted to the penalty box. Our guy disappeared behind the bench. Another Thunderbird in a blue and orange jersey, who hadn't been involved in the play at all, skated over to sit down in our penalty box.

I must have looked confused, because Zack explained. While they cleared the ice, the crowd quieted down, but they were still pumping in loud music over the speakers. It was easier now to hold a conversation without shouting, but that didn't keep him from leaning in a little closer to me than was absolutely necessary while he talked. "Matching majors, but since Beckel is getting patched up, someone has to sit for him."

"Huh?" I asked. When I'd enthusiastically agreed to attend a hockey game, I didn't realize that the rules were apparently written in some gibberish language I'd never heard before.

"Five for fighting," Zack said.

"Oh! Like the band," I said.

Now it was Zack's turn to look confused. "What?"

"You know, if you want to get into the record business, you're going to have to expand your musical knowledge," I told him.

"I *am* in the record business. I already own one record store, Rhythm and Brews in Galveston, remember?" he said.

Like Sip & Spin Records, Rhythm and Brews sold music and coffee drinks. Unlike our shop, their drinks had boring names like cappuccino and espresso. Ours had musically themed names, like Bohemian Frapsody. Zack and his partner Savannah were investors in Rhythm and Brews, which made them part owners.

Zack, like Beau, was a year or so older than me, which put me around twenty-nine or thirty. We'd been classmates at University of Texas. I majored in computer languages and software development. He'd majored in beer bongs and wild parties. We ran in very different circles, except for a few weeks during the fall of my sophomore year when he dated, and eventually cheated on, one of my study buddies. To be completely honest, I barely remembered him from college but when he called the shop out of the blue last week, he swore I'd left quite the impression on him.

He was an average-height, average-weight, average white frat boy, the kind who wore khaki shorts and polo shirts with the collars popped up. He came from money and wasn't shy about making sure people knew it. Zack was the guy who'd park his BMW—always this year's model, of course—in the reserved spaces because, according to him, a ticket was just the cost of doing business. His business was owning other businesses, and now he had his sights set on mine.

Not that my sisters or I were interested in selling Sip & Spin Records. Granted, we'd been open for six months and we'd barely made enough to cover the cost of rent and stock, but we had a steady stream of customers. If we didn't have any more major setbacks, we might be in the black by the end of the year. At least, that's what my middle sister, Maggie, claimed. She was the numbers person in the family and if she said we'd eventually turn a profit, I believed her.

In the meantime, I was living in my oldest sister Tansy's spare bedroom, riding a lime-green adult tricycle around town instead of making payments on a car, and wearing a steady stream of vintage denim and concert T-shirts, some from bands that broke up before I was born. Although, to be fair, I'd ride the trike and wear the tees even if I was rolling in cash. It's kinda my brand. Today, I had on a Red Hot Chili Peppers T-shirt under my new Austin Thunderbirds jersey that Beau had insisted on buying for me. It matched my blue glasses I'd worn for the occasion.

Even though my sisters and I definitely weren't considering selling any share of Sip & Spin, when Zack offered us tickets to the game I couldn't say no. I was drinking free beer and eating free snacks, and had been enjoying the game up until the fight. Yes, hockey was confusing at first, but the enthusiasm of the crowd was contagious and before long, I was cheering along. The Thunderbirds were up four goals to the Yetis' two, but then in the aftermath of the fight, the Yetis scored, filling the stadium with boos.

"You gotta be kidding me!" Zack said, surging to his feet quickly enough to spill his beer all over my new jersey. He swiped at the spilt liquid on my chest. Beau swatted his hand away. Zack didn't seem to notice. He continued arguing, "That was interference all day. You saw that, right?"

"Sit," Savannah said from the other side of him, dragging him back down to his seat by his elbow. "We're still up, and the Yetis always fall apart in the third."

She leaned around him so she could address me directly. Savannah looked like she ought to be hanging out on a party boat instead of at a hockey game with a finance bro. She was tall, blonde, and tan. Her makeup was perfect, her eyebrows were a work of art, and she wore a simple diamond pendant around her neck that probably cost more than I made in a year even back when I was bringing in a computer programmer's salary. It was certainly more than I made as a small business owner.

She handed me a handful of paper napkins. "He forgets his manners sometimes," she said to me, with a wink, as if we were sharing a secret. "But don't worry about him. Zack is very hands-off. You'll be dealing with me most of the time."

From what I'd seen—and felt—tonight, Zack wasn't nearly as hands-off as his partner wanted me to believe.

Zack took a swig of his beer. Realizing the can was empty, he tossed it on the floor. "Anyone else need a re-fill?" he asked, swaying as he stood. For a moment, I was worried that he might tumble over the railing. Savannah shook her head. So did I. I'd had enough beer, but was eye-ing the platter of wings. "Bro?" he asked Beau.

"I'm good," Beau said. He was seated at the end of the row, so he stood. "Sit. I'll grab you something." He dis-appeared into the back of the suite.

The box was designed to seat a dozen or more fans, but tonight, it was just the four of us. "You're enjoying your-self, right, Juniper?" Zack asked. He put his arm around my shoulder and leaned closer. I scootched over to the other side of my chair, as far away from him as I could get without climbing over the armrest into Beau's seat. "You think any more on what we were talking about earlier?" He'd used the two intermissions between periods to give me the hard sell. He had numbers and folders and all sorts of graphics to go along with his pitch. None of it made a lick of sense to me.

"Like I said, my sister Maggie is our numbers person." I was running out of polite ways to say no. Out of my two older sisters, Tansy, the oldest, was the responsible one. Middle sister Maggie was the organized one. And I was the baby, just over here enjoying my hot mess life and the free nachos.

"There's more to it than numbers," Zack insisted. Around us, a loud roar went up. I glanced over at the giant monitor mounted over the scoreboard to see a replay of our goalie stopping a puck that had almost gone into the net. I'd been so busy trying to fend off Zack, I'd missed the play. I wasn't terribly invested in it, but I was enjoying the game and I was happy that we were winning. "At Fjord Capital, we're family," he continued.

"Funny you should mention that," I told him. "At Sip & Spin, we're *actual* family. It's just me and my sisters. It doesn't get much more family-owned than that."

"Yes, but as I was saying, the numbers aren't in your favor. Did you know that ninety percent of small businesses fold within the first year?" He slurred his words a bit, and his breath smelled of beer as he inched closer. "Your coffee's good, but that's never going to be a money leader. At best, it gets customers through the door. And the records? Sure, there's a huge market right now, but the vinyl bubble can't last forever."

He wasn't telling me anything I didn't already know. To be completely honest, it was something that kept me up at night. I'd already experienced the collapse of the vinyl record market firsthand once before, back when my grandparents had owned the shop. They'd pivoted to tapes and CDs as they rose in popularity, but they couldn't stay afloat once music went digital. My sisters and I were taking a big bet that the same fate wouldn't befall us, but it was a constant shadow looming over us.

"Not to mention a string of bad luck," he said. "If you know what I mean."

"Yeah, I do," I said. Not that it was our fault a woman got killed in our supply closet during our grand opening party. Or that the mayor of Cedar River happened to be drinking a cup of Sip & Spin coffee when he dropped dead during last spring's Bluebonnet Festival. "But I'll have you know, there hasn't been a single murder in Cedar River in almost six months."

"Good thing, too," Beau said. He'd returned and was standing over me. "Any more suspicious deaths around my girl, and I was going to have to take a hard look at our little Junebug."

I bit the inside of my cheek. I loved the affectionate nickname, but wasn't a fan of Beau referring to me as his girl, not that this was the time or place to point that out to him. He knew as well as I did that I wasn't ready to define our relationship in such concrete terms. Beau was great. Better than great, if I was being honest. He had the ability to make me melt like a scoop of ice cream on the sidewalk in June with no more than a look. And worse, now I was blushing just thinking about it.

In another life, we'd probably be married with a little house overlooking the river, two point five kids, and a dog. But in this life, he'd broken my heart years ago and I wasn't sure I was ever going to get past that. I wasn't even certain I *wanted* to get past it. Maybe, if he was the only man in my life, I would have found a way to forgive and forget, but nothing was ever that simple, was it?

Beau had been a hothead back when I'd met him in high school, but he'd mellowed with age. So far, he'd been willing to let me take the time I needed to figure out what—and who—I wanted, but apparently sharing me with one other man was his limit. The way he was glaring at Zack made me worry I was going to witness another fight tonight, this one off the ice. He took Zack's wrist and moved his arm so it was no longer draped around me before tossing a bottle of water to him.

"What's this?" Zack said, looking down at the bottle in his hand. "I asked for a beer, bro."

"You've had enough, *bro*," Beau replied. "Game's almost over, and you've already had too many."

"Who are you, the fun police?" Zack asked with a pout.

Beau lifted the edge of his jersey where his badge was, as usual, clipped to his belt. Just shy of his thirtieth birthday, he was relatively young for a detective. He'd gone into the academy right out of high school and already had ten years on the force. "I don't know about the fun police," Beau said, forcing a little extra Texas drawl into his voice even as he shouted to be heard as the crowd exploded in applause. While Zack and Beau had been facing off in whatever this display of machismo was, the Thunderbirds had scored. He tapped his badge. "Cedar River Police Department."

Savannah's eyes went wide. When she gazed up at Beau, it was with a coy smile on her face. If I was the kind of person to get jealous, or if I had any claim on him, I would have been offended. As it was, I thought it was funny.

Despite Beau's rugged good looks and imposing physical presence, Savannah had barely given him the time of day since we'd arrived at the game. Now she was practically drooling. It was a phenomenon I'd seen often. Savannah was a badge bunny.

"Well now, this has been great, but it's time Juni and I get going." He reached a hand out to me and I took it. Even after I stood, he continued to hold my hand. "Nice meeting y'all."

"But the game's not over yet," Zack protested.

"You can't leave now," Savannah said, batting her eyelashes. "Not while we're up."

Beau shrugged. "This way we can beat the rush." He glanced down at Zack and the pile of empty beer cans at his feet. "You're not driving, are you, man?"

I hadn't been paying close attention to how much he'd had to drink, but now that I thought about it, over the past two or three hours that we'd been in the suite with Zack and Savannah, I hadn't seen him without a beer in his hand even once. Yes, his breath smelled like beer, but the whole arena smelled like beer and popcorn.

"I'm good, bro," Zack said.

"Don't worry, I've got his keys," Savannah said. "Nice meeting you both. Hope we get a chance to do this again sometime real soon." The look she gave Beau was the same one a cheetah might give a bucket of fried chicken.

I waved at her. She seemed nice enough. Zack was, if I was being totally honest, not the kind of person I'd normally hang out with. Back in college, he'd been obnoxious, and beer or no beer, he wasn't much better now. I appreciated the seats and had enjoyed the game, but I wasn't tempted in the least bit to get into business with either of them. "Maybe," I said, non-committedly. I squeezed Beau's hand. "Let's get out of here."

CHAPTER 2

"Seriously, what was that?" I asked Beau as we made our way out of the arena. With several minutes left in the game and the home team winning, we were the only ones sneaking out early. Other than the vendors packing up their wares, we were alone on the concourse.

"What was what?" he asked innocently.

"Don't play dumb with me, Beau Russell," I said. "For a moment, I thought you were gonna throw down back there. I thought you'd outgrown all that macho nonsense."

"That jerk had his hands all over you," Beau said as he led the way out the doors and toward the nearby garage where he'd parked.

"He had his arm over the back of my seat. No big deal. You're just jealous," I said teasingly.

"I'm not jealous," Beau insisted. "He was being fresh and you looked uncomfortable."

He had me there. "I was a little uncomfortable," I admitted. "I'd forgotten how annoying he could be. And I'm glad you got back when you did. I was about to move seats if he got any closer. I mean, there was room for what, a dozen in that box? Why'd he have to sit right next to me?"

"Because it's kind of difficult to grope you when you're on the other side of the suite. I wish your sisters had agreed to come with us. He'd have been so busy trying to sell to them, he would have left you alone and let you enjoy your first hockey game."

Zack had invited all three of us sisters to the game to give us his pitch. Tansy and Maggie had turned him down flat. I'd only gone because I wanted to see what all the hype was about surrounding the Thunderbirds, and I was glad I did. "I had fun."

"Maybe we'll do it again sometime," he said. "But next time, I'll pick the seats."

"I hope they're good, because I'm spoiled now."

"Don't worry, nothing but the best for my Junebug," he said, squeezing my hand. We walked the ramp of the parking garage and got to his big, black truck. I'm glad he was driving because I would have probably taken up two spots trying to park that monstrosity. He opened my door for me.

As soon as we exited the garage, he turned on the radio and tuned in to the game. Traffic was light as he easily navigated through Austin. "It'd be a shame if we missed the end," he said. I had to admit that listening to the hockey game wasn't nearly as exciting as watching it in person. I didn't know any of the players, and I barely understood what the announcer was saying. It was easier to follow the action in person, even if I couldn't always follow the puck or understand the calls on the ice. But the guy on the radio? He made no sense at all.

"Do you think that guy's alright?" I asked. We were on the long stretch of highway that separated Cedar River from the rest of civilization. As we chatted, I stared out my window into the darkness.

Beau didn't have to ask who I meant. "He's a goon, Juni. He's always getting into scrapes on the ice. I'm sure he's fine."

"Scrapes? I thought that Yeti guy was gonna murder him. What was it Zack called him? Killer?"

"Don't let his nickname fool you. Miller's no monster. He just plays hard. One of the best blueliners in the league."

I didn't ask what a blueliner was. I wasn't sure I wanted to know. "I didn't realize you actually follow hockey," I said instead.

"A little. Here and there," he admitted.

It was a good thing that he was a detective and not an elected sheriff, because most Texans had very strong opinions when it came to sports. Football was sacred. Baseball was a close second. Then there was basketball, soccer, pool, darts, pinball, competitive underwater basket weaving, and then, finally, hockey. "Don't let anyone in Cedar River hear you talking like that, or they'll run you out of town," I teased.

"I'll take my chances." Beau had been the local high school football hero before he became a cop. He didn't have much to worry about, reputation-wise. "Speaking of chances, you're not buying into their investor nonsense, are you?"

I shook my head. "We'll never sell Sip & Spin." Though I had to admit that his proposal had been attractive. Zack and Savannah had offered to buy us outright for a staggering sum, or if we didn't like that idea, they were willing to invest capital into our admittedly struggling business for a fifty-one percent controlling interest. "There was never a chance of that."

"Is that why your sisters didn't come to the game?" he asked.

"Yeah. Well, that, and neither of them are big on hockey."

"And it has absolutely nothing to do with the fact that Tansy would rather dangle me from my toes over a pit of hungry gators than sit next to me long enough to finish a beer?" he asked. His tone was light, but I could tell he wasn't completely joking.

"Tansy will come around," I assured him, but I wasn't sure I believed that. My oldest sister hated Beau with the fury of a thousand suns, and had ever since he'd broken my heart. Via a text message. I might have forgiven him, but my protective oldest sister wasn't the forgiving type. If Beau and I ever did end up together, it would be an up-hill battle to get Tansy on board. "Eventually."

Maggie, on the other hand, was #TeamBeau all day long. My middle sister was a romantic right down to her pink toenail polish, and the idea of a second-chance romance with my childhood sweetheart was enough to have her doodling little hearts and flowers in the margins of her many list-making notebooks. Whereas Tansy was perpetually single and my love life could best be described as complicated, Maggie had been happily married to J.T. since I was a teenager. I wouldn't be surprised if she'd started a wedding scrapbook for me already.

As much as I hated to disappoint either of my sisters, this was *my* life. I had two amazing guys vying for my affection. It would be so easy to pick up where Beau and I had left off. Our chemistry was off the charts, but I wasn't sure I could ever trust him again. And then there was Teddy, the other man in my life. He'd been my best friend for as long as I could remember. He was the sweetest guy I knew, and he knew me better than anyone. Whatever I decided was going to hurt someone I cared for, so I was going to take as long as I needed to make up my mind.

The game ended. The Thunderbirds won. Beau slapped the dashboard when Austin made the final goal—an empty netter, whatever that was—and let out a whoop. "Now that's what I call a game," he said, before tuning the radio to a local college station I liked because of their eclectic selection of music, much of which they bought at our shop. If he'd been alone in his truck, he would have been content with the country playlist on his phone, but he knew how I felt about streaming music.

We exited the highway and drove down Main Street. It was getting late. Everything was closed. The Sip & Spin Records sign glowed, but like the other storefronts, it was dark inside. Cedar River rolled up the sidewalks by nine o'clock on weekdays.

Beau drove his truck down the streets into the neighborhood where I lived with my sister. "I had fun tonight. Thanks for inviting me."

"Technically, Zack invited you," I said. Sure, I guess I could have picked someone else as my plus-one, but I knew Beau would enjoy the game. I unwound his scarf from my neck. October in Texas meant it was still warm, but between my beer-soaked jersey and the AC blasting, it had been a comfort. "And thanks for the jersey." I held out the scarf.

"Keep it. Looks good on you." He pulled into my sister's driveway. It had been a cloudy day, and now a few fat raindrops splattered on his windshield. Ignoring the rain, he glanced over at the mother-in-law cottage in the side yard where my mom lived. It was dark. "It's late, but I don't see your mom's car."

"Yeah." I unbuckled the seat belt and shifted uncomfortably in my seat. "She's staying with Marcus more and more these days."

"You wanna talk about it?" he asked.

I didn't remember Beau being that perceptive back when we were silly teenagers. I guess I wasn't the only one who'd grown up in the intervening years. Then again, he was a detective. It was his job to pay attention. "Not really," I admitted. Then I took a breath. I'd made a commitment to Beau that we wouldn't keep secrets from each other.

At the time, it had been because I'd stuck my nose into one of his murder investigations and hadn't shared what he considered to be vital information, but in any event, it never hurt to be truthful. "I'm not a hundred percent comfortable with the whole situation."

"With your mom dating Marcus Best, or with your mom dating, period?"

My dad had passed away unexpectedly almost two years ago. I wasn't nearly close to getting over it. The fact that my mom was spending all her time with a man who wasn't my father, well, that was going to take a little getting used to. "I've got nothing against Marcus." That was the truth, mostly. He wasn't a bad guy once you got to know him, but he was a used car salesperson and sometimes lived up to the pushy stereotype. "It's just a lot, you know?"

"I get it." He reached over and patted my knee. Outside, it began to rain in earnest. He reached for his door handle.

"What do you think you're doing?" I asked him.

"Um, walking a lady to her door?"

"You'll get soaked."

"I don't mind."

"Weirdo." I leaned over and kissed his cheek. "Stay in your warm, dry car. I'll see you later."

"You betcha," he said.

I let myself out and dashed for the front door. I was soaked by the time I got there. As I was fishing my keys out, my sister Tansy opened the front door. "I thought I heard something." She watched Beau's truck back out of the driveway. "What? He couldn't be bothered to walk you to the door?"

I rolled my eyes. With the way she'd yanked the door open, I know that she'd been hoping to spoil something. A goodnight kiss, perhaps. My dad used to pull that move all the time. Tansy was out of luck, though. As long as I was still torn between Teddy and Beau, there wouldn't be any lingering goodnight kisses on the porch for either of them. "It's raining cats and dogs, if you haven't noticed," I said.

In the short time it had taken me to run up to the door, the rain had gone from enthusiastic to angry. It was pelting the walk so hard that it was splashing onto the covered front porch. "You gonna let me inside?" I asked, since she was blocking the door.

Tansy eyed me with caution. "You're dripping wet."

"I noticed," I said with a shiver. Along with the rain, the temperature had dropped since we left Austin. That was common this time of year. It could be eighty one minute and forty the next. I pulled my soaking wet scarf and Austin Thunderbirds jersey over my head and held them out so when they dripped, it would be on the entryway tile, not on the carpet.

My sister moved aside so I could come in. She took the scarf and jersey from me and hung them on the hall tree to dry. She followed me down the hallway. Tansy's house was a modest ranch with three bedrooms. She had her own ensuite bathroom in the primary bedroom. I shared the hall bathroom with any guests we might have. I snagged a towel and wrapped it around my long hair.

"How was the game?" Tansy asked.

"I had a blast. You should have come."

"Not my scene. How was that investor guy?"

"Zack?" I asked, as if we'd had meetings lined up with multiple investors this week. People weren't exactly knocking down our door to buy out a records-slash-coffee shop in the middle of a nowhere town like Cedar River. Which was fine, because we weren't eager to sell. "He was fine. A little pushy, maybe." I wrinkled my nose. "Got worse after he'd knocked back a few beers. His partner, Savannah, seems okay. I think she has a thing for Beau."

"There's no accounting for taste," Tansy said. She leaned against the doorframe as I washed my makeup off. I didn't wear makeup often, and my eyeliner was running from the rain. She started to say something else, but I'll never know what, because the lights surged and then went out with a pop, plunging us into darkness.

When the lights didn't come back on after thirty seconds, I said, "I'll check the breaker."

The flashlight app on my cell phone was sufficient to light my way toward the breaker box. Halfway there, I heard Tansy call out, "Don't bother. Light's out on the whole block."

Following the sound of her voice, I found her in the darkened kitchen, peering out the window over the sink. Outside, the storm raged. Other than an occasional flash of lightning, there was no illumination. No headlights. No porch lights. No flickering TVs. Nothing.

"You think it's all over town or just us?" I asked, pulling out my cell phone to call our sister, Maggie. She lived on the other side of the town—the wealthy side of town—across Main Street and down by the river. "I've got no bars."

For all that Cedar River was a small, hick Texas town, one thing we did have was reliable cell service. "Cell tower's down," Tansy said. "That means power's out all over."

Without cell service, it was impossible to tell how far the blackout stretched. Did it go all the way to the municipal airport on the outskirts of town? Did it spread to the nearby towns? Maybe even all the way to Austin? The more widespread the outage was, the longer it would take to restore power. Cedar River, with its small population, wouldn't be high up on the priority list compared to some of the bigger suburbs closer to Austin.

Tansy opened the coat closet near the front door,

and I followed her, nearly slipping on the puddle my wet Austin Thunderbirds jersey had made on the floor. It was oddly quiet in the house, without the faint hum of electricity, the near-constant whirr of fans, or the background noise from television and radios. But the roar of the storm outside made up for the eerie silence inside.

"Where on earth are you going?" I asked. "Don't worry about Mom. She wasn't in the cottage, not when I got home." 'The cottage' was what we called the mother-in-law cabin in the side yard where our mother took up residence after deciding that her house was too big and lonely after Dad died. It was essentially a detached studio apartment with a single room, a bathroom, and a tiny kitchenette.

"Yeah, I've been meaning to talk to you about that," Tansy said. Outside, thunder crashed ominously. "Have you noticed that she's never at home anymore?"

Our mom was a grown woman, perfectly capable of making grown-woman decisions. It was none of my business where she spent the night, I told myself, even as I wished I could put my fingers in my ears and la-la-la this conversation out of existence. "First Beau and now you? Is there anyone in Cedar River that doesn't want to talk about Mom's private life tonight?"

As expected, that shut her up quickly. There was nothing like hinting that Tansy and Beau might be in agreement about something to get her to change her mind, or at least to change the conversation. It was a dirty trick, but it worked wonders.

"You're right, this isn't the time," Tansy muttered. She pulled a raincoat out of the closet and put it on, tugging the hood snugly over her head.

Tansy was seven years older, several pounds lighter, and a few inches taller than me. Her skin was lighter than mine, probably because while she spent more time outdoors than I did, she always remembered the sunscreen. I was hit or miss. She had super-short hair that complemented her sporty lifestyle. More often than not, my sister could be found training for her next marathon.

The oldest of us three sisters, Tansy was the most serious but also the most practical. If I'd come up with the idea of investing our savings in a vinyl record shop, my family would have dismissed it as a flight of fancy. But when Tansy suggested it? We were all on board immediately. Then again, I couldn't tease her for being the responsible one. After all, she'd bought this nice house all by herself, and I lived in her guest bedroom.

"If Mom's not home, where are you going?" I asked. The yard was likely underwater by now, but there was nothing she could do about that. The long Texas summers baked the earth into impenetrable clay. The rare times that we had a significant rainfall almost always resulted in flash floods since the water had nowhere to go.

"Gonna check on the shop," she said.

With the power off, that meant that the alarm was off, too. It wouldn't hurt to double-check that the doors were closed securely and locked. "No one's going to be out in this weather," I pointed out. "We should wait until after the storm."

"I'm more worried about Daffy," she said.

Daffy, short for Daffodil after the family tradition of naming us after flowers, was a big orange-and-white cat that had adopted us soon after we took over the lease for Sip & Spin. It took him time to warm up to people, so much so that most of the town didn't even realize we had a cat. Which was probably for the best, in the event that the health inspector dropped by unannounced to inspect the coffee nook. Daffy came and went as he pleased, with that magical ability some cats seemed to possess that made them

CHAPTER 3

The drive to Sip & Spin was harrowing. The streetlights were out. Water covered the streets almost to the curb, even as more rain poured from the sky. "Can you bump the heater?" Tansy asked. The defrost was on high, but the windshield was still fogging up faster than the heater could clear it.

Her hands were at the perfect ten and two position. She was gripping the wheel so hard that her knuckles were turning white as she concentrated on keeping us on the road, so I reached over to adjust the temperature.

I knew how she felt. Occasional flashes of lightning illuminated angry clouds all around us. My fingernails dug into the palms of my hands even as I tried to stay calm. It didn't work. I nearly jumped out of my seat at the next crack of thunder.

"It's okay, sis," Tansy said. "It's just a thunderstorm."

Thunderstorms were just a part of life in Texas. They were to be respected, but not necessarily feared. The problem was, it wasn't the thunderstorm that had me on edge. It was the other thing that Texans knew so well— the horrible funnel clouds that sometimes accompanied thunderstorms. A day like this, when the temperature had been in the high eighties all day until the storm popped up seemingly out of nowhere, had the perfect conditions for a tornado.

Tornados weren't as common here in Central Texas as they were closer to the Oklahoma border, but they weren't a rarity, either. You couldn't outrun a tornado. The best you could do if you heard the tornado siren or an alert popped up on your phone was to shelter someplace solid and hope for the best. A car provided no shelter at all and my phone had no service.

As if reading my mind, Tansy said soothingly, "Don't worry. I'm sure the tornado siren has a backup generator."

"Sure, but what if the storm knocked out the feed from Austin and they don't get the radar notification in time?"

"I'm sure they've thought of that," she said. "Besides, it's just rain."

I'm sure she was right. Unlike Tansy, who'd never left Texas for longer than a few weeks at a time, I'd spent the last six years in the Pacific Northwest, where tornados were a once-in-a-lifetime occurrence. During that time, you'd think I would have learned to relax but instead I'd built them up in my head as terrifying monsters.

"Seriously, Juni. Chill. If you grind your teeth any louder, I won't be able to concentrate," Tansy admonished me.

I didn't think I was freaking out that bad. And honestly, I doubted she could hear anything over the rain pounding the car and the windshield wipers struggling in vain to keep up with the deluge of water. "I don't grind my teeth," I told her.

"Sure you don't," she replied. "Just like you never borrowed my shoes to play dress-up when you were a kid and then returned them scuffed or mud-splattered."

She had a point. Tansy and Maggie were just shy of three years apart. When I came along as a surprise baby five years later, my sisters were already in elementary school. While I was learning my simple addition, Tansy was in driver's ed. By the time I was experimenting with makeup, she was off at college. The age gap resulted in a lot of what I liked to call misunderstandings, but my sisters insisted on calling it me being a brat. As if.

We pulled up in front of Sip & Spin Records, and I realized that by changing the subject, my sister had successfully distracted me from my fears. Did I have the best big sister in the world or what?

Our shop, like everything else in Cedar River, was dark. Even the sign and the overhead streetlights were dark. The rain fell in sheets, turning anything more than a few feet away into a blurry blob. "You ready for this?" Tansy asked. Without waiting for my reply, she opened her car door and plunged into the storm.

"Ready as I'll ever be," I muttered. In spite of my raincoat, I was drenched as soon as I got out of the car. Rain beat in through my open door, soaking into the upholstery. I jumped out and slammed the door behind me. Several inches of muddy water swirled around my feet as I dashed for the shop. The curb was an angry eddy of flood waters, but I was just grateful I could still make out the difference between the curb and the street. Another inch of water and I wouldn't be able to.

I made it to the entryway just in time for a burst of wind to howl up the sidewalk, almost snatching the front door out of my sister's grasp. "Come on!" she shouted.

We made it inside. It took both of us to drag the door closed. Tansy threw the deadbolt. The floor was wet, and not just because we were dripping all over it. The rising water from the sidewalk was finding its way in under the front door.

As we shed our raincoats, Tansy said, "Find Daffy. I'll deal with this."

"Daffy, where are you, buddy?" I called into the dark

shop. I shone the flashlight app on my phone around racks of records. "I'm gonna check upstairs."

Sip & Spin Records was a storefront on Main Street sandwiched between Cedar Spines Bookstore and Boot Scootin' Dance Studio. It was deeper than it was wide, with the cash register and barista station along the back wall. Tall tables were scattered throughout to provide patrons with a comfortable place to sip their delicious caffeinated beverages while being surrounded by good music.

Behind the cash register was a hallway leading to a small supply closet, an even smaller bathroom, and a stock room that was about a third the size of the main floor. The stock room, as could be expected, was crammed from floor to ceiling with the vinyl records we didn't have room to display.

The best part about our space, in my opinion, was the second story. I took the stairs up. There was a wide balcony on either side of the sales floor below, and in the back, a room that ran the width of the building was filled with shelves and bins of even more vinyl records.

"Daffy, baby, where you at?" I asked. As convenient as it was to have the app on my phone, it wasn't a great substitute for a real flashlight. What I wouldn't give for one of those enormous, heavy Maglites—the kind that could light up an entire warehouse—right now.

Just when I thought I'd never find the cat, I heard a plaintive meow. I swung my phone in the direction of the noise, and two floating orbs on top of the highest shelf greeted me as the light reflected off his eyeballs. "Daffy, how's my favorite kitty?"

He jumped down and wound his way around my legs. "Sorry, buddy. I hope you weren't too scared." I didn't know if cats got scared during bad storms, but I knew *I* did, and I was enjoying his comfort at least as much as he was enjoying mine. "Got him!" I yelled down to my sister as I scooped him up.

I made my way carefully down the stairs. I went up and down these stairs so often on any ordinary business day that I often joked that I could navigate them in the dark, but I hadn't had a chance to put that theory to the test before now. The front of the shop was all glass, which normally meant my path would be lit by the ambient street light, but tonight there was none of that.

When I finally managed to make it downstairs without tripping or dropping the cat, I found my sister hard at work mopping the wet floors. She'd shoved something against the bottom of the door, and no more water was coming in, which was a relief. "What'd you find to block the water?" I asked.

"Packing blankets," she said. "While I take care of this, do you mind making sure that all of our stock is up off the floor?"

Vinyl records were water-resistant, but their labels and covers were not. Luckily, all of our shelves and display cases were several inches off the floor, but now I found myself with a new concern. I looked up into the darkness. If our roof leaked, we could lose everything. "That's what insurance is for, Juni," I muttered to myself.

"Cat carrier's on the counter," Tansy said.

I made my way to the back of the shop and found the carrier right where she said it would be. We hadn't had much use for it up until now. It wasn't like we had the time off—or the money—for long vacations. As a result, the only time that Daffy had occasion for the carrier was when he was going to that dreaded place, the V-E-T. I don't know why I spelled it out in my own head, maybe so that if Daffy could read my mind he wouldn't hear that word, but the trick didn't help.

As soon as he saw the carrier, he hissed and tried to jump out of my arms. I tightened my grip on him. "A little help here?" I called out, even as he tried to claw his way to freedom.

"Turn around," Tansy said.

Daffy wiggled out of my arms and climbed onto my shoulder, his claws digging into me. He leapt. There was a thud followed by an angry howl. Tansy had managed to get the carrier up at the same time as Daffy had launched himself over my shoulder, and he landed squarely inside. She slammed the door shut. "Teamwork!" she said, triumphantly.

"Makes the dream work," I agreed.

Inside the cat carrier, Daffy was scratching and spitting, trying to find a way out. "And you were afraid of a little tornado," Tansy said. She handed me the rocking carrier. I put it gently down on the counter. "I promise, Daffy, this is for your own good. Really, it is," she tried to assure the cat. The cat was not convinced. He glared at me. "He's never gonna trust us again, is he?"

"Let's hurry up and finish, so we can get him home before he hurts himself," I said. I wasn't sure what he'd think about Tansy's house—he'd never come home with us before. But it had to be better than being left alone in the shop or getting stuck outside in the storm.

We mopped up as much as we could and emptied the bucket into the sink in the back. "Ready to leave?" Tansy asked.

I glanced outside. If possible, it was raining even heavier now than it had been when we arrived. "No time like the present," I said.

I turned my back on her to pick up the cat carrier when I saw my own shadow race along the wall. I spun back to find the source of the light and noticed a car headed down Main Street at a speed that wouldn't have been safe even in normal conditions. Its headlights flashed along a wall of records, and then there was a loud crash.

"If they hit my car, so help me . . ." Tansy grumbled as she jerked her raincoat into place and marched outside, heedless of the raging wind.

"Hold on, Daffy. We'll be back for you," I promised the furious cat as I dashed outside, my raincoat only half on.

There was a car turned sideways, half in the middle of Main Street and half up on the sidewalk. Its headlights pointed into the record shop. The driver's door hung open, but I only saw Tansy standing outside. She was bent over, examining the front end of her car, which looked to be fused with the rear side panel of the other car.

It figured. The *only* driver out on a night like this had to slam into Tansy's car, the *only* car parked on the street. Just our luck. Yes, it was my sister's car, but since I didn't have a car of my own, I relied on it almost as much as she did. I couldn't see how bad the damage was from here, but it would be a challenge for the two of us to get around if her car was out of commission.

"How bad is it?" I had to yell to be heard over the storm. Between this and the hockey game, I'd be lucky if I had any voice at all tomorrow.

"It's bad, Juni," Tansy yelled back.

She moved to the open driver's side door of the BMW that had collided with her car. The interior light was on. I could tell that there was no one behind the wheel, but through the shattered windshield I could see someone in the passenger seat.

I slogged through the swiftly flowing creek forming on the sidewalk. It was slippery with mud. A tree branch the size of my forearm raced toward my feet. I dodged it, hoping the tree it had broken off from hadn't come down on top of someone's house.

By the time I reached the BMW, the water was up to

my ankles. "Where's the driver?" I asked, crowding Tansy out of the way.

"No idea, but the passenger's not looking too good."

I leaned in for a better look. The passenger was slumped against the dashboard. "You okay?" I asked. Even if he'd been conscious, I doubted he could hear me over the rain pounding the car. Water poured in through the broken windshield. It rushed over the back of his head to pool around his feet. "Hey," I said, louder this time. I reached in and shook his shoulder.

He didn't move. He was wearing a seat belt and was covered in safety glass from the windshield, but he was doubled over with his head on the dash. "Please be alright, please be alright," I said to myself as I climbed into the driver's seat.

I gently pushed the man back into an upright position and got a better look at him. He was wearing a blue and orange Austin Thunderbirds jersey, similar to the one I'd been wearing earlier. His face had been cut in several places.

A week ago, I hadn't thought about Zack Fjord for years. I wouldn't have recognized him if I'd passed him on the street. But after spending the better part of the evening with him at the hockey game, there was no way I would fail to recognize Zack now.

Tentatively, I reached out and touched Zack's neck. I couldn't find a pulse. I checked his wrist. Nothing.

I backed out of the car.

"Is he okay?" my sister asked. "I'd call an ambulance, but my phone is dead."

I shook my head. "It's too late for that." I glanced back at the car. Maybe I was mistaken. Maybe I'd imagined the whole thing. But no, Zack was still right where I'd left him, not moving. Not breathing. "He's dead."

CHAPTER 4

While my sister did her best to secure the car by taping up a tarp we found in the stockroom over the busted windshield, I went in search of Beau. "Of all the nights to lose cell service," I muttered to myself as I tried to see over the wheel of Tansy's car.

I knew we should have left it where it was, but I wasn't about to walk all the way to Beau's in this mess, and with the internet down, it wasn't like we could order an Uber. There was a loud grinding sound coming from the front passenger side of the car, where Zack's car had hit it. I was likely doing more damage by driving it in this condition, but what other choice did I have?

Beau lived in the only apartment building in Cedar River. It was a four-story building on Armstrong Street, just shy of half a block long with six units on each floor. I found a parking spot and hurried into the dark lobby. There was an elevator, but like everything else in town it was out of order until power was restored, so I followed the glow of the exit sign to the stairs. Emergency lights cast a glow into the concrete stairwell as I hurried up the stairs.

Of course Beau had to live on the top floor, I thought, huffing and puffing as I exited the stairwell. The carpet squished beneath my wet sneakers as I left a trail of water in my wake. I should have shed my windbreaker-style rain-coat in the lobby, but hadn't thought about it at the time. Now, in the stifling hallway, I yanked it over my head and balled it up as best I could to keep it from dripping any more than it already had. There was nothing I could do about my soaking wet jeans and shoes, though.

Beau's unit was at the end of the hall. I'd only been here a handful of times. More often than not, if we were going to stay in for pizza and a movie, we ended up at my sister's place. Beau had a better television, but Tansy's had the benefit of a hovering chaperone intent on making sure that nothing untoward could develop. If I'd been sixteen, I would have resented the intrusion, but nowadays I appreciated it. Nothing did the job of making sure Beau stayed on his side of the couch quite like an overprotective sister sitting three feet away, clearing her throat anytime he scooted too close to me.

I knocked, expecting a quick response. It had already been late when Beau had dropped me off after the game, but he was a night owl. And an early bird. Come to think of it, I wasn't sure if Beau ever slept. I guess it came with the cop territory.

When there was no answer, I knocked again, louder this time. Beau and I had been casually seeing each other for nearly six months now, but we hadn't progressed to the key swapping phase yet. I tried the door handle. It was locked. I banged on the door.

The door on the other side of the hall popped open and a sleepy voice said, "Do you have any idea what time it is?"

The hall was lit with the soft glow of emergency lights, so I could make out the familiar face of Officer Jayden Holt glaring at me. Jayden was a Black woman about my height. She wasn't physically intimidating, but had an un-mistakable air of authority about her even when she was off-duty, the kind that made me straighten up and call her ma'am, even though she was a few years my junior.

But tonight I wasn't thinking about manners. I jerked my thumb at Beau's door. "Don't suppose you have a key?"

"Don't suppose I do," she said, relaxing her stance once she realized it was just me making all that noise. "Surprised you braved the storm for a late-night rendezvous."

I blushed, realizing how this must look to her. "Oh no, it's not like that," I stammered. Then I realized how odd it was to be having this conversation with Jayden in the middle of the night. I hadn't known that she and Beau were across-the-hall neighbors. "You live here?"

She nodded. "I do. And last time I checked, you did not." She stepped into the hall and let the door close behind her. "What's up, Juni?"

"There's a dead guy," I blurted out.

"Again?" she asked evenly. Nothing rattled Jayden.

"I found him," I clarified.

"Of course you did."

I should have expected her reaction, or lack thereof. This was the third dead body I'd found since moving back home. Maybe it was time to take a long look at my life and see what I might be doing wrong.

"Power's out. Phones are down. I couldn't call nine-one-one," I explained.

"So you came here, instead of the station?" she asked.

Jayden had a good point. The police station was technically closer to Sip & Spin, but it had never even crossed my mind to go there first. When I was in trouble, I went straight to Beau. I shrugged.

"And where exactly is this alleged dead man?"

"Main Street. In front of Sip & Spin. In his car."

"You didn't kill him, did you?" she asked.

"What? No," I sputtered. "There was a car accident."

"Had to ask." She opened her door. "Come on inside while I get dressed."

She picked up a hand-held radio from a table next to the entrance. She clicked a button and a green light came on. "Officer Holt. Copy?" Someone said something on the other end of the connection. I could barely make out their words over the static. I didn't recognize the voice, but I assumed it was someone at the police station. "Car wreck with possible fatality on Main, near the record shop. Send a unit." She glanced over at me. "And dispatch Detective Russell, will ya?"

I followed her into her apartment and left the door open. The light in the hall didn't reach far, but it was better than nothing. I couldn't see much, but her apartment smelled like lilac and vanilla. "Beau's at the station?"

"I don't keep track of your boyfriend." Jayden's voice floated back to me from the other side of the apartment. If her layout was anything like Beau's, it was a decent-size living room, a small dining nook, and a shiny kitchen, with a single bedroom and bathroom down at the end of a short hall.

I stood near the entrance, afraid I would bump into something or drip water all over her carpet. "He's not my boyfriend," I said automatically.

"Have you ever told *him* that?" she asked. She sounded closer now, and I caught a flash of light as she adjusted her equipment belt. Jayden had apparently gone from sound asleep to fully clothed in her uniform in the time it normally took me to make a cup of coffee.

"All the time," I told her. "I figured he'd be home."

"I'm sure when the power blew, he went to work."

"And you didn't?" I asked. Cedar River had a small police force. There wasn't a lot of major crime, or at least there hadn't been until I moved back home last spring. Not enough to employ a detective full time. Rather than share one with one of the nearby towns, they hired Beau as part-time plain-clothes detective and part-time uniformed officer. Jayden, on the other hand, was full-time uniform. Beau outranked her, and I was surprised that he'd gone in while she'd stayed home.

"I just got off a double. I was getting my first sleep in two days when you started banging on Russell's door," she said, with a hint of annoyance.

"Sorry."

"Not your fault that you find dead bodies the way most people find pennies," she said. She reached past me and I scooted over to stay on the small tiled area near the door while she rummaged through the closet. She pulled out a plastic bonnet that she snapped over her hat. Next came a thick raincoat. I could see the word "Police" in large, reflective letters across the front as she put it on. "Stay here. I've got some dry sweats that should fit you. Help yourself to anything in the fridge."

"Thanks, but I'm coming with you," I said. "Warm, dry clothes sound tempting, but Tansy's back at the shop."

"Your sister's a big girl. She'll be fine without you."

"I'm sure she will be. But I'm still not leaving her alone to deal with the fallout." I followed Jayden out of the apartment, down the long hall, and down the stairs.

She paused for a second at the lobby doors. The rain hadn't let up any. "No need for you to go back out in this mess," she said.

"Wouldn't be the first time tonight. I'll follow you." If Beau had been there, he would have insisted on driving us, but then I'd be stranded downtown with my sister and our cat, without a car.

She shook her head. "Suit yourself." Jayden headed out in the storm. I was close on her heels.

The streets were treacherous. There were a couple of low spots that if I hadn't seen Jayden successfully navigate,

I would have turned right back around. Fortunately, there was no other traffic on the road until we got to Main Street, where emergency flashers lit up the night.

I parked half a block away so I wouldn't get pinned in by emergency vehicles and then hugged the side of the buildings, dashing from the protection of one awning to the next until I got to the record shop. Gusts of wind kept blowing the hood of my raincoat back. I probably looked like a drowned rat and I felt worse. There were times that having long hair was a blessing. This was *not* one of those times.

The scene was surrounded by the usual suspects: an ambulance, several patrol cars, and Beau's familiar black truck. The dome light was on inside the ambulance. Through the fogged-up windshield, I saw Rocco O'Brien and Kitty Harris, two local EMTs, in an animated discussion.

Kitty was Maggie's husband's cousin, which practically made her family. She'd moved to town last spring and we'd quickly become friends. She was bold, sarcastic, and an absolute font of information. Plus, she could always be counted on to liven up our already entertaining family dinners, and I absolutely adored her. I waved, but she didn't see me.

Outside in the street, Beau was easy to recognize, even in the driving rain. He was crouched down in front of the passenger side of Zack's car with water pouring over his cowboy hat. It looked like they'd tried to erect a tent over the car, the kind that I was used to seeing at the local farmer's market, but the wind must have blown it down, because there was a lump of white canvas and metal on the sidewalk. I stepped over the mangled tent and ducked into the shop.

Inside, Tansy was sitting at one of the tall café tables near the window. Daffy's cat carrier was in the middle of the table. Plaintive yowls drifted out of the carrier, but his heart was no longer in his complaints. "Ahh, buddy, I'm sorry," I said, patting the top of the carrier. His paw darted at me, claws flashing out. I snatched my hand back before he could draw blood. "I probably deserved that, but trust me, it's for your own good."

Between the storm and the investigation outside, emergency personnel would likely be traipsing in and out of the shop for the next hour or more. Daffy hated having strangers in his home, and likely would have dashed out into the storm as soon as the front door opened. "Trust me, that crate is the safest place for you right now," I assured him.

"Thanks for notifying the cavalry," Tansy said. "It's weird. I can't even offer them coffee."

I glanced toward the back of the shop, where everything was, of course, dark. We wouldn't be able to open for business until all the power was restored. Depending on how long the storm continued to rage and how many outages there were, that could be hours or even days.

I pulled up a chair next to my sister. "Tonight, at the game, I was just thinking about what Maggie had said about us being able to make it if there were no more unforeseen emergencies between now and the end of the year."

Tansy laughed wryly. "I guess the universe has other plans for us." We sat in the dark and silence for a while, watching the police work. "I don't suppose we should call Zack's associate back? See if he's still interested in investing in Sip & Spin?"

"I don't think that's a great idea," I told her.

"Hear me out. I know we agreed to stick it out, but we're barely limping along here as it. One more setback, and we're done for unless we get a cash infusion to guide us through the rough patch. Mom's tapped out. So's Uncle Calvin. Maggie and J.T. are struggling to pay their mortgage and car leases. Unless we have some rich relative I don't know about, it's time to ask for help."

"That's not what I meant," I said, but Tansy cut me off before I could finish.

"You and I have to be on the same page on this. Maggie's going to be the holdout, but if the two of us stick together, we can convince her. She's too proud to admit that we need assistance. But what that investor was offering wasn't just a short-term loan. He said he had ideas to turn this place around. I don't know if I believe him, but it wouldn't hurt to hear him out."

"Tansy, that's great, I just—"

She interrupted me again. "Trust me, baby sis. I know what I'm talking about."

This time I really did grind my teeth. I loved my sisters with my whole heart. My entire family, really. They're the absolute best and I wouldn't trade them for the world. But sometimes they looked at me and saw the bratty little kid who refused to eat anything that wasn't shaped like dinosaurs or the annoying baby sister who followed Tansy and Maggie around everywhere they went. I was a grown-up now, even if they didn't always see me that way.

"I'm not arguing," I said. This time it was me not letting Tansy finish. She gave me an annoyed look and started to talk again, but I kept speaking, talking right over her. "But we can't call Zack Fjord." I pointed at the car. "Because that's Zack Fjord's wrecked BMW. And that's Zack Fjord dead in the passenger seat."

The door to Sip & Spin opened with a tinkle of bells. Ignoring the intrusion, my sister asked, "If that's Zack's car, what's he doing in the passenger seat?"

"And what's he doing here in Cedar River?" Beau asked from the doorway. "Can someone grab me a towel or something? I don't want to track water all over your store."

It was dark, so he didn't notice that a few more drips wouldn't matter. We'd had to move the blanket keeping the water out so the door would open freely, and there was a puddle of standing water by the door. "Careful," I told him. "It's slippery."

"Here, let me help," Tansy said, jumping up. She hurried over to take his coat and hat as I went back to the supply closet to grab a roll of paper towels.

"Sorry, it's the best we can do," I said, handing him the roll.

"Better than nothing," he said, tearing off a few towels to dry his face. Unlike mine, his hair was relatively dry since he'd had the forethought to wear a cowboy hat tonight. Then again, with the exception of the hockey game, Beau almost always had a hat on. "Juni, Tansy, I don't suppose I can get a hot cup of coffee?"

"No power," Tansy said, gingerly hanging his dripping outerwear on our coatrack.

"Figured as much," he said affably. He turned to me. "Third time's the charm, Junebug."

I hung my head. "This is *not* my fault."

"Uh-huh," he said. He didn't sound convinced. "Before we left, his partner, Savannah something, said she was driving him home since he'd had one too many. I'm assuming she was behind the wheel when the car wrecked?"

"Goodwin," I supplied. "Savannah Goodwin."

"Any idea where she is now?" he asked.

Tansy shook her head. "No clue. We heard a crash and ran outside. Saw the car had hit mine. The driver's side door was open."

"The door was open," he repeated.

"I closed it to keep out some of the rain, but it was open when we got there. We didn't see anyone else around. Just the guy in the passenger's seat," Tansy said.

"Zack Fjord," I said, trying to help.

"Yeah, Zack," Tansy agreed.

"They hit your car?" he asked.

Tansy nodded. "Looks like they lost control in the rain and spun out. The rear panel behind the driver connected with my front end. Most of the damage is to their car."

Beau ran a hand through this short hair, making it stand up. "I wish you hadn't moved your car."

"But—"

He stopped me by holding up a hand. "I know, I know. Phones are out. You went to get help. You did the right thing. Glad you didn't wait for the storm to pass. And taping the tarp to the windshield? Genius. It's still a mess, but at least some of the scene is protected that way."

"That was Tansy's idea," I said quickly, giving credit where it was due. I didn't know that I could ever heal the rift between my oldest sister and my, well, my Beau, but every little bit helped.

"Thank you, Tansy," he said with a nod. I noticed he didn't follow it with his trademarked grin, the one that reduced most women—myself included—to a puddle of goo at his feet. Maybe he knew it was powerless in the dark. More likely, he realized that grin didn't work with my sister.

She mumbled something that sounded a bit like "You're welcome." It was an improvement. Last time he'd tried to give her a compliment, her reply hadn't been fit for polite company.

"And y'all didn't see anyone else? No other cars?"

I shook my head. "None. But to be fair, we couldn't see

three feet in front of our faces." I glanced out the big front window separating our record shop from the sidewalk. The rain was still coming down in a deluge.

"There's not a lot we can do here until we talk to the driver. We're finished up here, but I need to go back to the station. I'll have an officer drive y'all home," he said, reaching for his wet jacket.

"We're okay," I said. "We've got Tansy's car."

He held out his hand. "Keys, please. I'll tow it to the garage so I can take a look at it. Besides, it's not safe to drive out there."

"She said we're fine," Tansy said, her voice cold. I knew that Beau was looking out for us, but all Tansy heard was her least favorite person on the planet telling her what to do, and that wasn't going to fly with her.

"Suit yourself," he said. "I'll come by tomorrow and get some pictures of the damage in the daylight." He turned to me and rested his hand on my shoulder. "Seriously. The roads are bad. I don't want you driving."

I agreed with him, but instead, I said, "Go on. And don't worry about me." There were times I had to side with Tansy to keep the fragile peace between them. This was one of those times.

"That's not ever gonna happen," he muttered. Beau put on his coat and hat, and went back out into the rain.

"Double-check the back door," Tansy said. "Then, we'll be on our way."

"Okay," I agreed. I knew it was closed and locked. It had been when we got here, and no one had opened it since. But I wasn't going to argue with my sister, not right now.

I headed down the narrow hall leading to the back alley. My phone was in my pocket. I didn't need the light to double-check a deadbolt I already knew was locked, and I might as well preserve my battery. There was no telling

CHAPTER 5

I shrieked.

"Juni, what's wrong?" my sister asked. I heard her footsteps running toward me. Tansy shone her phone light at my back, illuminating our intruder.

"Savannah!" I exclaimed, recognizing her. At the hockey game, she looked glamorous and put together in a way I could never pull off, but now her hair was a frizzy mess, her makeup had run down her face, and her soaking wet outfit hung shapelessly on her shivering body.

She held her hands up in surrender. "I'm so sorry. I didn't mean to scare you."

"Savannah?" Tansy asked. "As in the missing driver? Zack's girlfriend Savannah?"

She dropped her hands. "Wait a sec. I'm not his girlfriend. Business partners, not life partners. Savannah Goodwin, at your service." She looked into the light coming from my sister's phone. Her tone came out polite, despite her chattering teeth. "And who do I have the pleasure of meeting?"

"Tansy Jessup," Tansy said as she lowered the light. Having grown up on the beauty pageant circuit, my older sister never missed a social cue, no matter the circumstance. "You're freezing. Let me get you something dry."

But we had nothing to offer her. Tansy was still damp.

I was soaked. With our house so close to the shop, we didn't keep spare clothes here. If anything ever happened, we'd just go home and change. We looked at each other. "I'm sorry. I don't know why I said that. We don't have anything," Tansy clarified.

"That's okay," Savannah said, hugging herself as she shivered some more. "I'm fine."

"Wait right here," I said. "I'm gonna grab Beau." I hurried off, but when I looked out the front window, the emergency vehicles were gone. Even Zack's car had been towed away. Only Tansy's car remained, half a block away. "That was quick," I muttered to myself. Then again, they'd all been working in the pouring rain for quite a while. They were no doubt eager to get somewhere dry. "He left already," I said.

"Thank goodness for that," Tansy added.

"That's fine, I'd rather not have to deal with cops right now anyway," Savannah said.

"You have to talk to them." I looked at my sister for confirmation. She nodded her head. "You were just in a wreck, and the passenger is dead."

Savannah burst into sobs. Tansy threw her arms around her and let her cry. When Savannah's tears subsided, Tansy managed to steer her to one of the café tables nearest the barista station. Then she took my elbow and pulled me to the side. "Maybe it's too soon," she said.

"Zack is dead," I said. "And she fled the scene."

"She's going through a lot. She needs a minute."

"*She* needs a minute?" I asked. "Time out. She was the driver. She ran away and hid when the cops showed up. How do we know she didn't kill Zack on purpose?"

"I didn't kill anyone," Savannah said between sniffles. My sister and I exchanged glances that were mostly lost in the dark. "Oh come on, it's not like I can't hear you."

"So tell us what happened," I prompted.

"When we left the game, Zack was in one of his moods, ranting and generally making as much sense as someone who'd just put away a twelve-pack would make. By the time we got out of the post-game traffic jam, Zack tells me we need to make a pit stop in Cedar River, then passes out in the passenger seat."

"What kind of pit stop?" Tansy asked.

"Who knows? I was too busy driving in horrendous conditions to worry about that, then someone stepped out in front of us."

"There was someone in the road?" I asked.

"Yeah. I didn't get a good look at him. The rain was coming down like no one's business. I could barely see beyond my headlights. There was a loud noise. The windshield shattered and I lost control."

"Wait, the window broke before you hit my car?" Tansy asked.

"I think the person in the street threw something at us. I swerved, and that's when I hit the parked car. I'm so sorry. I was so scared. I didn't know what was happening. I know, it sounds nuts." She shook her head. "I looked over at Zack, but he was slumped over and there was blood and glass and rain everywhere and I panicked." She looked at my sister for a beat, and then at me. "I wasn't thinking. I just had to get out of there, and I saw your door was open."

The timing was suspect. Tansy left the shop first and Savannah wasn't in the car. I was right on her heels. For Savannah to slip into Sip & Spin without us noticing, she would have had to be awful sneaky. Then again, the rain was loud and visibility was null. All my attention was on the wrecked car. I could have passed Sasquatch without noticing.

"You could have said something earlier," Tansy insisted. "We would have taken care of you."

"I'd just been attacked." She sniffled again. "I needed a safe place."

"It was a lot safer once the cops showed up," I said.

"I guess I was in shock," she said. Considering that Savannah was pale and trembling, I had to assume she was *still* in shock. I didn't blame her.

"I can imagine, after all you've been through," my sister said, putting her arm around Savannah's shoulders. "But now that you've calmed down, you need to talk to the police."

"Can I trust them?" she asked. "I've heard some awful things about small-town cops."

Tansy grimaced as if she'd smelled something foul. "Well, I don't know about all cops, but I guess if push comes to shove, you can trust Detective Russell."

In my attempt to hold back a laugh, I accidentally snorted. I covered it—poorly—by faking a cough. "Dear sister, that might be the nicest thing you've ever said about Beau."

"Wait, Beau? Like the hot cop you brought to the game? The guy that couldn't keep his hands off you?" Savannah asked.

I turned to Tansy. "Before you ask, there were no hands."

"Oh please, you should have seen him," Savannah said. "Zack started to get a little too friendly, you know, like he always does, and I thought that Beau guy was gonna rip his face off."

"It wasn't anything like that," I insisted.

"He was just defending you. It was sweet."

"Toxic masculinity is anything but sweet," Tansy muttered.

I gave her a warning look. "We all know how you feel. And even you said that Savannah can trust Beau. Let's go talk to him while everything's still fresh in your mind." I stood up and scooted my chair in.

It was still pouring outside. Tansy offered her raincoat to Savannah. I draped mine over Daffy's carrier. Together, we hurried to the car. Once Savannah and the cat were settled into the back seat, we took off toward the police station, which was only a few blocks away. Jayden had made a good point earlier. The station was a lot closer to Sip & Spin than Beau's apartment. It definitely said something that I'd thought of Beau himself as my particular port in this storm.

The waiting room was crowded with wet, anxious residents huddled around candles that had been set up along the reception desk. As far as I could tell, half of the town was here, which was bad news. During a storm, even a bad one like tonight's, most people were wise enough to shelter in place at home if they could. A night without power wasn't enough to drive them out of their houses. But Cedar River had sprung up around, well, a river. When it flooded, the river liked to creep into low-lying homes.

The police station was built on higher ground. Judging by the looks of my neighbors, with soaking wet shoes and wet pajama legs sticking out beneath their emergency blankets, I could only assume that their homes were at least partially underwater. "Oh no," I said, looking around. "This is a disaster."

"Take care of Savannah," Tansy said. "I'll see if there's anything I can do to help."

I waded through the assembled crowd to take a place in line to speak to the clerk at the front desk. When it was our turn, I didn't recognize the person behind the desk, so I introduced myself. "Hi, I'm Juni Jessup and this is Savannah Goodwin. We need to talk to Detective Russell."

"Russell's got his hands full tonight. Him, and everyone else on the force," they said.

"Yeah, I know, but Savannah here was involved in a car wreck where the passenger died at the scene." I pleaded with the clerk. I knew they had their hands full, but this was important and their dismissive attitude wasn't helping anyone.

"You don't say?" They reached for the phone on their desk and went so far as to pick up the receiver before realizing that all the phones were dead, even the landline ones. Or, it was a VoIP phone, and when the internet went out, it died too. They shook their head. "Two in one night. What are the odds?"

"Oh no, it's the same case that Beau's already working on," I assured them. "Savannah was the driver."

"In that case, that guy's not going to be any deader in the morning. How about you come back then? Next!"

I started to protest, but Savannah dragged me out of the line.

"See? They don't need to talk to me."

"Yes, they do," I insisted. "But the clerk's right. We'll try again in the morning." Since she didn't have anywhere else to go, it seemed clear that Savannah would have to come home with us tonight.

"Hey! Juni!"

I altered my course toward a cluster of familiar people calling my name. I recognized several Cedar River residents, many of whom I'd known my entire life.

"Everyone okay?" I asked, worried about them. Even with everything that had happened with Zack, I counted myself lucky.

"River overflowed again."

"But no one's hurt?" I asked.

"Just our property values," Carole Ackers said. We'd

gone to school together. "Please tell me we're still on for karaoke this week."

"I don't know. I haven't thought that far ahead," I admitted. In the grand scheme of things, hosting karaoke at Sip & Spin didn't seem that important right now. "I guess it depends on when we get power back."

"If there's anything I can do to help, just ask," Carole offered. Everyone around her bobbed their heads in agreement. "Times like this, we need something to look forward to."

I hadn't thought of it like that. Entertainment was more important than ever after a night like tonight. "I'll see what we can do. In the meantime, y'all have someplace to stay tonight?"

Carole nodded. "Hank's folks are gonna put us up. We're just waiting on our ride."

"Can we give you a lift?" I offered. It would be crowded in the car, and we might have to make multiple trips, but it wasn't any trouble.

"Thanks, but we're good." Carole gave me a spontaneous hug. "Stay safe, Juni."

"You too," I told her.

Savannah and I made our way back through the crowd. Near the front door, I spotted Tansy speaking with an elderly Black woman draped in a foil emergency blanket. "Miss Edie!" I exclaimed as we got closer. "You okay?"

"I've had better days," she said. "When the river started to rise, they brought a bunch of vans out and told everyone we had to evacuate, and then they brought us here. They told us we had to leave everything behind, even pets, but I couldn't leave Buffy, now could I?"

That's when I realized that she was holding a quivering dog under the blanket. Buffy, a tan puggle, weighed about thirty pounds. She wasn't very big as far as dogs went, but Edie was a tiny woman in her late seventies. "Can I take her from you?" I asked, reaching out for the dog.

"Hey, I already told y'all! You can't have a dog in here!" the clerk yelled.

"Where are we supposed to go?" Edie demanded.

Miss Edie was the heart and soul of Cedar River. I've known her ever since I could remember. She used to baby-sit my mother and Uncle Calvin when they were little, and often watched me after school, along with half of the other kids in town. She was the first person to lend a hand when anyone needed it, and there wasn't a single person in town who wouldn't do the same for her.

I hugged the dog closer to my chest. "You're coming home with us, of course," I said. "You and Buffy."

Tansy echoed me. "Of course you are."

"Any news about Calvin?" I asked. Our uncle lived across the street from Edie. As the self-appointed neighborhood watch, she knew all the comings and goings on the block.

"He wasn't at home," she said. "He was probably out with that pretty girlfriend of his."

"He's at a fishing tournament out of town with Samuel Davis," Tansy corrected her. "Assuming, of course, they didn't call it off for weather."

We got everyone settled into the car. Miss Edie sat up front with Buffy the puggle on her lap. Savannah and I were in the back, with Daffy's car carrier on the seat between us. We headed for home, with the damaged car protesting all the way. We weren't doing the car any favors by driving it in its current condition, but we didn't have much of a choice.

"I have half a mind to turn this car around and have a word with that clerk about how they treated Miss Edie," Tansy grumbled.

"Let's just get home and dry off," I said. "We can always launch a complaint in the morning when we take Savannah back to talk to Beau."

When we finally made it home, Tansy let Daffy out in her bedroom, where he promptly disappeared into her closet. I found some dry clothes for Edie. She and Buffy settled into the guest room. I offered to take the couch so Savannah could have my room, but Tansy had a better idea. "She can have the cottage. It's not like Mom will be home tonight," she suggested.

"She's a stranger," I said in a whisper.

"So you'd make her sleep in the pigsty you call a room when the cottage is just sitting empty?" she whispered back. "What kind of host would that make me?"

"Good point," I agreed. Manners were everything to Tansy, and it would take more than a little disaster to change that.

Savannah happily took an umbrella, a change of clothes, and the spare key, and headed across the yard to the cottage. Alone at last, Tansy asked me, "Is it just me or is she acting strange?" she asked.

"How is someone supposed to act in her situation? She's just been in a car crash and now she's surrounded by strangers."

"I don't know but it was weird, right? How she ran away? Her boyfriend's dead and she's hiding in the back of our shop?"

"Hey, I thought it was weird from the start," I reminded her, before adding, "I guess she's in shock. She said herself that she was scared. And I don't think Zack was her boyfriend. She was very clear that they aren't, weren't, a couple."

"There is that. But when your boyfriend came by to check out the scene . . ."

I interrupted her. "Beau's not my boyfriend."

Tansy grinned at me. "Which is almost exactly the

same thing Savannah said about Zack. And I don't believe either of you for a single minute."

"Back to the subject at hand," I said quickly. I didn't want to get into it with Tansy, not after the night we'd already had. "Savannah was just in a wreck, and she lost her friend. She's bound to be a little off."

"Maybe you're right. Zack was in no shape to drive, so she was behind the wheel. Even with the weather being a factor, she probably feels responsible."

"She saw someone in the road, right? She claims they threw something at the windshield, and that's why she lost control of her car. Which means it's not her fault."

Tansy shook her head. "I don't buy it. We would have seen them if someone else was out there."

"Not necessarily. It was raining too hard and we didn't go outside until after the accident. We didn't see Savannah run into the shop, and she had to have slipped right past us. There could have been a whole parade of elephants down Main Street and we might have not seen a thing in this weather," I said.

"I don't know. It's a little too convenient, if you ask me. The passenger is passed out and dies. Then the driver, the only witness to any of this, takes off and hides until after the cops leave? I smell something fishy."

"Fine," I admitted. "It's fishy. And why was Zack passed out? I'd just seen him at the hockey game, remember? When we left, there were only a few minutes left in the last period. Zack had been drinking, agreed. Was he obnoxiously drunk? Yes, but he was also obnoxious when he was sober. He wasn't stumbling around, soon-to-be-passed-out drunk."

"Savannah said he'd put away a twelve-pack," Tansy said.

I shook my head. "He was drinking, but I didn't notice him drinking anywhere near that much. Maybe he downed a whole lot of beers quick after we left."

"Hmm." Tansy tapped her chin. "So you're telling me Savannah lied."

I sucked on my bottom lip. "I don't know. Maybe?"

Tansy yawned, and I gave her a hug. "What was that for?" she asked.

"It's been a wild night, and I am glad you were there with me."

"Do me a favor, Juni, and next time you find a dead body, don't get me involved."

"What makes you think there's gonna be a next time?" I asked.

"Because I know you too well. 'Night."

"Good night," I told her, then headed for my room. Out of habit, I checked my phone for missed messages, even though I had no service, and plugged it into the charger, even though the power was off. Old habits die hard. Then I stared at the ceiling and listened to the storm until the rain finally stopped. Every time I closed my eyes, I saw Zack Fjord's face. While I lay there in the dark, unable to sleep, Beau's words rattled around in my head on repeat like a broken record.

Third time's the charm.

If he was right, then Zack's death wasn't an accident. Which meant I had another murder to solve.

CHAPTER 6

Having installed good-quality blackout curtains in my bedroom, I was no longer at the mercy of the sunrise—not that I'd gotten much sleep last night. As I lay in bed, wide awake, a dog started yipping at my closed door. Which was weird because last time I checked, we didn't have a dog.

I got up, pulled on a robe, and opened the door. Miss Edie's puggle, Buffy, greeted me enthusiastically before jumping up on my bed and starting a wrestling match with one of my fuzzy blue throw pillows.

"Sorry," Edie said, shuffling into my bedroom. "Buffy, drop that!" The dog abandoned the pillow and started rolling around in my covers. "She's a morning person. Or dog. You know what I mean."

"I do," I agreed. I flicked my bedroom light switch on. Nothing happened, so I flicked it off again. "I guess the power didn't come back."

"I guess not," she said.

"I'd offer you coffee or something, but until we get electricity, we're out of luck," I said.

"Not so." Edie grinned. "I thought you girls might be hungry, so I made us breakfast."

After dressing hastily in an oversized Backstreet Boys concert T-shirt and denim shorts, I followed her into the kitchen, where I was greeted by the heavenly smell of fresh-brewed coffee and a couple dozen muffins. "I hope you don't mind, but with the power out, everything in your fridge is going to spoil unless we eat it. So I started baking."

"Mind? Miss Edie, you can bake for me anytime." I sat down at the table, peeled the wrapper off a muffin, and took a bite. It was cinnamon streusel. I didn't know we even had the ingredients for cinnamon streusel muffins. Then again, I was always more interested in eating than I was in baking. "Oh my gosh, this is amazing."

"Glad you think so," she said, patting the top of my head like I was five years old again.

"I didn't realize that we had muffin mix in the house," I said.

"Muffin mix?" Edie said, shaking her head. "Blasphemy."

"In my defense, the last time I tried to make muffins, I couldn't have been much more than twelve years old. I followed the directions on the package to the letter until I realized I didn't know where the muffin pans were."

"I don't know where your mom kept them when you were little, but Tansy had them stashed in the warming tray under the oven," she said.

"Apparently, that's where my mom stored them, too. At the time, I didn't realize there *was* a warming tray under the oven. Anyway, I couldn't find the muffin tins so I used the waffle iron instead."

Edie raised an eyebrow at me. "And how did they turn out?"

"Messy, but edible. Almost. It probably would have worked better if I'd sprayed the waffle iron first."

"You didn't . . . ?" She shook her head. "Some folks shouldn't be allowed in the kitchen." She turned back to the stacks of muffins cooling on the counter. "Do you mind if we take the leftovers to the police station, or the community center, or wherever everyone ended up last night? It was absolute chaos yesterday, and who knows if anyone has figured out how to feed all those poor, displaced people."

"That's a fantastic idea, Miss Edie," I said. "Let's pack them up and take them over right now."

"Take what over where?" Tansy asked, coming in the front door.

"Were you out for a run?" I asked. I knew she liked to get her roadwork in early, before it got too hot, but we'd stayed up last night and I was surprised that she'd kept to her routine this morning.

"I wanted to assess the damage around town," she said. "Is that coffee I smell?"

"Hot and fresh," Edie confirmed. She walked over to a pot on top of our gas stove, and poured coffee into one of Tansy's mugs. "One of the advantages of being old is I remember how we used to make coffee back in the good old days, before your fancy cappuccino machine did all the work."

"This is delicious," Tansy declared, taking a sip. She plucked a muffin off one of the stacks and sniffed. "Orange?"

"Apricot," Edie said. "Try it."

Tansy took a bite and declared it "perfection." "There's good news and bad. The river overflowed. Most of the backyards on the east side of town are underwater. Edie, your neighborhood fared better than expected. Your front yard is a swamp, but I peeked through the windows and I don't see any standing water inside. That's not to say that it's safe to return until public works checks it out, but your house looks good."

"That's such a relief," Edie said, touching her hand to her chest.

"But in the meantime, you and Buffy are welcome to stay with us as long as you need," Tansy offered.

"That's awful sweet of you, but what about your cat? The last thing I want is my dog causing problems."

My sister and I looked at each other. "How is Daffy this morning?" I asked.

"I don't know. When I woke up, I couldn't find him anywhere. He either slipped out when we weren't paying attention, or he's the hide-and-seek champion of the world."

"With cats, you can never tell," Edie said sagely.

The front door opened again. "Knock, knock." Savannah walked into the kitchen. She didn't look as put together as she had when I first met her. I could tell that she'd been crying. Her hair was tousled and her eyes were red, but she still managed to pull off socialite-pretty even without makeup and expertly styled hair. If I were in her shoes, I didn't know that I could have even gotten out of bed, much less gotten dressed. "Do I smell coffee?"

"Take a seat and I'll fix you a cup," Edie told her.

"Thanks, but don't put yourself out for me," Savannah said, walking around her to select a mug out of the cabinet. My sister collected funny and interesting mugs. The one Savannah picked was shaped like a kitten on its back. She poured the coffee, careful not to spill a drop.

"Muffin?" I asked. "Miss Edie made a ton."

Savannah waved me away. "I don't have an appetite."

"More for the rest of us," I said, reaching for another. Then I thought about all the folks we'd seen at the police station the night before and changed my mind. "Maybe later. Let's pack these up."

I heard the front door open again. "Morning!" Beau called out from the door as he let himself in. He looked around the crowded kitchen and helped himself to a seat at the table. "I didn't realize y'all were having a party."

"Who invited you?" Tansy asked.

He shrugged. "I needed to take some pictures of your car for my files, remember? Plus, your front door was unlocked."

"And the riffraff just walks right in," Tansy grumbled.

"If you want to keep the riffraff out, you could lock your door," he said with a forced grin. I knew he was just looking out for us, but if he had it his way, he'd install a high-tech security system in our house that paged him every time there was a problem.

Not that it would work without power. I wasn't sure if it was creepy or cute how overprotective he was of me. "Have a muffin," I said, tossing him one.

He took a bite. "Okay, where did you get these? The bakery's closed, Tansy doesn't make junk food, and you don't bake."

"Miss Edie made them," I told him. "And they're not junk food. They're breakfast."

"They're amazing." He took another bite. "Miss Edie, if you ever want to come over to my place for breakfast, I'd let you make an honest man out of me."

She grinned at him. "Be careful what you wish for, Beauregard. I might just take you up on that."

Beau finished his muffin in one more bite before turning his attention to the fourth woman in the kitchen. "You must be Savannah Goodwin. Just the person I wanted to talk to." He glanced over at me, then back at her. "Imagine bumping into you here."

"We found her after you left," I said. "She was in shock." I didn't mention she was hiding in the back of the shop, because even I had to admit it sounded suspicious. "We brought her by the station, but it was a circus."

"That it was," he agreed. "The front desk let me know that you stopped by."

"Where did all those folks end up last night?" Edie asked.

"A few went home with friends. The rest got cots at the high school gym."

"Well, then I suppose we ought to be heading for the gymnasium," Edie said. We wrapped the muffins in cellophane and filled a few shopping totes. "Give me a hand, Beauregard?"

"I've got you," Tansy said, grabbing one of the totes.

"I'll help y'all out to the car," Beau offered. "Juni, Savannah, sit tight. I need a word with you two."

"Aye aye," I said, giving him a snappy salute.

"What about Buffy?" Edie asked.

"Leave her here. I'll keep an eye on her," I offered.

"You're a good egg, Juniper," she said, and followed Beau and Tansy out to the car. The little puggle whined at the door, then lay down on the tile to wait for Miss Edie's return.

As soon as they were out of earshot, Savannah asked, "All that and he flirts with little old ladies, too?"

I got up to pour the rest of the coffee into a travel mug. I added sugar and cream. "Beau flirts with any woman with a pulse," I said.

"It's all part of my evil plan to drive Juni jealous until she realizes that she can't live without me," Beau said. I hadn't heard him re-enter the kitchen. I blushed at the comment and handed him the giant mug of coffee. He took a sip. "I should have known the Jessups would have the only hot coffee in town. It's stronger than what you normally make. I like it."

"Edie brewed it," I told him. "On the stove, like a pioneer woman."

"She's a marvel. You better be careful. If I can't get you to finally admit that you're madly in love with me, I might set my sights on Miss Edie."

"Good luck with that," I told him. "She's already buried four husbands. I'm sure she won't mind burying a fifth."

He took another sip of coffee before setting it on the table in front of him. "As much as I'm enjoying—what did you say, Juni? Flirting with any woman with a pulse?—we've got business to discuss." He pulled a small notebook out of his back pocket and flipped to a clean sheet of paper. He patted his pockets and looked concerned, until I handed him a pen out of our junk drawer. "Always looking out for me," he said with a smile.

But when he turned his attention to Savannah, his expression was all business. "So, tell me, Miss Goodwin, what happened last night?"

She repeated the same story she'd told Tansy and me, nearly verbatim. Beau interrupted her several times with questions, but her narrative never wavered. "Let me get this right. You were driving. Someone stepped in front of your car and threw something at the windshield. You swerved and struck Tansy's car. Then you got out and ran because you were afraid they might come after you?"

"That's about it."

"And when the police arrived on the scene, you stayed in hiding why?"

"I told you. I was scared."

"Of the cops? Of me?" Beau asked. He scratched his head and pulled out his best good-ole-boy drawl. "Not quite sure I follow."

"I wasn't thinking straight," she admitted. "I was in shock."

Beau looked at me, then jerked his head toward the hall. "A minute?"

I followed him. Instead of stopping in the hall, he continued into my bedroom and closed the door behind us. He blinked at me. "What did she tell you last night?"

"The same exact thing."

"The *exact* same thing?" he asked.

"Pretty much word for word," I confirmed.

"And so naturally, you invite her home for a sleepover."

"She needed somewhere to stay. It's not like she's a serial killer, Beau."

He pursed his lips. "I agree." Then he laughed at my expression. "Don't look so surprised. You've got good instincts. We did find a brick at Zack Fjord's feet, and glass inside the car, which confirms her story."

"Does this mean she can go home now?" I asked.

He shook his head. "I'm afraid not. None of the roads out of town are passable. We've got trees down, mudslides, and hip-deep rushing water. We've got calls into public works, but every crew in the county is already booked. It might be a few days. In the meantime, I'll be happy to drop her off at the gym on my way back to town."

"No need," I told him. "She can stay here a little while longer. We don't mind."

"Sounds like it's gonna get awful crowded up in here." He wiggled his eyebrows at me. "If you need to get away, you can always stay at my place."

"Nice try," I said. I leaned into him and gave him a peck on the cheek. "But she's staying in Mom's cottage."

"And Bea's okay with this?" he asked. Like my sisters Tansy and Maggie—whose full name was Magnolia—and me, my mother was named after a flower, the Begonia. Grandma was Rose. What could I say? We're suckers for a good tradition.

I shrugged. "I'm assuming she's with Marcus in Austin. Until the roads are clear or the phones are working, there's no way of knowing what she thinks."

"She's still a suspect."

"My mom?" I asked.

"You know that's not who I'm talking about," he said.

"Savannah's not a very good suspect." I didn't know her well enough to defend her innocence, but last night, she had seemed genuinely scared.

"Well, she's the only one we have right now," Beau said.

"What about that guy, what's his name?"

"Oh yeah, him," Beau deadpanned. "Can you be more specific?"

"The hockey player who got into a fight last night," I clarified.

"Miller?"

"No, the other one. Zack bragged that he dated his wife, while she was still married to him, remember?"

"Beckel," he said.

"Yeah, Beckel. He's a big dude with anger management issues, if the fight during the game was any indication. I bet he could throw a brick through a windshield, easy," I suggested. "Especially if he knew the passenger had slept with his wife."

"I doubt Beckel could throw anything right now. He could barely stand up after that fight, and he never did make it back into the game. I'll look into him, but I don't expect much will come of it."

"Thanks," I said. I couldn't tell if Beau was taking me seriously or not, but I appreciated the gesture.

"And Juni?"

"Yes?"

"That's the extent of your involvement in this case, okay? No more suspects. No more theories."

"Whatever you say," I agreed.

Beau took out his key ring and unwound one of the keys. He put it into my hand, and closed my fingers around it. "If you change your mind about needing someplace to stay," he said. "But do me a favor. Be careful, okay?"

"You know me," I told him.

"That's why I'm worried, Junebug. Seriously, whoever

killed Zack is probably running scared right now and if they feel backed into a corner, they could lash out again. Someone else could get hurt, and I don't want it to be you."

"Yeah, okay," I agreed, nodding to show I understood.

"I'm serious. This was no mere accident. A man is dead. That's manslaughter, at the very least. Worse, if the wreck was intentional. We'll know more once we catch the perp."

"Oh." I hadn't considered that. Whoever caused the wreck was responsible for Zack's death, even if that wasn't their original intention. "Good luck with that."

Beau let himself out of my bedroom. I heard muffled voices as he said goodbye to Savannah, and the sound of the front door opening and closing. Only then did I look down at the key in my hand.

I guess I was wrong. Apparently, we *were* at the key exchanging portion of the relationship, whether I was ready for it or not. I dropped the key into a shallow bowl on my dresser, next to my hairbrush, where I could deal with it later.

Savannah was hard at work doing dishes when I got back into the kitchen. "It's lucky you still have hot water," she said, scrubbing one of the muffin pans.

"Gas water heater and stove," I said, taking the pan from her to dry it before putting it back. "And good thing, too, or Edie couldn't have made all those muffins."

"She seems nice," Savannah said. She found a few muffin crumbs and fed them to the grateful dog. "She's your friend?"

"Friend. Neighbor. Honorary aunt to us, and everyone else in town," I explained. I looked down at the puggle, who had such a hopeful expression on her face. "We don't have any dog food, or cat food, come to think of it." We had plenty of cat food for Daffy at the shop, but in all the excitement last night, neither Tansy nor I thought to pack any for him. That was assuming he hadn't bolted the first chance he got.

I was still a tad surprised Savannah hadn't taken off this morning before the cops could question her. Then again, Beau had shown up unannounced and taken advantage of her being unprepared. He was good at that.

Maybe a similar sneak attack would work for me, too. "How'd you meet Zack?" I asked.

She took a deep breath before answering, "We've known each other forever. Family friends and all that."

"Ahh," I said. Back when we were in college, I'd gone to a party at Zack's house in Port Aransas, a beach town a few hours away. It was by far the nicest house I'd ever seen in person. It was only after I realized that it was just one of their many vacation houses that I figured out that Zack's family weren't just rich, they were loaded. If Savannah grew up with him, it stood to reason that her family was in the same tax bracket.

Zack had always been a lot. He'd worn a different expensive watch every day of the week and paid other students to take his tests for him. Savannah seemed a little more down-to-earth. At least she wasn't afraid to literally roll up her sleeves and do the dishes by hand. "And how long have you been partners?"

"I told you, it wasn't like that," she said defensively. "We weren't romantic."

"I meant business partners." I grabbed a stack of dry plates and shoved them into the cabinet, hiding my face so she didn't see my grin. Tansy was onto something. If Savannah and Zack weren't an item, why did she sound so defensive?

"Gosh, what is it, four, five years now? Zack had plenty of capital, and he was an absolute shark when it came to sniffing out businesses that were ripe with potential, but he, uh, lacked that certain, um, well, you know."

"It's okay, you can say it. He came off as a little obnoxious," I supplied.

"Zack wasn't a bad dude!" Savannah jumped to his defense. "He was a straight shooter. Didn't candy-coat things. Some people found that off-putting. So yeah, I was there to smooth things over and keep feathers from getting ruffled."

"I can see how you'd be very good at that," I told her. Her presence should be weird or awkward, but she fit in like she belonged, despite only having met her yesterday. "You up for some fresh air?" I clipped the leash to Buffy's collar and we stepped outside. I assumed that Edie had already taken her for a walk, but it would be good to stretch our legs and the last thing I wanted on top of everything else going on was to have to clean up after a puggle.

All over the neighborhood, trees were down. Bushes were uprooted. Lawns were under standing water. The sidewalk was covered in mud and debris.

"If you're the face of Fjord Capital, why is it Zack's last name on the company?" I asked as Buffy thoroughly sniffed every single blade of grass we passed.

"Like I said, he was the money guy. I mean, it was his daddy's money, but that well was bottomless, you know?"

No, I most certainly did not know. My parents gave me a lot of things. Love. Stability. An appreciation of music. Two wonderful sisters. But what they didn't have was money, much less the kind of money that could be described as "bottomless."

"You're easy to talk to," I told Savannah. "Zack could be a little overwhelming. Why, if you're the smoother-over, was Zack the one giving me and my sisters the hard sell for Sip & Spin?"

"Oh my goodness, don't even get me started," Savannah said. "We bickered for days about that. Three sisters with their own niche business in a cozy little town like Cedar River? I knew you ladies would never buy into Zack's brand of, um, well, you know."

As I unfurled a small bag from the container clipped to Buffy's leash to pick up after her, I assured Savannah, "Yeah. Trust me. I know."

"But Zack swore that you two had a 'connection.'"

"A connection?" I repeated.

"Because, I mean, because you two hooked up in college," Savannah said. At least she had the good sense to look sheepish.

"What?" I sputtered. I'd made some questionable decisions in my life but nothing like that. "First off, let me set the record straight. I have never hooked up with Zack Fjord. Not in college. Not before. And not since. We ran in the same circle for a hot minute when he was two-timing a friend of mine. But we never dated."

"Are you sure?" Savannah asked.

"Am I sure?" I nodded my head vigorously. "One hundred percent. Zack? Not my type. Besides, I was in what I thought at the time was a serious relationship all throughout college."

Savannah gave me a sly grin. "Oh please. You'd have me believe you dated the same guy for four straight years and never once strayed? Not even just a little?"

I realized she was teasing, but the implications cut deep. "More like six. I met my first boyfriend in high school. Fell hard. Dated him most of high school and all through college. Thought he was The One. I was twenty years old and ready to settle down and call it a day. So no, I didn't cheat on him. Not even 'just a little,' and especially not with a jerk like Zack."

I know, I know. I shouldn't speak ill of the dead. But the absolute nerve of this woman to accuse me like that.

I wanted to go back home and take a nice long shower to scrub that thought out of my head.

"What happened to Mister The One?" she asked, her voice still light. She had no idea how many bad memories she was stirring up.

"I got an offer to intern with my dream company out of state. He knew I wouldn't take it if we were together, so he broke up with me." I took a deep breath. That was his story, and I really did believe it. But it didn't make the hurt I'd felt at the time any less real. "Over a text," I added. Even if what he'd done was understandable, forgivable even, how he'd done it was not.

"Ouch. So you killed him and buried the body, obviously." A light went on in her eyes. "Oh my gosh, you know what you should do? You should sic that hot cop on him. I see the way he looks at you, like you're a chocolate bar and he's starving to death. When that Beau Russell is done with him, there won't be enough left of your ex to fill a bucket."

"I don't think that's a very good idea."

"Sure it is. Trust me." She pulled her phone out of her pocket and swiped to unlock it. Savannah had gotten so carried away with her revenge fantasies that she'd forgotten there was no cell service and no internet. "What's his name? I'll google him."

"Beau Russell," I said.

Her face fell. "Oh."

"Yeah. Oh." I wasn't sure if I wanted to laugh or cry, but one thing was for certain. Savannah certainly had a bloodthirsty streak when it came to avenging scorned women. I'd been mad at Beau for a long time for dumping me, but I'd never once fantasized about killing him.

Savannah might have been joking about murdering him and burying the body, but it seemed like a pretty tasteless thing to say when her business partner had just died. I was starting to wonder if she was as innocent as she appeared. Despite what I'd said to Beau earlier, Savannah was back on my list of suspects.

CHAPTER 7

As much as I suspected Savannah might be capable of playing avenging angel and killing Zack, I had a hard time wrapping my head around the logistics. Her story fit the evidence. The windshield was broken inward, and, according to Beau, the police found a brick by Zack's feet. Unless she'd put the car in park, jumped out of the car, hurled a brick through the windshield, jumped back in the driver's seat, and then deliberately crashed into Tansy's car, she was off the hook.

I needed to expand our suspect pool.

Fortunately or unfortunately, depending on how I looked at it, the pool was literally contained to Cedar River. While the storm was raging last night, driving conditions had been treacherous. I could personally attest to that. And now, between mudslides, downed trees, and the overall negligence to vital infrastructure like roads and bridges, Cedar River was cut off from the outside world. Beau had said as much this morning. The roads in and out of town were impassable.

With the roads closed, the person who killed Zack couldn't jump on the highway and disappear. There was a killer in our midst who had already struck once. I forced myself to see that as an opportunity. We were trapped in town with a killer, but at the same time, the killer was trapped in town with me.

Yes, I know I'm not a PI. I'm not a cop. I'm not a vigilante. I don't even own a car. But I do have a keen sense for a good mystery, a direct line into the local gossip mill, and two equally dogged sisters. Not to mention that I make a mean cup of coffee.

"Why Cedar River?" I asked Savannah as I trotted to keep up with Buffy. Apparently, the little dog had two speeds: slug and full throttle. It made conversation difficult.

"Why Cedar River, what?" Savannah asked in return.

I tried to recall the details of the proposal Zack had presented during one of the intermissions at the hockey game. "Y'all already invested in another record shop in Galveston," I started.

"Rhythm and Brews," she supplied helpfully.

"Yup. And a bar in San Antonio."

"Taps on Top," Savannah said.

"A lingerie store in Fort Worth."

"Undressed for Success," she said.

"Obviously, you're all over the map. How did Cedar River get on your radar?" I asked.

"Believe it or not, you're not the only mom-and-pop here that caught our eye. You know Blow Your Own Horn?"

"The musical instruments place owned by Frankie Hornsby?"

"Not exactly. Zack and I own a controlling interest," Savannah said.

"How is that possible? The Hornsbys have owned that place forever. I remember getting a flute from them when I was in middle school band," I said. I hated that flute. One semester in band had taught me a valuable life lesson. Just because I loved music didn't mean I was destined to make music. To be completely honest, that was the main reason I never tried to learn how to cook. I enjoyed eating too much to ruin the experience by failing as utterly in kitchen as I had in band.

"That's the thing with businesses," she said with a casual shrug. "One bad year can threaten decades of dedication, especially if you were just scraping by to begin with. Sometimes, an influx of capital from a small, motivated investor can mean the difference between living to fight another day and an everything-must-go sale because you've lost your lease."

"That's depressing," I said. She'd hit a chord. If Sip & Spin Records wasn't in exactly the same boat, we were at least in the same fleet. "I still can't believe the Hornsbys sold."

"Juni, that was nearly three years ago. Think about it. Not only is Blow Your Own Horn still in business, but you didn't even realize it was under new ownership because everything stayed exactly the same. That's what Zack and I offer . . ." I heard a hitch in her voice. Her face fell as it dawned on her that she was still giving the sales pitch even though, without Zack, there was nothing left to sell.

Ironically, she was now in the same desperate situation as many of the small businesses she sought out. I guess it's true that a really bad day can wreck years of hard work. I wondered if Fjord Capital would crumble without Zack, and what that meant for the businesses they'd invested in.

Tansy's house came into view. "If you'll excuse me," Savannah said. Without waiting for my reply, she made a dash for Mom's cottage. I didn't blame her. I wouldn't want to have a meltdown in front of a stranger, either, and she was overdue for one.

I looked down at the puggle, who was exhausted from

our walk. Her tongue was lolling out and it looked like she was ready for a long nap. "Looks like it's just you and me, kiddo," I said. I practically had to drag Buffy the last few feet into the house, where she collapsed on the tile and refused to move another inch.

With the dog sufficiently worn out and Savannah mourning the loss of her partner in the privacy of the cottage, I had work to do. I left a note for Savannah on the table in case she came out before I got back.

When I stepped outside, there was a man sitting on my front porch. His hair was dark, his shoulders were broad under a long-sleeved flannel shirt, and his smile was infectious. "Teddy!" I squealed as if I hadn't seen him in months instead of a day and a half. "I wasn't expecting to see you today."

I'd first met Teddy Garza a gazillion years ago, and we had been fast friends since about the time we were first learning our ABCs. Of course, back then, he was just a geeky little kid with too-big ears who liked to chase fireflies with me. I hadn't realized his romantic potential until recently, but he'd been one of my favorite people on the planet for about as long as I could remember.

These days he wasn't so little, geeks were cool, and he'd long since grown into his ears. Lanky Teddy was now a tall, lean Hispanic man with a rich tan and the longest eyelashes I'd ever seen. Ever since I'd moved back home to Texas, he was more interested in chasing me than fireflies. Which was just fine with me, because now that I'd started thinking of him as more than just a friend, I had half a mind to let him catch me.

Which, come to think of it, was the root of most of my problems, at least the relationshipy ones. My heart couldn't figure out what it wanted. Until it could, I was determined to straddle the line between the two very patient, and suspiciously understanding, men in my life.

"Howdy," he said in return, looking up at me with a slow smile. "I knocked. There was no answer, but your trike is still here so I thought I'd give it a few minutes."

"Sorry, I didn't hear you. The door's unlocked. You could have come in."

"I don't mind waiting for you," he said and I grinned back at him. Beau would have let himself in, grabbed a beer out of the fridge, and made himself at home—all without knocking first. Teddy was different. He was a gentleman. He reached out his arm toward me. "Lend me a hand?"

I took his hand. He got to his feet gracefully, without pulling against me for counterbalance. I looked down at our clasped hands. "You know, I'm starting to think you didn't need any help from me at all," I teased.

"Everyone wants to feel needed," he said, squeezing my hand before letting go. He dusted off his jeans. They were dirtier than they could have gotten just sitting on the bare porch.

"Everything okay at the farm?" I asked.

Teddy's family had run a dairy farm on the far edge of town since even before Texas was a state. These days, the Garza farm was mostly managed by his mother and his younger sister. Teddy didn't officially work on the farm, but he lived in an apartment over the garage and lent a hand whenever it was needed.

"Not bad," he said.

"And Buttercup?" Buttercup was a cow I'd accidentally adopted last spring. She was a very sweet cow, but I didn't have room for a cow in my sister's suburban backyard, so I'd gifted her to the Garzas. Every time I was at the farm, I made sure to say hi to her. Either she recognized me or she really liked my shampoo, because she always trotted up and tried to eat my hair.

"Buttercup is fine, but she misses you. A lot. She thinks

you ought to visit her more," he said with a sparkle in his eye.

"If I didn't know any better, I'd think you were making that up. Are you sure you're not the one that wants me to visit the farm, and you, more often?" I teased.

"Guilty as charged," he admitted.

"I'll keep that in mind. Don't get me wrong, I'm really glad to see you, but I'm surprised you made it into town," I said. "How were the roads?" The road out to his family's farm wasn't paved. It was a challenge to traverse on a normal day. I couldn't imagine what it was like after the storm.

"I drive it so often I could probably do it with my eyes shut," he said. "Even if the road gets washed out, that's what four-wheel drive is for."

"I thought with the weather last night, it would be all hands on deck at the farm," I said.

"It was a rough night, but no major damage. We got lucky. A couple of fences came down, but no cows got out and no one was injured. Plus, we're used to frequent power outages. Silvie convinced our folks to invest in solar a few years ago, and we haven't had a problem since." Silvie was Teddy's younger sister. She was also the future heir to the Garza farm, since Teddy had no interest in the dairy business. He surveyed my yard. "I knew y'all were on high ground, but I wanted to stop by to check in on you and bring you something."

"That's sweet, but you didn't have to do that," I said. That was just like Teddy. Even when he had his hands full, he always managed to make time for me. It had been like that even when we were kids, and he'd drop everything to help me with my math homework. To this day, I still didn't fully understand differential equations, but I'd passed the class, thanks to Teddy.

"Okey doke. I guess I'll just take this genny back to the farm then . . ." He turned and started to walk away.

I caught his elbow. "No need to be hasty."

A generator was worth its weight in gold during an extended power outage. We had banks of them at the hospital and other emergency services. Most average families that owned one would let their neighbors stop by to bask in their air-conditioning for an hour or two on a hot day, but they wouldn't just go giving them away.

"Oh, so you *do* need me?" he teased.

"Yes, Teddy, I need you. You're my knight in shining armor," I said. And I meant it. How had such a great guy been right under my nose practically my entire life, and I'd barely noticed him before recently? "Happy now?"

"Very," he said with a solemn nod.

I'd only been planning on going downtown to check on the shop to make sure we didn't take any damage in the storm. But now, with a generator, we could actually open, in a limited capacity at least. "Thanks for this. There's no telling how long it will take to get power back. Without power, we can't make coffee."

"Can't have that, now can we?"

"It would be a crime," I agreed. "I'll make you a deal. In exchange for loaning us the genny, I'll make a Cherry On, My Wayward Son just for you." Teddy preferred his caffeine the old-fashioned way: hot and black. He was the only person I knew who wouldn't even sample my creative coffee combinations. But if anything was going to tempt him, a chocolate cherry latte with a pinch of sea salt ought to do the trick. "If you're not in the mood for coffee, I can get you a There'll Be Teas When You Are Done, or if you're feeling adventurous, I could whip up a Don't You Chai No More."

"Sounds great, but plain coffee's fine. Come on, hop in." He gestured at the Jeep that was parked on the curb.

"Actually, I was planning on riding my trike downtown," I told him. With Tansy's car damaged in the crash last night, it wouldn't hurt to have reliable transportation readily available. My lime-green market tricycle was just what we needed. Not only was it good exercise and easy on the environment, but also, I didn't have to worry about whether or not the gas pumps were working.

"Suit yourself. See you at the shop?"

"I'm right behind you," I said. He got in his Jeep and headed downtown. I hopped on my trike and followed.

By the time I caught up to him, he was already parked behind the shop's rear entrance. The generator looked relatively new. It was mounted in a wheeled housing that made it easier to move, but it had to weigh two hundred pounds empty. Teddy had somehow managed to get it out of the Jeep by himself. He'd set it up by the back door and was adding fuel when I pulled up on my trike.

"Extension cord?" he asked. He'd been wrestling with the heavy generator, but barely sounded out of breath and hadn't broken a sweat. I'd only ridden a few miles from the house to the shop, but I'd been pedaling fast and I was winded.

"Coming right up."

I unlocked the back door. He followed me inside. I rummaged around the dark supply closet until I came up with a sturdy extension cord. "Will this work?"

"That'll do just fine."

He fired up the generator. It was a loud but welcome sound. Teddy connected the extension cord, and I plugged in our fancy barista machine.

I checked the shop and was happy that there was no real damage from the storm. After mopping up the puddles and drying the floor as best I could, I propped open the front door to let everyone know we were open for business. Before the first beans had brewed, we already had a line of customers. I handed the first cup to Teddy. "Thank you.

You're a lifesaver. We'll bring the genny back when we're done with it."

"No rush," he said. He glanced over at the waiting customers. "You think we'll have power restored in time for karaoke night or will you have to postpone?"

Back when our grandparents ran the shop, it was enough to sell records and the occasional poster. These days, that barely kept the doors open. The coffee café brought customers in. We relied on special events to bring in extra cash. Once every few weeks, we hosted Arts & Crafts nights, where we taught do-it-yourselfers how to re-purpose vinyl records as anything from bowls to wall art. But our real moneymaker was karaoke.

"I hope we go on as planned," I said. I didn't tell him how worried I was that the power outage was one more setback we couldn't afford. It was hard enough keeping the lights on—figuratively, if not literally—when everything was normal. "You gonna sing for us?"

"How else am I gonna impress you?" Teddy asked. "I was thinking 'Rock You Like a Hurricane.'"

I grimaced. "Too soon. After last night's storm, that might be in bad taste. How about 'Girls Just Want to Have Fun?' That's always a crowd-pleaser."

"Thanks for the suggestion. And the coffee." He tipped an imaginary hat at me and let himself out the back door.

"Okay folks," I said to the growing crowd. "No dairy today, so it's back to the basics." Frankly, it was a good thing Teddy had turned down the chocolate cherry latte. We had plenty of soy, rice, and coconut milk in shelf-stable cartons, but I didn't trust anything in the fridge since we hadn't had power all night. And Teddy, who'd spent his whole life on a dairy farm, was deeply suspicious of any milk substitute.

"Who wants a Never Gonna Give Brew Up?" I asked,

and got an enthusiastic response from the patiently waiting customers.

The first person in line wanted to know what was in a Never Gonna Give Brew Up. I explained that it was a simple drip coffee made with mild roast beans. When I asked if they wanted a small, medium, or Ariana Grande, they ordered the grande. How could they not?

We'd only been open a few minutes when one of our regulars dropped off a few big bags of ice he claimed were going to waste. I set a giant pitcher of tea to brew so I could add Sweet Dreams Are Made of Iced Teas to the menu.

Our customers usually paid with a touch of their phones or a swipe of their cards, which was problematic when the power was out. But my neighbors were resourceful. Those with cash paid for themselves and the next person in line, and those without promised an IOU. When word got out that we were low on fuel for the generator, a dozen gas cans showed up without me even asking.

Of course, not everyone who stopped in was looking for a caffeine fix. Apparently, what we lacked in options today we more than made up for with the local scuttlebutt. "Did you see the accident?" "Are you going to be okay?" "Is it true that that the passenger was knifed before the car wrecked?" "How are you going to get by without him?" "I think the driver did it, don't you?" were the most common questions I received.

"You should totally be more careful," Kennedy said when it was their turn at the front of the line. Kennedy ran the counter at the bakery across the street, as well as moderating several on-line conspiracy forums.

I braced myself for their latest colorful theory. "Careful?" I asked.

"When the men in black engineer a town-wide blackout, then shut down the roads in and out of town just so they can tighten the net around the alien invaders that have been hiding in Cedar River, you really shouldn't be drawing attention to yourself with that noisy generator."

"Oh, that kind of careful," I replied. I should be used to Kennedy's nonsense by now, but they never failed to surprise me. "Will that be cash?"

"Nah, that's how they track you," they replied.

"So you're gonna be paying for your coffee today with . . . ?" I let the question hang in the air.

Kennedy leaned closer and whispered conspiratorially. "With the most valuable currency in the universe. Information. Watch out for the shadows. That's where they like to hide."

"Okay then," I said, and poured a Sweet Dreams Are Made of Iced Teas. "Enjoy."

"You look like you could use a break," my sister's familiar voice said once Kennedy left. I'd been on my feet for a few hours, which wasn't unusual, but I was used to my sisters and me rotating in and out all day long. With Tansy running around with Miss Edie trying to feed the good folks of Cedar River and Maggie who-knows-where all morning, I had been on my own so far today.

I looked up and grinned. "Maggie! You're a sight for sore eyes."

My middle sister, as always, was in a pretty floral dress with short sleeves and a full skirt. Her hair was in perfect roller curls and her makeup made her look as fresh as the daisies on her dress. I, on the other hand, had my long hair pulled up in a rubber band I'd found in the drawer beneath the cash register, and I didn't want to look in a mirror.

"I hear you had an interesting night. Want to talk about it?" Maggie asked.

"Not really," I admitted. While Zack's death was the foremost thing on my mind right now, I was getting a little tired of playing question-and-answer with everyone in town. At least Kennedy's wild theory broke the monotony. "What I really need is a break." With the steady stream of customers, I hadn't been able to step away all morning.

"It's a shame. I was really rooting for you two crazy kids."

"Huh?" I asked her.

"Oh, poor Juni." Maggie sniffed, then hugged me. "I'm here for you."

"Really, I'm fine," I assured her. I had an idea why she was getting overly emotional. Maggie was the stereotypical middle child. FOMO was baked into her DNA. She and Tansy had been as thick as thieves growing up, but ever since I'd moved back and was staying with Tansy, I suspect that Maggie was jealous of the new closeness between me and our oldest sister, and was feeling left out that we'd found a body without her.

"If anything, it's happened so many times now I think I'm getting used to it." That was a little white lie. I'll admit it. But I didn't want Maggie to think she was being cheated out of some grand adventure. "I'll fill you in on all the gory details when the line dies down."

"Well, if you ask me, he got what he deserved."

I looked at my sister in shock. Maggie was one of the kindest, most big-hearted people I knew. She hadn't been Zack's biggest fan, because even more than Tansy or me, she was convinced that Sip & Spin was going to turn a profit sooner rather than later, and resented the idea of outside influences coming in and messing with our dynamic. But she'd never even met Zack. "I can't believe you'd wish that on anyone," I sputtered.

"Um, excuse me, can I order now?" The next person in line had gotten impatient and decided to assert themselves.

"Just one minute," Maggie said. "Juni?"

"You know what, we'll talk about it after my break." I

stomped off, feeling like a petulant teenager. I didn't understand my sister's reaction. Zack wasn't a saint. Yes, he was a privileged jerk who went around bragging that we'd hooked up in college even though we hadn't. He was a loudmouth who couldn't hold his beer and pawed at me during the game. But he didn't deserve to die.

Maggie turned to the next person in line. "Coffee or tea?" she asked pleasantly.

I rolled my eyes. Maggie really had everyone fooled. And here I was, thinking Savannah was the bloodthirsty one.

I navigated around the record aisles, ducking a volley of questions from customers milling around. It felt weird that we had no music going. I'd thought about hooking one of the record players up to the generator, but I was worried about drawing too much power. In the end, the line was noisy enough that we probably couldn't have heard the music anyway.

Outside, there was a crispness in the air that promised apples and pumpkins and homecoming dances. I took a deep breath, willing myself to think of haunted hayrides and pumpkin spiced everything instead of dead financiers in BMWs. It didn't work. I found myself staring at the spot where his car had collided with Tansy's.

There was no sign of last night's activity. The storm had washed it all away as if it had never happened. I wished I could do the same with my memories. I turned to walk away from the scene and smacked right into Teddy again.

He'd changed since I'd seen him this morning, swapping his jeans and flannel for an official Cedar River mail carrier uniform. He had a mail sack slung over his shoulder. I had to admit it was a good look on him, but then again, I always had liked a man in uniform.

"Fancy bumping into you again," I said. "They got you working?"

He nodded. "I assumed we'd be closed today, but you know what they say. Rain, snow, yadda, yadda, yadda. Hey, I'm just about finished with my downtown route. Wanna come with and keep me company?"

"Sure. I'd love to," I agreed. He dug into his bag and pulled out a bundle of letters, flyers, and other advertisements, all addressed to Sip & Spin Records. The mail was neatly organized with a rubber band identical to the one currently holding my hair back. He handed it to me. "Such service."

"Just doing my job. Walk with me." We matched each other's pace down the sidewalk toward the next business. Teddy had gone to school for environmental engineering, but found his true calling in delivering packages to the good folks of Cedar River. He said it was the only job he could think of that let him be outside all day, surrounded by people instead of cows. "Be right back."

He ducked into Boot Scootin', the dance studio next to Sip & Spin. I watched through the window as the instructor taught a bunch of folks around my mom's age line dancing. Teddy dropped the mail on the counter, waved at the instructor, and came back out. When the door opened, I could hear a familiar country song playing from the boom box in the middle of the room.

"Everyone said streaming music was the way of the future," I told Teddy. "But look at us now, scrambling to find a bunch of D batteries for our old tape decks."

"What is it you're always saying about vinyl records?" he asked me. "Everything old is new again? Speaking of out with the old, I hear you finally came to your senses and told Beau Russell to take a hike. Good riddance. Can't say I'll miss having him around."

"Huh?" I asked. Back when I first started dating Beau in high school, Teddy hadn't been his biggest fan. Eventually, it drove a wedge into our friendship. Now that I was back home and casually dating both of them, he wasn't enthusiastic about sharing me with Beau any more than Beau liked sharing me with Teddy, but up until now, they'd both managed to be civil about the arrangement. I wonder what had changed.

"Hold that thought." Teddy stepped into the next storefront. When he returned, he picked up the conversation again. "Rumor has it y'all had a knock-down drag-out at his apartment last night."

I shook my head. "How do these things get started? There was an, um, incident at Sip & Spin last night, after the power went out. I went to Beau's to get his help. Banged on his door a couple of times. He wasn't home. But his partner was. She took care of everything. Did you know that Jayden Holt lives across the hall from Beau?"

Teddy gave me a sympathetic smile. "Juni, I'm the mail carrier. I know where *everyone* lives."

"Oh. Yeah. Right." I liked to think of myself as basically honest and forthright. Which was why I was completely up-front when I realized I couldn't—or didn't want to—choose between sweet, easygoing Teddy and foxy, charismatic Beau. But it was times like this I was relieved I'd never considered sneaking around with either of them. Between Beau's detecting skills and Teddy's access to absolutely everything that went on in town, I would have been caught in a heartbeat.

"So you and Beau didn't get into a fight and break up?" he asked, his customary grin slipping.

I shook my head and grimaced. "Sorry, no." That might have made things easier, I admitted to myself, but I never had been the kind of person who took the easy way out.

"I knew it sounded too good to be true. One sec." Teddy stepped into the last storefront on the block. Standing there on the corner, I watched a steady stream of traffic turn on and off Main Street. There had been talk of putting a stoplight up at this intersection, but now I was glad it had never made it through the town council. Without power, there would probably be a bunch of cars driving all willy-nilly without the stoplight telling them what to do. Thank goodness for good old-fashioned stop signs.

"Why Miss Jessup, I was hoping I'd bump into you," a woman said as she walked toward me, dragged behind an enormous black Great Dane.

"Mayor, you're looking well," I said. Mayor Leanna Lydell-Waite was on the beauty pageant circuit back in the day with my sister Tansy. Even now, heavily pregnant and walking the dog in her sweats, she looked like she'd just stepped out of the glossy pages of a fashion magazine. "Hey, Hamlet, how's my buddy?"

The big dog nuzzled my hand and then started sniffing my shoes with interest.

"Miss Edie and her dog are staying with us. He probably smells Buffy on me," I explained.

"That's actually what I wanted to talk to you about. I pulled a couple of strings and have some engineers coming in later this afternoon to give the all-clear before we let everyone back into the lower-lying neighborhoods. Can you pass that info along to Edie, your uncle, and anyone else you know that lives on that side of town?"

"Sure will, but how'd you get the engineers in if the roads are blocked?" I asked.

"A bunch of folks showed up with chainsaws this morning and took care of the downed trees. Some of the ranchers brought in their skid steers and cleared up the mudslide. Roads aren't great, but most of them are passable."

"That's great. You know, a couple months in office and you've already done more than the previous mayor's twelve-year stint."

Leanna flapped her hand dismissively. "I can't take

credit. It was everyone pulling together." Teddy came out and joined us on the sidewalk. "And a good day to you, Mr. Garza. Has Juni been regaling you with tales of her adventures last night?"

"Adventures?" Teddy asked with a furrowed brow. I guess he wasn't as tuned in with the town gossip as I'd assumed.

"You know our Juni, always getting herself in trouble," she said. "Y'all have a good one." She took off down the sidewalk with Hamlet, the Great Dane, in tow.

"Adventures?" he repeated to me, as soon as she was out of earshot.

I took a deep breath. "Last night, during the storm, a man died outside of Sip & Spin. That's why I needed Beau and Jayden's help."

Teddy nodded. "I see. And when I stopped by this morning with the genny, you didn't think to mention that you stumbled across yet another dead body?"

"I was so happy to see you that it must have slipped my mind," I confessed. "Besides, you didn't ask," I added with an exaggerated shrug.

"Well, that'll teach me. You okay?"

"Not exactly," I admitted.

"Want to talk about it?"

I shook my head. "Not really. I'd rather not think about it, to be honest."

"If you change your mind, I'm here," he offered.

"Thanks. I don't get it. Every tongue in town is wagging about a death that I want absolutely zero to do with, and all you hear are rumors about some fight between me and Beau that didn't even happen? What's wrong with the rumor mill around here?"

"Maybe we should try turning it off and then turning it back on again?" Teddy suggested.

And then everything clicked.

"Are you going to be okay?"

"How are you going to get by without him?"

"It's a shame. I was really rooting for you two crazy kids."

The gossip mill was hit-or-miss on a good day, but with the normal channels of communication knocked out along with the power, all the wild stories flying around were even more mixed-up than normal. Well, maybe not Kennedy's stories, but their theories about Bigfoot and alien abduction were pretty far out there even on a good day.

Half the town was gossiping about Zack's death and the other half was talking about Beau and me supposedly breaking up. I hadn't realized there were two completely different rumors about me making the rounds. Which meant Maggie might not be as hard-hearted as I'd thought. "I gotta go," I told Teddy. I gave him a quick peck on the cheek, then took off in a sprint back toward Sip & Spin.

CHAPTER 8

I burst into Sip & Spin and bypassed the line as I hurried to the back of the shop. "I'm so sorry!" Maggie and I said at the same time, and then we both burst out laughing.

"I heard you and Beau broke up," she said. "I didn't realize someone was dead."

"Beau and I didn't have a fight. A man was killed outside the shop," I said at the same time.

"I told you he got what he deserved!" Maggie said. She clasped her hands over her mouth. "You must have thought I was a monster."

"The thought did cross my mind," I admitted. "Wait a second. I thought you *liked* Beau?"

"I do, but I like my baby sister more," Maggie said. "And I don't want to see you get hurt."

"I just assumed you were talking about Zack."

"Wait, Zack? Zack Fjord? That pushy finance creep you went to college with? What does he have to do with any of this?"

Instead of answering, I gave my sister a beat to put it all together. Her eyes went wide.

"No!"

I nodded. "Yeah."

"Sorry folks, but we're gonna take a quick break," Maggie said, projecting her voice to the people in line.

"Come on, I've been waiting forever," one of the people grumbled. I recognized the speaker as Jen Rachet, town gossip extraordinaire. Jen loved our coffee, but she loved the information she picked up from hanging out at Sip & Spin even more.

Come to think of it, she'd been in line when I left to take a break. I hadn't been gone long, but the rest of the customers who had been in the shop when I left had been served and had gone on their way, only to be replaced with new customers. All but Jen.

"You're not even in line," I said. I walked around the corner and pointed at her hand. She was holding an empty cup. "I served you less than an hour ago. You've just been loitering, hoping to hear something juicy."

"Well, I'll be. Is that any way to talk to a loyal customer?" she asked, puffing herself up.

"Gee, Jen, I'm sorry for the mix-up," Maggie said, maneuvering around me. "I just need a quick second with my little sis. We'll be back before you know it. But how about I get you a refill, on the house, for the road?" She snatched Jen's cup and handed it to me. I poured her a refill and passed it back. "Okay now, have a great day!" Maggie said as she ushered Jen and the rest of the patrons out the front door.

She thumbed the lock to closed and slid the "Back in 5 minutes" sign into place before turning to me. "That woman. I swear she lives for trouble."

"Right?" I agreed.

"Start from the very beginning," Maggie demanded.

"Do I have to?" I'd told the story so many times I wasn't sure I could keep it straight anymore.

"Yes. You absolutely do."

"Fine." I settled myself at one of the tables near the window overlooking Main Street. "Pull up a chair." I told her everything, or at least everything I could remember.

"And now this Savannah lady is staying in Mom's cottage?"

"I just told you that a man was killed right outside Sip & Spin. A man we know. A man that was trying to buy us out. And that's what you're hung up on?"

"It's Mom's cottage. And where is she, anyway? Have you heard from her? Should we be worried?" Maggie asked.

"Her car's not at home. With all the time she's been spending with Marcus lately, I assume she's with him. And no, she hasn't sent a pigeon to let us know she's okay, but I'm sure she is," I said.

Maggie might be the romantic of the family, but in her opinion, the only romance Mom was allowed was the one she shared with Dad. I'll admit I was a little sus of Marcus when I first met him, but he really did care about our mom. He made her happy, so who was I to stand in their way? My middle sister did not agree.

"You said the roads are passable now. So, let's go see for ourselves," she suggested.

"Sure thing. Just one problem," I said. "Do you know Marcus's address?"

She shook her head. "Of course not."

"Neither do I. Phones are down. I can't even google him. How exactly do you propose that we drop by his house when we have no idea where he lives?"

"The phone book!" Maggie exclaimed.

"The phone book? Really? When's the last time you even saw a phone book?"

Maggie propped her elbows on the table. "Is this what the world's come to?"

"Yup," I said.

"You're really not worried?"

"I'm really not," I told her, but in the very back of my head, I knew she had a point. It was kinda scary not knowing where Mom was, or if she was safe after last night's storm. "Look, I've got an idea about how we can get ahold of her, okay?"

"Really?"

"Really." I knew exactly who to ask for help. "While I do that, do you mind looking into Fjord Capital a little deeper?"

"Why?" Maggie asked. "We all agreed that we weren't interested, and now with Zack gone, the offer's off the table, right?"

"Right, but I'm having a hard time understanding how the whole investment model works," I admitted. "You always were better with numbers and contracts than I am."

"You think Zack was killed over a contract?"

"I don't think we can rule that out as a possibility," I hedged. "Historically, most people are killed over love or money. Zack's a money guy . . ." I trailed off.

"Of course. I printed out a copy of their proposal." She began rummaging through the drawers below the checkout counter where we kept miscellaneous items like pens and sticky notes. "It should be around here somewhere."

"Thanks, sis. And can you mind the shop a little while longer?"

Maggie nodded. "Of course."

She unlocked the front door and removed the "Back in 5 minutes" sign. I went out back, where my trike was parked, and headed to the police station for the second time in as many days. This time, the clerk let me in to see Beau right away.

When I appeared in his doorway, a slow grin spread across his face. "Well, lookie who's dropping in on me at work. Aren't we supposed to be broken up or something?"

"You heard that rumor, too?" I asked.

"Apparently, we had quite the row last night at my

place. And now you're here to kiss and make up?" he asked, hopefully.

"Not exactly."

Hearing the seriousness in my voice in response to his teasing, he stood. "Tell me you didn't find another dead body. Because you've already exceeded your quota for the month."

"There's a quota?" I asked. "What is it?"

"For you? None. Your quota is none."

As I sat down in one of the chairs in front of his desk, he sat back down. I thought about what he'd said at the hockey game about me being a convenient suspect since I always ended up in the middle of murder investigations. At least he wasn't investigating me. Yet. That I knew of. "Zero doesn't seem very fair."

"Life isn't fair, Junebug. But seriously, my hands are kinda full right now . . ." He let the unspoken question of what I was doing at his office hang in the air.

I realized that as often as he visited me at Sip & Spin or walked into my kitchen like he owned the place, this was my first time ever barging in on him at work. "Any chance you've got an update on the brick-and-run case for me?"

He gave me a steely glare. "You know I can't comment on active investigations."

"Never hurts to ask," I said brightly. "But the real reason I came to see you is I need your help finding Marcus Best."

"Used car salesperson Marcus Best?" he asked. "Your mom's boy toy Marcus Best?"

I cringed. "Please, never say 'my mom' and 'boy toy' in the same sentence ever again."

"Noted. Why?"

"Why don't I ever want to hear the word 'boy toy' in

connection with my mother?" I asked. Just because I accepted that she was an adult who deserved to be happy didn't mean I wanted to think of her with a boy toy. "That should be self-explanatory."

He laughed. "No, not that. Why do you want to find Marcus Best?"

"Because I haven't heard from Mom since before the storm. I'm sure she's fine, but what if she's not?"

He nodded. "That's fair. And I'd love to help, but I don't see how."

"Don't you have, like some kind of database? Of people's addresses and stuff?"

"You mean, like a phone book?"

"Yes," I said sheepishly.

"The database is down. And no, we don't have a phone book."

"Don't you have an UPS?" I asked. Like most techies, I pronounced it as a single word, "ups," not three separate letters.

"U-P-S? I'm pretty sure we're not going to get any packages until the rest of this mess is sorted out."

"No, not U-P-S, the delivery service, UPS, as in 'uninterruptible power supply.' Battery backups for computers and servers," I explained. Sometimes I forgot that not everyone was a computer nerd like me. Before I'd invested everything to run a record store with my sisters, I'd been a software developer. I had more experience with coding and computer languages than I did with hardware and operating systems, but I knew my way around a server room.

Beau made a motion with his hand, waving it over his head. "You forget. While you and all the other smart kids were in computer club, I was getting hit in the head with footballs and football players."

"I was never in computer club," I protested. "Chess club. Model UN. Academic Decathlon." Come to think of it, Teddy was in all those clubs with me. "But not computer club."

"Whatever. Let me go introduce you to the geek squad. Maybe they'll understand you."

It turned out that the Cedar River P.D. tech department consisted of one sixty-year-old former janitor who had tech support on speed dial for a dozen different companies, and a part-timer they shared with three other police stations. The part-timer was in Round Rock today. "What's your UPS situation?" I asked the on-site tech.

He blinked at me. "Not sure U-P-S or FedEx is getting through until they clear the roads, but I hear the post office is open."

I mentally slapped my forehead. "Can you show me your server room?"

He looked over at Beau.

Beau nodded. "Go ahead."

"Sure, whatever."

The server room wasn't much more than a closet. When I got inside, every machine in the rack was beeping and flashing, and it felt like a sauna. "Let me guess, your air handler's not hooked up to the generator?"

"Genny's for emergencies only," he said lazily.

"Okay, so a town without power and a police force without any kind of tech doesn't constitute an emergency, I guess." I walked around reading the labels on the servers. "You've got a choice to make," I told him. "We can get all the servers up, but without the AC running, they're going to overheat and fry the circuits. Or we can gracefully power everything down and hope there's nothing on any of these servers that anyone needs for the next who-knows-how-long until power is restored. Which is it?"

He shrugged. "How should I know?"

One of the big UPS battery units stopped beeping, and an entire rack of servers went dark. "So much for gracefully powering down," I muttered. The final remaining UPS beeped once more and died. The last few remaining servers turned off. It was now completely silent and pitch black in the server closet. "Well, on the plus side, you don't need to worry about the temperature anymore," I said, backing out of the room. "But you should really think about moving to the cloud."

I left him standing in the open door as I retraced my steps back to Beau's office. "Any luck?" he asked.

"Does bad luck count?"

"I take that as a 'no'?"

"Take that as a 'you need to reassess your computer support situation.'"

"Any chance you want the job?" he offered. "It comes with benefits." He winked.

I shook my head. "Tempting, but I've got my hands full at Sip & Spin. Besides, I'm a coder, not a cabler. You need a good sysadmin."

"I have no idea what any of that means. Maybe you can help us with interviewing some additional tech support?" Beau asked.

"That I can do," I agreed.

"Sorry you didn't get what you needed." He stood and walked around his desk. He picked up his cowboy hat from the rack next to the door. "Come on, let's hit the road."

"Where are we going?" I asked. "I didn't find Marcus's address."

"Nope. But we know where his dealership is, right? We pop on by, I flash a badge and ask for his home address. Or, if that doesn't work, we'll pay a visit to Austin P.D. They're bound to have better IT support than we do. Maybe one of their databases will point us in the right direction."

"You'd do all that for me?" I asked.

"Yeah, Juni, I'd do all that for you," he said, as if it were the most obvious thing in the world. Then he added, "But you're buying dinner."

"Deal," I agreed.

I followed him back to the lobby, where I heard a familiar voice raised in anger. "Yes, I heard you loud and clear. I just don't think you're hearing me. You're gonna let my daughter go right this very minute or you'll regret the day you put on that uniform!"

I looked at Beau. "I'm thinking that trip won't be necessary." Then I hurried into the lobby, where my mother looked like she was fixing to strangle the poor clerk. "Mom! Calm down!"

She looked at me and blinked like she'd just seen a ghost. "Juniper!" She ran over and threw her arms around me, squeezing me until I thought I would pop. When she finally let me go, she looked over her shoulder at the confused clerk. "Now that's what I'm talking about." She held me at arm's length. "They treat you okay in there?" She turned to Beau. "And you? What were you thinking? Treating my daughter like a common criminal."

"Mrs. Jessup, let's talk outside, shall we?" Without waiting for her to agree, Beau steered us to the exit. Once outside, he reached over to shake Marcus's hand. "Marcus, nice to see you. And Bea, you too."

"Don't you Bea me," my mom said, still looking like she was going to spit fire. "I can't believe you had the nerve to arrest my baby."

"Mom, calm down. No one was arrested."

"But Jen Rachet said . . ."

I cut her off. "Mom. Really? She's lying."

"You weren't arrested?"

"Not even close," Beau said. "If anything, Juni was a witness." I elbowed him in the ribs and he let out a pained puff of air.

"A witness to what, exactly?" Marcus asked.

"Hey, can we not hash this out in the police station parking lot?" I suggested. "Beau, thank you very much for your help, but I think the situation is resolved."

"Situation?" Mom asked.

"That's my cue to go," Beau said before going back inside.

"Juniper, what's going on?" Mom asked.

I took a deep breath and repeated the story for the fifth—or was it the sixth?—time for Mom and Marcus. Before today, I'd always hated the family chat thread. My phone beeping thirty-seven times a minute because of everyone's responses and reactions had seemed excessive until now. What I wouldn't give to have been able to summarize the last twenty-four hours into a single text, hit send, and be done with it.

"And this Savannah woman is staying in my cottage?" Mom asked.

"That's what you got out of that story?" I asked, repeating the question I'd asked Maggie in the same situation and rubbing my temples, where a headache was forming. No one seemed to care that a man was dead and the person responsible was in the wind. "If you'll excuse me, I need to go let the dog out."

"What dog?" she asked. "When did you get a dog?"

Instead of answering, I jumped on my trike and peddled away before she could stop me. I wasn't sure if Miss Edie, or Buffy, would be at the house when I got there. I wasn't even a hundred percent certain Daffy would be home. After the night he'd had, I wouldn't blame him if he made himself scarce for a while. Either way, after making sure my mother was fine, I needed a bit of a break from all humans. But I couldn't go home empty-handed. The grocery store was closed, but Sip & Spin was on the way.

Wanting to avoid Jen Rachet and anyone else who might

be lying in wait, I peddled down the alley. It was eerily silent. It took me a minute to realize what was wrong. The constant hum of the generator was gone.

I parked my trike and headed in the back door. "Hello?" I called out. The sun was starting to set and it was getting dark inside the shop.

"Hello!" Tansy called back.

Both of my sisters were in the shop. Maggie was cleaning the barista station. Tansy was counting the bills in the cash register. "It got too dark in here to see, so we decided to close early," Maggie said as she scrubbed the hard-to-reach places.

"We should drop that by the bank," I suggested. Normally, most of our sales came from credit cards, and it made me nervous to see that much cash on hand.

"Bank's closed because of the power outage," Tansy said.

"The night drop isn't," Maggie said. "Here, I'll fill out the deposit slip if you'll finish cleaning the machine." They swapped places smoothly. Running the shop had become an easy routine for all three of us, and while we each had our primary responsibilities, most of the jobs were interchangeable.

"Mom and Marcus are back in town," I said.

"That's a relief," Maggie replied.

I looked at Tansy. "What about Miss Edie?"

"As soon as she got the all-clear, I drove her home to pick up Buffy before dropping her at her house. The carpet's a loss and she might need some new baseboards, but it could have been worse."

"It certainly could have been," Maggie agreed. We all watched the news. We've seen earthquakes, wildfires, hurricanes, and ice storms destroy homes all over the country. Sometimes, it felt like we were living in the first fifteen minutes of a disaster movie.

"And Calvin's house?" Our uncle lived across the street from Edie. He and his best friend Samuel were off at a fishing tournament at Lake Palestine. They never checked their phones when they were off on one of their adventures, much to the chagrin of their friends and family. They probably didn't even know about the storm yet.

"About the same," Tansy said. "I popped my head in and took a look around. There's water damage, but nothing insurance won't cover. Frankly, it's about time he got new carpet. That shag in his living room needed to go."

"Agreed," Maggie said. "And Savannah?"

Tansy shrugged. "She wasn't at the house. I thought she was with you, Juni."

I shook my head. "Haven't seen her since this morning. She was in the cottage when I left. I think she's having a hard time dealing with the death of her partner."

"As can be expected," Maggie said. "What should we do about the generator?"

"Teddy said we could keep it as long as we need it, but we ought to bring it inside for the night." My sisters followed me to the back door.

"Looks heavy," Maggie said. She reached for her phone before stopping herself. "I was gonna call J.T. and ask for a hand," she said with a chuckle.

"And where has my favorite brother-in-law been all day?" I asked. Maggie was right, it would be easier to muscle this inside with a few extra hands, but it was nothing we couldn't manage. Plus, it didn't hurt that it was on wheels. We only had to lift up one end and push it, not drag the whole thing by ourselves.

"Everyone with a working chain-saw, shovel, or ATV, J.T. included, has been clearing debris since the rain stopped," Maggie said.

"That's nice of them," Tansy said.

"Sure is," I agreed. J.T. had never struck me as the

chain-saw-and-shovel type. He was more the three-piece-suit type. He didn't mind getting his hands dirty, metaphorically, in the courtroom but when it came to mowing the lawn, he hired someone to do that for him. Learning that he didn't hesitate to roll up his sleeves and pitch in when the town needed him made him an even more perfect match for my middle sister.

Together, we got the generator inside far enough that we could shut the door.

"I better get a move on," I said. I didn't usually mind riding my tricycle at night. In fact, I loved it. Between the cooler temps and less traffic on the road, it was the perfect time for me. But with all the streetlights and porch lights I'd come to rely on out, and Zack's killer on the loose, I wanted to make it home before it got much darker. Before I left, I grabbed a stack of cat food cans and a bag of litter for Daffy and stowed it in the market basket behind the seat.

"Later," I called out to my sisters before taking off.

The ride home was quieter than normal. With nothing better to do, it seemed like the whole town of Cedar River had collectively decided to turn in early. Last night's clouds had dissipated and the stars were out in full force. With no haze from streetlights or nearby Austin light pollution, I could pick out clusters I normally couldn't see. It was beautiful and serene, at least until the coyotes started to serenade me.

CHAPTER 9

By the time I pulled up to the house, I was out of breath. I knew the coyotes hadn't actually been chasing me. It just sounded like that. Coyotes wouldn't go after a full-grown adult, not on a big, noisy tricycle. Or, at least that's what I told myself as I peddled faster than I ever had before.

"You okay?" a voice drifted out from the darkness of the covered front stoop as I wheeled my trike up the driveway. I saw Savannah stand and stretch. "You look like you just saw a ghost."

"Just spooked myself, I guess," I admitted. "What about you? Are you alright?"

"As good as one can be under the circumstances." I noticed she was holding Daffy. "This your cat?"

I nodded, then realized she probably couldn't see me in the dark. "That's Daffy. He doesn't usually like strangers."

"Cats love me."

The fact that Daffy liked her was a point in her favor. Cats were usually very good judges of character. "I left the door unlocked for you so you could come and go."

"I know, but I wasn't sure if the cat was allowed inside, so I hung out here with him."

"Come on inside," I offered. "Both of you." I grabbed

the litter and cat food and opened the front door. I'd hated to leave it unlocked, especially with everything that was going on and no way to call for help if there was an intruder, but I hadn't wanted to lock Savannah out either. Like the rest of us, she didn't have a phone. She also didn't have a car or know anyone else in town.

Or was that really the case? "This morning, when we were talking, you mentioned how Fjord Capital was the majority owner of the local musical instrument shop," I said, trying to not sound like I was interrogating her.

"Did I?" Savannah asked.

I opened a can of cat food. Daffy jumped up on the counter and meowed loudly. At least my fears that he'd run away and never come back were unfounded. "Blow Your Own Horn?" I prodded. "Frankie Hornsby's place?"

"Oh, yeah. Guy's kinda an odd duck but he knows his way around an instrument."

"Have you invested in any other local businesses I might have heard of?"

"Why?" Savannah sounded suspicious. "Have you changed your mind about taking on an investor?"

"I don't know," I said. "I'm on the fence about the whole idea."

"Well, it's too late now," she said. "With Zack out of the picture, there is no more Fjord Capital."

"And what happens to the businesses you've already invested in?" I asked.

"Everything reverts back to the Fjord family."

"What? That doesn't sound fair. Aren't the Fjords already one-percenters?" The Fjords weren't just rich. They were the kind of rich that took their helicopter to their yacht to take them out to their bigger yacht rich. When Zack was doing poorly in school, his family paid for a new library and suddenly, he was making straight As rich.

She moved to the fridge and opened the door. "I don't

know why I'm surprised that the light didn't come on," she muttered to herself. She fished around and pulled out a beer, which was room temperature by now. "Want one?"

"I'm good. I'll get some candles." We kept a box of them in the pantry for emergencies. I lit one and placed it on the kitchen table. I lit a few more and lined them up along the counter. It gave the kitchen a nice glow. "Have you eaten?" I asked her. I hadn't had anything since Miss Edie's muffin at breakfast, and I was not in the habit of missing meals.

"I don't have an appetite," she said, picking at the label on her beer. I handed her a bottle opener magnet from the refrigerator. "Thanks."

"I do. Mind if I fix something?"

"Knock yourself out," she said.

While I pulled out the fixings for a sandwich, I wondered if I should make enough for the rest of the family. Where was Tansy? Mom? Marcus? That thought stopped me in my tracks. When had I started thinking of Marcus Best as family?

"Juni?" Savannah asked.

"Huh?"

"You kinda zoned out there for a second."

"Sorry about that." I realized that I was standing frozen with a jar of mustard in one hand and a dinner knife in the other. I started assembling my sandwich. "Where were we? Oh yeah, you were telling me about how all the businesses revert back to the Fjord family."

"We were twenty/eighty partners," she explained. "Zack provided the cash, so he was the eighty, naturally."

"Naturally," I agreed.

"Sometimes that worked out in my favor. Sometimes it didn't."

"How is that ever good for you?" I asked. From what I could tell, Zack was investing his father's money, not his own. They were both contributing to the business. It didn't seem fair that they weren't equal partners.

"Take Cedar River Casuals. You know it?"

I shook my head. "Can't say that I do. Is it new?"

"Nope. Just the opposite. It used to be a dress boutique owned by the Elbys. Jackson, and his wife, um, Liz? No, Sheila."

"Name doesn't ring a bell. Cedar River Casuals, you said?"

"That's funny, it was right where your record shop is now. Folded about nine months ago. Soon after that, you and your sisters took over the lease."

"Fortunate timing," I mused.

My grandparents once leased that very storefront for the original family record shop. I knew that the space had hosted a lot of tenants since then, but I hadn't thought about it much. My sister Maggie thought the location was cursed. Tansy was too sentimental to care even if it was. I personally thought it was kismet that the exact storefront opened up right when vinyl was making a comeback, and just as I got laid off from my old job and was able to move back home. Though I'd be willing to bet Jackson Elby wasn't quite as pleased about the timing as I was.

"For you, maybe. When Casuals folded, Zack took a bath. I mean, Jackson and Sheila did, too, but honestly that place was in such bad shape before we came in, it's a wonder it lasted as long as it did."

"And you?" I asked.

She shrugged. "I didn't have any skin in the game. I didn't make money on the deal, so there's that, but I didn't lose any, either."

"We should go talk to this guy. Sounds like someone who might have reason to throw a brick at your car."

"Don't worry about him," she said. "Jackson's harmless."

"How can you be so sure?"

She shrugged. "What's in it for him? Even if he carried a grudge, Zack's death wouldn't bring his shop back. We're all empty-handed now."

I wished Maggie was here to help me make sense of the financial aspect. "What you're telling me is that with Zack gone, the investments dry up and you end up with nothing?"

Savannah let out a distinctively unladylike snort. "That's putting it mildly. Not only have I lost my partner, but everything I've worked so hard for over the last few years is gone. And now I've got to figure out a way to start all over again." She shook her head. "I'm just so tired. I don't know if I have it in me to start from scratch again."

"I'm sorry." It was unfortunate for her, but it also made her look innocent. She had no motive. Savannah was better off with Zack alive than she was with him dead.

"Not your fault I hitched myself to the wrong wagon." She clinked her empty beer bottle down on the table.

"You want another?" I asked, reaching for the fridge.

"No, thanks. I think I'll just turn in for the night." It was hard to tell without clocks and televisions and cell phones, but it couldn't have been much later than eight p.m. "Mind if I take one of those candles with me?"

"Help yourself," I told her. "Want me to walk you over to the cottage?" It was only a few yards away from the front door, but the thought of coyotes still had me spooked, and I wasn't the one who'd had a brick thrown at them less than twenty-four hours ago.

"I'm fine." She rubbed Daffy's head. "'Night, cat." She took her candle and left.

I got up and locked the door after her. Then I finished my sandwich. I was doing the dishes when Tansy came home. "Where've you been?" I asked her. "I was sure you'd beat me home."

"We stopped by to check on Miss Edie, and got to visiting."

"What are we going to do about Savannah?" I asked.

Tansy pulled back the curtain to get a better look at the cottage. We could see a light moving about, probably the candle I'd given her. "Marcus's power has been restored already, so he and Mom are going to stay there. They offered to let us stay with them, of course. I'm sure we can find room for Savannah, too."

"I'm good here," I said. What was more inconvenient? Being without power for a couple more days or sleeping on my mother's boyfriend's couch? "You can go if you want, but I'll stay here with Daffy."

"Personally, I'd rather sleep in my own bed tonight and I'll reassess in the morning. But since Mom's in Austin, Savannah is welcome to stay here another night."

"About Savannah," I said. "I don't think she killed Zack."

"I don't either," Tansy agreed. "If I did, I never would have welcomed her into my home."

"But someone killed Zack."

"Juni . . ." she said with a warning tone. "We are *not* getting involved in this. And we don't even know for sure his death wasn't an accident."

"Did someone mean to kill him?" I asked. "I don't know. But a man—a man we know—is dead and someone's at fault. He was killed outside our shop and his partner is staying with us. We're already involved, like it or not."

"A man *you* know," she pointed out. "I never even talked to him."

"Exactly. I've known him for ages, ever since college. Sure, I haven't thought about him in forever, but I do know him. He calls me with a proposal to take over our family record shop. He treats me, and Beau, to a private suite at a hockey game so he can do the hard sell. He gets a little drunk and handsy. And an hour later, he's dead. Outside our shop. Think about it. I'm as good of a suspect as Savannah. Better, maybe. Who better to clear my name than me?"

"You're not a suspect," Tansy said.

"The only reason I'm not is because Beau would never accuse me of anything, not even manslaughter, much less murder."

"Because you're not capable of murder. Beau, and everyone else, knows that," Tansy argued.

"Everyone is capable of murder, under the right circumstances."

"Be that as it may, you didn't kill anyone. I can testify that I was with you when Zack died."

"Yeah, but everyone knows you'd lie to protect your baby sister," I pointed out.

"I would, but I don't have to. Where are you going with this, Juni?"

I thought about it for a second. "The Cedar River P.D. doesn't exactly have the best track record when it comes to catching killers." I shrugged. "We do. We're two for two."

Tansy let out a long-suffering sigh. "Juni, you're too much sometimes." She yawned. "I know it's early, but it's been a long day. Let's talk about this in the morning, okay?"

My sister had a point. It had been a long day, and I hadn't slept well last night. "'Night, sis," I told her, and headed off to my room.

As soon as my head hit the pillow, I started to relax. Maybe Tansy was right. Savannah wasn't being accused of anything. I wasn't a suspect. No one I cared about was in any danger. To be completely honest, it was a shame that a man was dead, but I wasn't planning to host a candle-light vigil for Zack Fjord anytime soon. We weren't close. I didn't even like him that much.

His death was—literally—none of my business.

Just as I was drifting away into sleep, another thought occurred to me. It was odd that Beau hadn't been home when I got to his apartment that night. It was late, and he wasn't scheduled to work. Jayden had assumed he'd gone into the station once the power went off, but I hadn't con-firmed that.

I had been worried that Beau was going to pick a fight with Zack in the suite for putting his arm around me. Which was weird because for the past six months, Beau had known full well that I was dating Teddy at the same time I was dating him, and he hadn't said a bad word about the arrangement. Where was that machismo non-sense when it came to Teddy? Or, did that have something to do with his overreaction at the game? Was he tired of sharing me with Teddy, and was taking it out on Zack?

Sure, high school Beau had a bit of a temper. Not a punching-holes-in-walls temper, but I'd seen him tackle guys after a play was over when our football team was down. He certainly seemed to be enjoying the fight at the hockey game more than I had. He'd been rooting them on, along with the rest of the crowd. And, hadn't I just been thinking that anyone was capable of murder under the right circumstances? Not that Zack groping me was cause for murder.

Besides, if Beau wanted to kill someone, why would he throw a brick at their car? He certainly had more ef-ficient means at his disposal.

Wait a second. What was I thinking? I was exhausted and my imagination was running away with me. Beau wasn't a killer. I was ashamed that I could think such a thing, even for a second. Beau would never accuse me of wrongdoing, no matter how strong the evidence was. I owed him the same courtesy.

What I needed was a good night's sleep. A rest would put everything to rights and chase away all these nagging suspicions. But first, I wanted a glass of cold water. I'd been too busy running around today to hydrate properly, and that was surely affecting me as well.

I realized as I padded down to the kitchen that after a day without power, cold water might be too much to ask. The house was quiet as I poured a glass of room-temperature water in the dark. My sister, always the responsible one, had extinguished the candles I'd lit earlier. I was tempted to light one up again, but then thought better of it. What if I forgot to blow it out before I went to bed? Instead, I pulled back the curtain over the sink, hoping that the night sky would provide enough illumination that I could at least see the hand in front of my face.

That's when I noticed the lights in my mother's cottage.

Except, it wasn't really lights, plural. It was more like one single light, bobbing around slowly. It didn't have the warm flickering glow of the candle I'd given Savannah, but instead had a steady beam. Someone was moving around the cottage with a flashlight.

It was probably nothing, I told myself as I fumbled around the dark kitchen for the knife block, but it wasn't in its usual place. Maybe Miss Edie had moved it to make room for baking and hadn't put it back. It was too dark to see, so I grabbed the next best thing. Armed with a flimsy Swiffer mop handle, I quietly let myself out the front door.

I snuck across the lawn. The damp ground sucked at my bare feet. Part of me wished I had reached the adulting phase where I wore house slippers, but if I had, they would have been caked with mud before I could cross the yard.

The guest cottage wasn't much more than a glorified shed raised up on short concrete columns with a narrow crawlspace underneath. It was a tiny house before tiny houses were cool. It was four hundred square feet, maybe a little more, including the bathroom and kitchen. Two wooden lounge chairs sat on the raised front stoop on either side of the steps leading up to the front door. There were windows framing the front door, another over the small kitchen sink on the side, and a large window facing the backyard. The front curtains were closed.

The kitchen window had a lace curtain covering it. It was through this window that I'd seen the light moving around. Even on my tiptoes, the house was elevated just enough that I couldn't easily peek through the window. I propped the Swiffer mop handle against the wall. Making as little noise as possible, I carried one of the heavy deck chairs around the side of the house and set it down in front of the window.

I stepped up on the chair and peered through the window only to see a face staring back at me. "Argh!" I shouted. "Argh!" the person on the other side of the window echoed. I jumped back, remembering too late that I was standing on a chair. I fell backward into the mud. At least the soggy yard softened the landing.

"Juni?" Above me, Savannah had opened the kitchen window and was staring down at me. "What on earth are you doing? Are you trying to scare me to death?"

"I, uh, saw a flashlight and thought there might be an intruder," I confessed. I got to my feet. Cold mud seeped into my pajama bottoms.

"I found a flashlight in the closet. I was afraid the candle was going to set off the smoke detector."

"Good thinking."

"Want to come inside?" she offered.

"I'm a mess," I told her. I was covered in mud. "My mom would hose me down before inviting me inside."

"Good thing I'm not your mom." She met me at the front door with a towel and we went inside. "What's that?" she asked, pointing at the Swiffer mop handle in my hand.

I shrugged. "What? You don't think I could scare off an intruder with this?"

Savannah laughed. She took the Swiffer from me and rested it against the wall. I cleaned my feet off as best I could on the straw doormat. I wrapped the towel around myself. Short of a long shower and a washing machine, I was as clean as I could get under the circumstances. "Sorry for disturbing you."

"Don't apologize," Savannah said, flopping back onto the couch. "I couldn't sleep."

"Is the bed too hard?" I asked. "Mom likes her mattresses to feel like concrete. Says it's good for her back." I remained standing, rooted to the spot near the front door. The last thing I wanted to do was spread mud all around Mom's cottage.

"The bed's fine. It's just, well, you know, everything."

I nodded. "I can't imagine what you're going through." She'd been in a car wreck, then lost her business partner and her job all in one night. And now, she was stuck in a stranger's mother-in-law cottage, without power, in the middle of nowhere.

"Every time I close my eyes, I see him."

"Him?" I asked. "Zack?"

She shook her head. "No. The guy in the street. Maybe if I'd swerved, he wouldn't have hit the windshield. I wouldn't have gotten startled and lost control of the car. Or, I could have hit the gas and run him down. Then I wouldn't have to worry about him still being out there."

"It was a man?" I asked. "You're sure about that?"

"I think so. But it was dark. They had a coat on with the hood pulled up. I guess it could have been a woman." She sighed. "They were standing right in front of me, and I can't even tell you if it was a man or a woman. I'm the worst. They could walk right up to me and I wouldn't even recognize them. What if they're out to get me?"

"You don't need to worry," I assured her.

"I don't? I'm a witness to a major crime. Zack died because someone threw that brick at his car. Whoever did it is looking at serious jail time, and they have no way of knowing that I can't ID them."

Hmm. She had a point. I just didn't want to agree with her and make things worse. "If there was someone after you, they would have made their move already, don't you think?" I asked before realizing that wasn't as comforting a thought as I'd hoped.

"Gee, I'll sleep better tonight now," she replied. "Instead of worrying about Zack's killer coming after me, I'll worry why they haven't come after me *yet*."

I was about to assure her that she was totally safe when something banged against the front door.

CHAPTER 10

"Bet you're glad I have my Swiffer now," I said, as I picked up the flimsy pole and held it like a bat. As far as improvised weapons went, I'd probably rank them fireplace poker, baseball bat, hockey stick, literally anything else, and then a Swiffer, but when there was a killer on the loose and someone was trying to break in, I'd take what I could get.

Savannah turned off the flashlight, and the room plunged into darkness.

"What did you do that for?" I hissed.

"Shh, if we pretend to not be home, maybe he'll go away."

There was more scratching and bumping at the door. I tried to remember if I'd locked the door behind me when I'd come inside. I didn't think I had. "I don't think that's gonna work," I said, willing my eyes to adjust to the darkness. Was the doorknob turning or was that my imagination?

I heard a thump followed by a grunt.

"Bar the door!" Savannah suggested.

"With what?!" The cottage was small. There was a bed, a love seat, and a pair of tall café chairs under the island-slash-counter-slash-breakfast nook. There wasn't even a dresser, just a closet with lots of shelves.

"The Swiffer!" Savannah touched the back of my

shoulder and I shrieked. "Shh!" But it was too late. The sounds outside stopped. A heavy silence fell over the cottage. Savannah and I listened to each other's ragged breaths as we strained to hear any other noises.

I was thinking hard, making a mental list and checking off each possibility. There was nothing to barricade the door—the door that opened outward—with. The cottage was so small that the builders thought having a door that opened out instead of in made more sense. Also, to save space, there was no back door, but the full-length window in the back popped out in an emergency. The design was substandard, and probably not up to code, but it was too late to do anything about it now.

I couldn't call the police. Even if I'd had it on me, my cell phone was dead; and until the towers came back online, we had no service. There was no landline in the cottage, and if there had been, I doubted there would have been a dial tone.

There were no guns in the cottage. Mom didn't like guns. She kept a can of pepper spray on her key chain, but her key chain was safely with her in Austin. There weren't any knives in the kitchen larger than a steak knife.

"Do you think he's gone?" Savannah asked, after a full minute of silence.

"Do I think the maniac outside got scared away because I screamed?" I whispered back. I shook my head, not that she could see it in the dark. "I doubt it."

We waited. Nothing happened. "I think he's gone," Savannah said.

I was starting to agree with her. I was ninety-nine percent sure that I hadn't locked the door. Besides, if someone had really wanted inside, they could have broken a window. "If they didn't know that the door opened outward, maybe they thought the door was locked," I muttered to myself.

"The door's not locked?" Savannah hissed. "There's a killer running around Cedar River, and you didn't lock the door?"

"We're in a glorified toolshed surrounded by windows," I responded, still whispering. "I don't think a thumb lock is going to deter anyone. If he wanted to get in, he would have."

"I should have gotten a hotel," Savannah said.

"There are no hotels in Cedar River," I told her.

We hadn't heard anything for several minutes. I crept to one of the windows next to the front door, took a deep breath, and peeked outside. "There's nobody out there."

"Are you sure?"

I pulled the curtain back completely. The moon had risen. It was nearly full. After sitting in the dark for so long, our eyes had adjusted, and the yard might as well have been lit up like a movie theater after the credits rolled. "See for yourself. There's no one out there."

Still holding my Swiffer like a lifeline, I twisted the doorknob. The door opened. I wasn't sure if I felt vindicated or mortified that it was unlocked. There was no one on the small stoop. No one in the yard. No one in sight.

"Maybe we were imagining things?" Savannah suggested.

"Hand me your flashlight." She did. I turned it on and shone it at the ground. My footprints were distinct in the muddy ground, but there were no other footprints, and least no human ones. "Look at that," I said, shining the beam on a set of tracks. Each pawprint had four long toe impressions with a hole at the tip where a sharp nail had dug into the mud.

"Raccoon?" she asked.

"I don't think so." I swept the light back, where a line ran down the center of the tracks. "See that? It's his tail."

"Raccoons have tails," Savannah said. "Don't they?"

"Follow me." I took off the towel I'd been wearing over my muddy clothes and draped it over the remaining chair on the stoop. The other chair was still around the corner of the house where I'd left it, under the kitchen window.

I took a few steps out into the lawn, bent down, and shone the light into the crawlspace under the cottage, illuminating a startled armadillo.

"It's so cute!" Savannah said. "Can we keep it?"

"You sound just like me when I was a kid," I told her. "I found a baby armadillo and snuck it into my room. I was going to raise it as a pet until my sisters dimed me out. Apparently, armadillos carry leprosy or something."

"No one's perfect," she said.

I turned off the flashlight. We'd traumatized the armadillo enough for one night. Although, to be fair, he had traumatized us, too. "I'm sorry you felt unsafe. Would you be more comfortable sleeping in the house tonight?"

Savannah shook her head. "Strangely, no. You made a good point. If someone wanted me dead, they've had plenty of opportunities. Just because I'm paranoid . . ."

"You witnessed a death," I said. "Last night." Okay, maybe it was the night before last. I wasn't sure what time it was. How soon I lost track of time without a phone in my hand. "Of course you're jumpy."

"Jumpy? I about had a heart attack because of an armadillo. You don't even know me, but here you are, putting yourself at risk to save me. Again. While all this time I've been lying to you."

"Excuse me?" I asked, blinking at her. She looked guilty. "About what?" I asked suspiciously, leaning forward slightly as if it would help me hear her better. Whatever Savannah was about to confess to, I had a feeling it was going to be good.

"Zack and I weren't old family friends, and we were

more than business partners. You were right. We were, um, romantically involved."

"What?" I tried my hardest to not sound disapproving. I was starting to like Savannah, and now I was seeing her in a completely new light. Sure, Zack was attractive. And rich. But he was also a serial cheater. And kind of a jerk. She could do a lot better. "But it wasn't serious, right?"

"Pretty serious," she admitted. "We were living together. I think he was about to propose." Her eyes filled up with tears.

Tansy was right. Savannah and Zack had been an item. My heart went out to her. It was hard enough losing a friend and a business partner, but a significant other? I couldn't even imagine what she was going through right now.

"I'm sorry for your loss," I said. It felt inadequate, but I had no idea what to say. I wondered how she managed to keep it together as well as she had. Was that all part of pretending that she and Zack hadn't been dating? What else was she hiding?

"I know what you're thinking," Savannah said, after she'd taken a moment to compose herself.

"I doubt that," I said.

"You're wondering what else I lied about."

"Yeah, okay, you've got me there. Anything else you're holding out on?"

"It wasn't my idea to keep our relationship a secret," Savannah said.

"Why hide it?" I asked. "Why lie?"

"His family already thinks I'm a gold digger. And our clients? It's hard enough to get taken seriously as a woman in finance without being the girlfriend of the money man. By the time you asked, it was a habit to lie."

I thought about how Zack had acted at the game. He'd hit on me right in front of her, and she hadn't said a word.

Spilling his beer on me and then groping me as he tried to clean it up could have been a drunken accident, but putting his arm around my chair and leaning in a little too close was intentional. "How did that make you feel?" I asked.

"Having to hide our relationship? It made me feel like dirt."

"I mean all the other women. I'm guessing he left a trail of jilted lovers and jealous husbands in his wake," I suggested. Of all the reasons to kill someone, that had to be at the top of the list.

"Zack was a magnet for every eligible woman in Texas. And some not-so-eligible women, come to think of it. He didn't *do* anything about it. Of course not." She didn't sound convincing. I doubted she believed it herself.

"Zack cheated on you," I blurted out.

"No, never. At least I don't think he did." She paused. "Okay, I had my suspicions once or twice, but he told me I was being silly. Swore he'd never do that to me."

"What about that hockey player? Beckel? Zack bragged about dating his wife while she was still married," I pointed out.

"That was just for show. He concocted that story because he thought it made him sound cool. Zack was all about appearances, but he was faithful to me."

Personally, I think Zack was more than capable of cheating on her. My memory was a little fuzzy on the details, but he'd cheated on my friend back in college. She'd caught him red-handed. Sure, people grew up and they learned their lessons, but it would be a lot easier for Zack to cheat on his girlfriend if the rest of the world thought he was single.

Then again, for all I knew, Savannah knew full well that Zack was a cheater. But sometimes death had a way of making saints out of people who didn't warrant it. Maybe giving him more credit than he deserved helped her deal with his sudden passing. Which made what I needed to ask that much more difficult. I had to tread lightly. "Is there anyone in Cedar River that Zack may have rejected? Or, perhaps, a significant other who thought Zack was interested in their partner?"

"Other than you?" Savannah asked. She looked miffed that I would suggest such a thing.

I shook my head. "Excuse me?"

"Come on. We both saw how that cute cop of yours pounded his chest at the hockey game when Zack paid too much attention to you."

"He's not *my* cop." I wasn't going to admit it, not aloud, not to Savannah, but my protests sounded almost as unbelievable as her earlier ones had. Plus, I'd thought this through already. Beau wouldn't kill a man in cold blood, at least not out of misplaced jealousy.

"We had clients here. Businesses we'd invested in," she said. "But nothing like what you're suggesting. If Zack was seeing someone else, and I'm certain he wasn't, it wasn't anyone in Cedar River."

"If you say so," I said. I wasn't convinced, but if Savannah wanted to close her eyes, put her fingers in her ears, and yell tra-la-la at the top of her lungs rather than consider the possibility that her secret boyfriend had cheated on her, who was I to stop her? "What about local investments? You told me about the music store, Blow Your Own Horn. And the dress shop, Cedar River Casuals. Any others?"

She had to think about it for a moment. I had about all I could handle with Sip & Spin Records. I wondered how she was able to keep her fingers in so many pies that she couldn't even name them all off the top of her head. "Rediscovered Treasures."

"That adorable second-hand shop run by Darlene

Daye?" I asked. Darlene and my mom have been friends since as long as I could remember. She was on the Cedar River softball team with Maggie, volunteered at the high school, and brought homemade pecan sandies anytime there was a bake sale. I loved her shop, but I'd been steadfastly avoiding it ever since returning to town. I had a hard enough time fitting all my belongings into my sister's spare bedroom without spending money I didn't have on more stuff.

"That's the one."

"I love her window displays. So unique."

"That was all me," Savannah said. "Lovely woman, but she doesn't have a bit of design sense. If Darlene had her way, she would have every bit of stock jammed onto a shelf or in a bin and hope for the best. It took me forever to convince her that by curating the floor, she could make twice as much on half as many sales. In fact, she's doing so well, she recently bought back a good chunk of our investment."

"She can do that?" I asked.

"It was right there in the prospectus that Zack was trying to present. Then again, you were so hung up on you and your sisters having sole ownership, I don't think you were paying that close of attention."

"I was too paying attention," I argued. Talking to Savannah felt a little like talking to my older sisters when they got it stuck in their heads that I was still five years old. "I must have missed that point."

"I think you missed the point completely," Savannah said. "Fjord Capital isn't, wasn't, a predatory firm. We only succeeded when our partners succeeded. And that's how we saw our investments. As partners. Practically family."

"Practically family isn't the same as actual family," I pointed out.

"You know what I mean," Savannah said defensively.

I did know what she meant, to an extent. I was lucky to be surrounded by a happy loving family. Others weren't born into a close-knit family like mine but found a different kind of family along the way. Then she surprised me by saying, "While we're getting things off our chest, I have another confession to make."

I wondered what bombshell she was about to drop. She was pregnant? She'd been cheating on Zack? Zack was secretly broke?

"We always do our research before approaching a business, so we know all about Sip & Spin." She paused a beat. "All about it. We know about the murders connected to your shop."

"None of that was our fault," I was quick to say.

"No, of course not! But you were able to find both killers before the cops were."

"My sisters helped."

"Of course they did," Savannah said. "When . . ." Her voice trailed off. Then she visibly composed herself. "When Zack died, I was scared and devastated and angry all at the same time. Even if I had a car and the roads were passable, I was in no shape to drive and had nowhere to go. You and Tansy were kind enough to take me, a stranger, into your home. I should be scrambling to find a way to repay you, but instead I need to ask you for another favor."

"What is it?" I asked.

"Juni Jessup, I want you to find whoever killed Zack and bring him to justice."

And then the power came back on.

The lights in the cottage and the main house flickered on even as the streetlights surged back to life. All around us, porch lights blinked on. The stillness of the night was broken by a neighbor who'd been listening to TV too loud when the power went out. I was so busy marveling at the difference a few light bulbs made, I'd forgotten that I was in the middle of a conversation.

"So? Will you do it? Will you find Zack's killer?"

"No promises," I told her. "But I'll do my best."

CHAPTER 11

After checking in on Tansy—she slept right through the power returning—I finally went to bed and slept like the dead.

I was still sound asleep when my oldest sister burst into my room on Friday morning. "Were you planning on getting up today, or are you going to sleep until noon like a teenager?"

"What time is it?" I rolled over and put on the closest pair of glasses, a pink pair, and checked my phone screen. I hadn't thought to plug in my phone last night after the power came back on, so it was dead. "Sorry. I didn't mean to oversleep."

"You're supposed to open the shop today," she reminded me.

"On it." I hopped out of bed. Before opening my own business, I don't think I was ever eager to get to work. But it was different now. I wanted to be at the shop. I enjoyed concocting delicious drinks and talking to customers about music. I didn't even mind being on my feet all day.

"How long do you think you'll need to get ready?" Tansy asked, looking at her watch.

Before today, I'd secretly thought it was weird that my sister wore an old-fashioned wristwatch when phones were everywhere. But after a few days of no power, I envied her watch. "I took a shower last night," I said. I didn't tell her about my adventures with the mud and the armadillo, not because I was hiding anything from her but because I was short on time. "Can I borrow the car?"

"It's all yours," Tansy assured me.

By the time I was ready to go, Savannah was waiting for me in the kitchen. She looked more composed than she had last night. "I'm going to be at the shop this morning, but when I get off this afternoon, I'll start poking around with you," I told her.

"Poking around?" Tansy asked.

"Juni agreed to help me find the person who killed Zack," Savannah said.

"I said I'd look into it," I said quickly. Tansy had been an integral part of my previous sleuthing adventures. She'd even encouraged me when I wanted to give up. But as the practical Jessup sister, I was afraid she would try to talk me out of investigating, especially when she'd already warned me that she didn't want to get involved.

"Good," Tansy said. "Cedar River's finest, Detective Russell couldn't find his—"

I cut her off. "Gotta run. Don't want to be late for work. Love ya, sis." I blew her an air kiss.

"Love you too."

I headed out the front door with Savannah on my heels. "You're coming along?"

"Might as well," she said. "Besides, I hear there's coffee."

"There is," I agreed. The drive to the shop was a short one, especially since I was used to riding my trike. We got there just before I was supposed to open.

I unlocked the front door. It was weird, not being greeted by Daffy as soon as I stepped inside. He was settling in well at Tansy's. I wondered if it was worth the trauma—to me and the cat—to try to wrangle him into the carrier and bring him back into town. I'd have to check with my sisters to see what they thought.

Still pondering what would be best for Daffy, I selected a record. AC/DC's *Back in Black* seemed appropriate this morning. I propped open the front door. Maggie had done a deep clean after the flood waters receded, but the faint smell of mildew lingered. Not only could the shop stand a little fresh air, but this would also let customers know we were open for business.

"I just love your fun coffee flavors. What's the special of the day?" Savannah asked.

"Hmm. It's finally starting to feel like fall," I said. I looked down at my T-shirt, from the Mellon Collie and the Infinite Sadness tour. I was born a couple of weeks before the album dropped, and this concert was the first time Mom had left me alone with my sisters. I guess the good part of having a surprise baby when your eldest is already seven is having built-in babysitters at home. It didn't hurt that when I came along, my grandparents lived next door. "How does Smashing Pumpkins Spice Latte sound?"

"Delicious." She flipped through a bin of records, stopping to examine any albums that caught her attention. "How'd you learn all this?"

"My grandparents had a record store just like this one when I was little. Almost exactly like this one. In this very storefront, actually. I grew up around music. I don't know that I'll ever be quite as knowledgeable as Tansy—she knows more music trivia than anyone I've ever met—but it's in my DNA."

"No, I mean the coffee part," she clarified.

"Oh." I selected a bag of beans and set them to grind. "The machine does all the hard work. I learned most of the features on YouTube, to be honest." I plugged my phone in behind the counter and started inventory. We were low on several things and out of dairy completely.

We'd had to pour out anything that might have spoiled while the power was out, but we had a good selection of dairy alternatives. I started a grocery list.

My phone must have gotten enough charge to power on, because a constant stream of notifications came flooding in as it finally connected after several days offline. "Network's back," I said.

"Thank goodness," Savannah said. "I was starting to feel like I was trapped on a desert island. No offense. Isn't it hard?"

"Being trapped on a desert island?" I asked. I was scanning my messages and was having a hard time following her train of thought.

"No, being a barista."

"It's a lot to learn," I admitted, putting my phone down. The messages could wait. "Take this latte. It's one part espresso and two parts steamed milk or milk substitute, with foam and whipped cream on top." I was using unsweetened soy instead of milk right now. Luckily, we had a backup stock of shelf-stable whipped cream that didn't need to be refrigerated, or I'd be making an emergency run to the market. "Add sweetened pumpkin puree into the mix, and a dash of our secret blend of spices on top of the whipped cream, and now it's a Smashing Pumpkins Spice Latte." As I talked, I made two cups. One was for her and the other was for quality control, which was how I justified drinking so much coffee.

"You make it sound easy." She blew on the top, then took a sip. "This is good. Even better than the one they serve at—"

"Shush." I put a finger to my lips. "We don't say that word around here."

She nodded. "Got it."

I heard voices and looked up as our first customer came into the shop. It was Jen Rachet. "Good morning, Miss

Jen. What can I get for you today?" I asked in my most pleasant tone, trying to make up for pointing out her gossip mongering yesterday. Jen was a descendant of one of Cedar River's first families and a legendary busybody. I was tempted to call her out for lying to my mom about me getting arrested, but if I was rude to her, everyone would hear about it. "We haven't had a chance to restock the dairy yet, but you prefer oat milk, right?"

"You remembered," she said, sounding surprised, as if she didn't stop into the shop almost every day for coffee and gossip.

"Special of the day is Smashing Pumpkins Spice Latte. Large, oat milk, no whip?" I asked.

"Sounds perfect," she agreed. She took a seat at one of the tables. "Who's the new girl?"

"Savannah Goodwin," Savannah said, offering her hand to shake.

Jen ignored her hand. "Don't you think you should be paying attention? Juni makes the best drinks in town, and if you want to be even half as good as she is, you'll want to take notes."

"I'm not a barista," Savannah said.

"And with that attitude, you never will be," Jen said. I rang her up and she tapped her phone against the machine. I was grateful the internet had been restored so we weren't cash-only like we'd been yesterday. I handed her the drink. "Better keep an eye on this one, Juni," Jen said. She took her drink and left.

"She's something," Savannah said, as soon as Jen was out of earshot.

"She's special," I agreed. "Sorry I didn't stand up for you and clarify that you're not an employee, but that's the nicest thing she's ever said about me, and I didn't want to ruin the moment."

"No worries. I spend a lot of time getting to know

the businesses we invest in. We don't just invest money, you know. We invest time. Resources. Knowledge. New ideas." Her face fell. "I mean we did. I still can't believe Zack's gone. It's hard to believe it's all over now."

I couldn't bring Zack back for her, but maybe I could still cheer her up. "Maybe it doesn't have to be. You said Zack's family supplied the capital, but you still own twenty percent of the investment company. Even if you can't convince the Fjords to invest in new properties, you have your existing portfolio. If you really lean in and try to grow those businesses, it might be enough to keep going."

Savannah shook her head. "You don't understand. Zack's dad only funded us because he couldn't ever tell his son no. But even more than he hated Fjord Capital, he hated me. I was never good enough. Trust me. He'll find a way to take it all and he won't care who gets hurt."

Another customer stopped in. They wanted to chat about a special vinyl release of several albums that had only been CD and digital before records started their comeback. We had two of the albums they were interested in, which they bought. I ordered the other one. They were tea drinkers, so I made them a Chai Can't We Be Friends and sent them on their way with a promise to call them once the third album came in.

"You were talking about Zack's dad hurting people?" I prompted Savannah after the customer was gone.

"He's gonna call in the markers." I must have looked confused, because she explained. "Seriously, were you paying *any* attention during the presentation?"

"In my defense, there was so much going on. It's hard to pay attention to anything during a hockey game. Maybe a noisy arena isn't the best place to do business."

"Which is why he only pitched you during intermissions." Savannah rolled her eyes skyward. "Anyway, once someone makes enough money because of our improve-ments, they can buy controlling interest back if they want."

"So it would be their company again?"

"Depends. We buy fifty-one percent up front. That way, if the original owner refuses to make the improvements we recommend—within reason—we can use store funds to make them ourselves."

"Within reason?" I asked.

"Look at this place. It's new. It's shiny. You've got a well-curated selection of music already. Your barista ma-chine isn't absolute high-end, but it meets your needs."

"The coffee's here to get people in the door," I told her, somewhat defensively. "The records are the money-maker."

"Exactly. It's good business. If anything, you need to work on your branding. You should have your logo on your bags, cups, and protective coffee sleeves. Maybe add some T-shirts or hats. I know you don't want to talk about that other coffee shop, but their branding is on point. Yours is an afterthought."

I nodded. "That's fair." It hurt to hear, but I didn't dis-agree. I'd like to make little changes like that, too, but we couldn't afford them. I guess that's where investors came in. It was starting to make sense why people might buy into the Fjord Capital model.

"When we come in, we're going to make your business thrive. We standardize everyone on the same accounting system and banks to reduce fees. We offer discounts on anything from insurance to appliances. That's all part of the service we offer. Once the money's rolling in, the original owner can buy out up to half of our share. We'd still get a return on our investment but they're back to hav-ing controlling interest."

"How would Zack's father hurt them?"

"There's a nuclear clause in our contracts. We can pull out of any investment for any reason or no reason at all. If we do that, the original owner has ninety days to buy back our percentage, at the current value of the business. If the business is worth more now because of our involvement—and it nearly always is—then they would have to pay more than our original investment, of course." She said this all matter-of-fact, as if she wasn't talking about generations of family-owned businesses that people had poured their life, not to mention their savings, into.

"And if they can't afford to buy you out?"

"We put the business up for sale. We get our money back. They get anything that's left over."

"That's rotten," I said.

"No. It's business. It's really the only way to guarantee we get our investment back if something goes wrong."

"But they lose everything," I argued.

Savannah shrugged nonchalantly. "Not my problem."

Another customer came in, and I tried to focus on them instead of worrying about Zack's investment scheme. Sure, it gave small business owners a way to save a floundering business, but there was little to no risk for Zack and Savannah, and nothing but risk for the original owner. The more I learned, the more I was glad my sisters hadn't been willing to entertain the idea. I thought it had been a matter of pride, but I was starting to think that Maggie had seen right through them. She'd always had a better head for numbers than I had.

Speaking of Maggie, she breezed through the door with her arms laden down with reusable totes filled with groceries. "Thank goodness you're here," I said. "Let me help you put that away."

"Take care of them," she said, indicating the customers who were currently debating between two editions of the same album, each with different covers. "I've got this."

After I rang up their purchases, I started a coffee for my middle sister. "You're an angel," she said.

"Sorry it took me so long. I had to borrow Uncle Calvin's truck to get out to the Garza farm to pick up fresh milk since they were swamped with deliveries." Teddy's family's farm had the best dairy in all of Travis County. It was great to be able to buy local, and even better to know that our suppliers were family friends. But the road to the Garza farm wasn't much more than a dirt trail. As much as I liked visiting with the Garzas—and Teddy—I hated that drive and was grateful my sister had made the dairy run for us.

"Did you say hi to Buttercup for me?" I asked. She was a sweet cow, but she looked different than the rest of the herd and I often worried that she didn't have enough friends.

"Of course I did," my sister said, with practiced patience. Maggie might not understand my attachment to a cow that had only been mine for a few hours before I rehomed her, but she knew to humor me.

"Wait a second. Calvin's back in town?"

"He and Samuel had to cut their fishing trip short because of the weather," she said.

"And he loaned you his truck?" I asked. "Am I the only one not allowed to drive it?"

"He'll forgive you . . . one day," she said. I wasn't so sure I believed her. I'd borrowed his truck once—once!—without permission. I'd ended up getting a flat tire—not my fault—and you would have thought the world was ending for the fuss he made over it.

"I doubt it," I said.

"Who's Calvin?" Savannah asked.

"Oh!" I looked between Savannah and my middle sister, realizing they hadn't formally met yet. "Savannah, this is Maggie, my other sister. And Calvin's our uncle. He's a character."

"You can say that again," Maggie agreed. "Nice to meet you, Savannah."

"Same," Savannah said.

"Juni, a minute?" Without waiting for me to agree, she took me by the arm and pulled me into the stockroom in the back. "So that's the infamous Savannah."

"She is," I confirmed.

"What's she doing here?"

"She just kinda invited herself along this morning."

"No, not what is she doing in the shop. What's she still doing here in Cedar River? She's not still staying with you and Tansy, is she?"

"It's just temporary," I told her. "I don't think Beau would be happy if she left town in the middle of an investigation. Besides, she just lost her boyfriend, and her business, and I'm not sure she should be alone right now."

"She looks fine to me." Maggie poked her head out of the stockroom, as if to confirm that Savannah wasn't listening in at the other side of the door.

"People grieve in different ways," I said. "It's impossible to know what's going on inside her head."

Maggie pursed her lips. "It's suspicious, if you ask me."

I thought she was going to say something else, but before she could, the stockroom door opened again. "Uh, Juni, there's someone here to see you," Savannah said.

We followed her back to the front of the shop, where Marcus Best was waiting for us. "Morning, girls," he said. I cringed. I hated how he called my sisters and me "girls." It was okay when Mom called us that. We would always be her girls. Marcus didn't get that right by proxy just because he was dating her. "Is that your uncle's truck parked out front? We'd brought a wrecker for Tansy's car, but while we're here, we can always hook that old Bronco up, too, and take it off your hands."

"Not on your life," I said. "Just try it," Maggie said at the same time.

Marcus laughed. "Just kidding. We all know how Cal feels about that hunk. Something smells delish. Can I get a coffee?"

I moved to the barista station and started making him a drink. Since he was dating Mom, I didn't charge him. "What wrecker?" I asked.

"Your mom asked me to take care of Tansy's car," he said.

I snuck a glance over at Savannah. She'd been the one driving when she hit Tansy's car, which had been legally parked at the curb. She'd had as good an excuse as any, but until whoever threw the brick that caused the accident was caught, technically, it was Savannah's fault. Which meant it was her responsibility to get Tansy's car fixed, not Marcus's. Then again, she was still grieving or she probably would have made the offer already. "I'm sure it will all get worked out," I said.

"No doubt it will, but in the meantime, I won't have Bea's daughters riding around in an unsafe car. My guys will fix it up, good as new. And don't worry about anything, we'll deal with the insurance."

I should have guessed Marcus wasn't doing this out of the goodness of his heart. Don't get me wrong. It was nice to have access to mechanics and an autobody shop, but if Marcus got the friends and family discount on our coffee, shouldn't he extend the same offer in reverse? Then again, he was getting a six-dollar coffee for free. The body work on Tansy's car could run in the thousands.

"Does Tansy know you're taking her car?" Maggie asked.

Marcus tossed her a key fob attached to a Best Used Cars key chain. It was red and shaped like a sedan, with the logo "If you need a car, you need the Best" printed on it in gold letters. Again, I was reminded that Savannah had a point. Sip & Spin Records could stand to brand better. "Don't worry, I'm leaving a loaner. Keys?"

If it had been Maggie's car, she might have been too stubborn to accept his assistance. It wasn't that she didn't like Marcus, it was that she didn't like Marcus dating Mom. But Tansy got along with him fine for the most part, and if anything, she would be grateful that one thing was off her plate. I pulled her car key off my key chain and handed it to Marcus. "Thanks."

"Don't mention it," he said. He saluted us with his free cup of coffee and went back out the front door.

"Kinda heavy-handed, don't you think?" Maggie asked.

"I think it's sweet," I said.

"Of course you do," she muttered. "Well, it's my shift now, if you've got other places to be."

I looked over at Savannah, who was trying her hardest to pretend she wasn't witnessing our family drama. "Actually, I do. Need anything before I leave?"

"Nope. I'm good. Now shoo," Maggie said.

Savannah and I hurried out of the shop before Maggie could change her mind. "Hungry?" I asked Savannah.

"Not really," she said. "It's not even lunchtime."

"Oh." I was always hungry. Or, to be more accurate, I could always eat. What could I say? I loved good food. "In that case, how do you feel about going shopping?"

The more Savannah revealed about her business model, the shadier it sounded. If I was a business owner caught up in that net, I might do anything to find a way out. If I didn't understand that killing Zack would make things infinitely worse, I might even be tempted to do something extreme. Not that I would kill someone, especially not for money, but family-owned businesses like Sip & Spin Records were about more than money.

Between Zack running around with other men's wives and yanking the rug out from under small business owners, frankly I'm surprised it took this long for someone to come after him.

"I'm game," Savannah said.

Blow Your Own Horn was only a few blocks away, but I decided to drive instead of walk. The loaner Marcus had left was nice, much nicer than Tansy's older sedan. It was a small, sporty SUV with the latest gadgetry and the upgraded interior package. Either Marcus was trying to spoil us, or he was not so subtly trying to sell us a new car. My money was on the latter.

"Your stepdad has good taste in cars," Savannah said.

"He's not my stepdad," I replied. A voice in the back of my head added *yet*. I ignored it.

I drove the shiny SUV to Blow Your Own Horn and pulled into a spot in the tiny parking lot. Sip & Spin was on Main Street, so we didn't have designated parking. Blow Your Own Horn was set back a few blocks, so it had a nice blacktop parking area. Other than one car parked in the farthest spot, we were the only car in the lot.

"Is it even open?" Savannah grumbled. I could understand why, as part owner, she might be frustrated at the apparent lack of customers. But if she'd done her homework before approaching Sip & Spin, she had to have done her due diligence here as well.

Blow Your Own Horn got most of its business from local kids joining school bands. They rented or sold flutes, clarinets, trumpets, and more. I remembered from my short stint in band that kids went through a lot of reeds, finger pads, and drumsticks, but the big sales would be concentrated at the beginning of a semester.

They also bought and sold instruments for all ages, from folks in garage bands to big musical groups on tour that found themselves in need of anything from amps to guitar strings. Since nearby Austin was the self-proclaimed Live Music Capital of the World, there was never a shortage of musicians in the area, and Blow Your Own Horn had a great selection in stock. But musicians weren't exactly early birds. Tansy had teased me about sleeping in, but professional musicians were never up and about this time of morning.

"I'm sure business picks up later in the day," I said.

"Oh, it does," Savannah said. She opened the front door and we stepped inside.

We were surrounded by musical instruments of all sizes and shapes, roughly organized by purpose. On the right were the traditional school band instruments, starting with the smaller woodwinds and working up to the giant brass ones. In front of us were the stringed instruments ranging from banjos to cellos and giant basses. Lined up along the wall behind that was a selection of pianos. To our left were guitars, keyboards, and synthesizers before getting to the drum sets along the back wall.

I was better at listening to music than I was at making it, but I could imagine how each instrument might sound in the hands of a well-trained musician. If I'd spent half as much time learning how to read sheet music as I'd spent memorizing album liner notes, Blow Your Own Horn might be my idea of heaven.

"How can I help you ladies?" A man a decade or so older than me appeared from behind a rack of electric guitars to greet us. He was a thin Black man with short hair and a neatly trimmed goatee. He was dressed, like me, in blue jeans and a concert T-shirt, but I didn't recognize the band on his shirt. Tansy would probably know them, but I was drawing a blank.

"Oh. Savannah. It's you." His enthusiasm waned as soon as he recognized her. "Thought I smelled sulfur."

I waved awkwardly. "Hi."

He turned to me. "I know you."

"I don't think we've ever officially met," I said. I put out my hand to shake. "Juni Jessup."

"Frankie Hornsby. And you're one of the Jessup girls. Of course. You look just like your sister." I didn't ask him which one. Personally, I didn't see the resemblance, but everyone else seemed to think all three of us were virtually interchangeable. "I wonder if she knows what kind of company you're keeping these days," he said, jerking a thumb at Savannah.

"I got a flute from your store in middle school." I didn't know why I was compelled to tell him that. I wanted to redirect his attention, and it just came out.

"Well, in that case, you're probably about due for an upgrade. I've got a good selection in stock. If you're looking for something specific that we don't carry, I can always order it for you. Flute, you said?" He headed into the woodwinds section.

"I don't play anymore," I told him hastily as I followed. Returning that flute at the end of the semester had been one of the highlights of sixth grade. Then again, as bad as I'd been, it was probably the highlight of my parents', my sisters', and my neighbors' year, too.

"That's too bad." He came to a halt halfway down the aisle. "Where's Zack? No, let me guess. He's off torturing kittens somewhere."

Savannah grimaced. "He, uh, well he . . ."

"Wait, no, it's Friday. That means he's probably curled up under a heat lamp waiting for someone to drop a live mouse into his aquarium."

Savannah cringed and turned to me. "A little help here?"

I'd known Zack for a long time, but I'd never known him well. I hadn't even thought of him since college. But Frankie deserved to know what was going on with his business partner and apparently Savannah didn't know how to tell him, so by default, it was up to me.

"I hate to be the bearer of bad news, but Zack Fjord passed suddenly."

"Passed?" Frankie asked, looking stunned and confused.

"He's dead, Frankie," Savannah said. As she said this, everything seemed to hit her all at once, and she broke into sobs.

CHAPTER 12

"Well, I'll be," Frankie said. "Zack Fjord, dead, you say? I didn't think the devil could die."

Savannah's tears redoubled.

I looked at her frantically. My heart went out to her, but I didn't know how to help. "Why don't you go get some air? It might make you feel better." She looked at me through red, watery eyes and nodded as she choked back another sob. "Come on." I put my arm around her and steered her out the front door. "Don't go far," I told her, realizing I didn't know her phone number. All I had was Zack's, for all the good that would do me now.

There was a bench a few feet away from the front door, next to a smoker's pole. Savannah collapsed onto the bench. I felt horrible leaving her like that, with her face in her hands and her shoulders shaking with sobs, but the best thing I could do for her was to figure out who killed Zack, and why.

With Savannah settled on the bench, I went back inside. "Sorry about that," I said, even though I wasn't even sure what I was apologizing for.

"Don't you worry yourself," Frankie said. "That came out harsher than I'd intended. He, well, Zack wasn't a good person. I shouldn't speak ill of the dead. But if you'd known him, you would understand."

I shook my head. "I actually did know Zack. Not well, but I knew him. He wasn't everyone's cup of tea."

"You can say that again," Frankie said with a wry laugh. "Dead, you say?"

"It's true." I didn't elaborate. If the rumor mill hadn't made it to Frankie yet, I considered that a stroke of fortune. "How long have you two been in business together?"

"In business together?" He snorted. "That's rich. More like extortion. This place has kept food on the table for generations. It's not printing money, but it pays my bills, and my parents' bills now that they're retired. Or at least it used to." He sighed. "Can I get you anything? Water? Coffee?"

"I'm fine."

"Oh yeah. You run that coffee shop that also sells records."

I grinned. "That's one way to put it. I like to think that Sip & Spin sells records and also has coffee, but you might have a point." Pound for pound, we sold more coffee than we did records.

"My dad needed to go into one of those fancy memory care facilities a while ago. Insurance didn't cover it. We were in a bind. I tried to secure a loan, but that fell through. I was starting to talk to other distributors and music stores about liquidation, but those sharks smelled blood in the water and start offering pennies on the dollar. I've got hundreds of thousands tied up in merch, and I couldn't sell a Gibson for more than five bucks."

I grimaced. "I understand. When my grandparents' record store went under in the early two thousands, they had more stock than they knew what to do with. They had their whole life savings tied up in the shop, but back then, you couldn't give away vinyl records."

"What ended up happening to them?" Frankie asked.

"Most of them sat in boxes for decades. We got lucky.

When vinyl came back, my uncle Calvin still had a bunch of records in storage, and some of them are worth a pretty penny now. But it could have gone the other way, just as easy."

"Exactly. Most of my inventory will never go down in value. Just the opposite. But when I was in a bind, everyone knew that if they just waited me out, they could get it all for free. And it was looking like Horn was going the way of the dodo when those two vultures swooped in."

"And saved your family business?" I asked hopefully.

"Seemed so, at first." Frankie shook his head. "My dad lived out his last days in comfort. I was debt free. Even when my water heater went out at home, it was no big deal. I had enough to cover it. Then, well, things went downhill."

"Business fell off?" I asked.

"Nope. Just the opposite. Business was going gangbusters. Savannah had some contacts in the Austin music scene. Convinced them to come to me for their gear. Then they started telling their buddies. Next thing I knew, stock was flying off the shelves."

"Sounds like a success story," I said.

"Sure, but then came the kickbacks to club owners and tour organizers. I'm half convinced Zack and Savannah were skimming off the top because there's no way they're letting these folks shake them down like this. And now there's the discounts to bands I've never even heard of. I'm still paying the same for merch, but I'm selling it at seventy, seventy-five percent and I'm only taking home half the profit after Zack takes his cut. I'm working longer hours and writing bigger and bigger checks to my distributers, but at the end of the week, my pay is a fraction of what it used to be."

I cringed. "Oof." Sip & Spin wasn't quite at the point where we were taking home paychecks, but it covered the bills at the shop and our living expenses. If that suddenly got cut in half, or more? There was no way we would survive.

"Exactly. It was like being stuck on a treadmill, but the incline kept getting steeper until every step felt like my last. Those vampires were sucking me dry."

"What did you do about it?" I asked.

"I tried to get out from under them. Friends and family chipped in, and along with my dad's life insurance, I offered to buy them out. They turned me down. Said their improvements had increased the value of this place. Had the store reappraised by one of their cronies at three times what it had been before Fjord invested. What I'd raised wasn't enough by half, and it was everything I had."

"So what are you going to do?"

"The way I see it, there's not much of a choice. I can work myself to death and still fail, or I can walk away. Sure, the store implodes but I'm no worse off than I was a few years ago. At least this way, it bites Zack in the pocketbook. Or at least it would have." Frankie shrugged. "Looks like that train's left the station. But I can still hit Savannah where it hurts."

"Too late for that," I told him. "She's in the same boat you are."

"Well, shoot," Frankie said. "I was looking forward to seeing the look on her face. Guess this time we all walk away losers."

"Guess so," I agreed.

After saying my goodbyes, I left. Savannah was still sitting on the bench outside, but she was no longer inconsolable. I sat next to her. "This is probably not the time, but Frankie was under the impression that some of the new business expenses since you and Zack took over weren't a hundred percent aboveboard."

She sniffled. "What? Frankie was the one who dealt with the distributors, not us."

"He's talking about payouts to the club owners, discounts to bands that no one's heard of, those kind of things."

"That's just the cost of doing business." Savannah smoothed her blonde hair back into place. "Think about it. He went from selling one guitar a day to three. Even after our split, he's still doing better than he was before we came along, and that's not even counting our initial investment. He wasn't complaining when he cashed that check. Not our fault if he spent it already. And you don't triple your profits without greasing a couple of wheels."

"And you weren't keeping any of that grease for yourself?" I asked.

Savannah scoffed. "What do you take me for? Up until a few days ago, I had it made. Zack contributed the seed money, and even that wasn't his. It was his dad's. I smiled a lot and made people comfortable. We sat back in Zack's penthouse and cashed the checks while everyone around us put in the work. We made a profit no matter what. I didn't need any grease, as you call it. I had the whole goose."

It was getting harder and harder to feel sorry for Savannah. I realized this all seemed like a victimless scheme for her, but there were real people on the other end of all that sweat and tears. Real people with real dreams were struggling to keep their heads above water while she and her already rich boyfriend made money hand over fist.

"I know that look," Savannah said.

"What look?" I asked.

"Disgust." She pointed at the loaner car in the lot. "What do you think that car costs? Forty K? Fifty? If you're like ninety percent of Americans, you can't afford that, not all at once. But you can afford a car payment. Interest rates are what, six, six and a half percent right now?"

I had no idea. The last time I bought a car, I was in college. Savannah continued, doing the math in her head with ease. "On a standard five-year loan, you're looking at eleven or twelve thousand dollars in interest alone. Business loans, student loans, mortgages, they're all the same. It's not the principle that kills you, it's the interest. Now that's predatory. What we and Zack do—did," she corrected herself, "is completely different."

"Only instead of paying your car off, in five years, you still owe as much as when you started even though you've been making payments."

"But that's the beauty of it not being a loan. After the cash changes hands, we're part owners. No one owes anyone anything. We're entitled to some of the profits to make our investment back. Yes, Frankie here is the one standing behind the counter all day, but now we're providing a CPA and a tax accountant and health benefits that he didn't have before. Plus, we're out there hustling, driving in business. We might not punch a clock, but we're working to increase the value for everyone. You know what the problem is?"

"Rampant capitalism?" I suggested. I wasn't a financial wizard by any means, but I was starting to think that even if the Fjord Capital model was legal, it wasn't very ethical.

Savannah blinked at me in surprise. "No. The problem is that Frankie Hornsby doesn't know a good thing when it lands in his lap. You should talk to Darlene Daye. She'll tell you what's what."

"Fine," I agreed. "Let's take a drive."

"You know, I'm really surprised you and I aren't on the same page on this," Savannah said as I drove to the secondhand shop.

"How so?"

"You're a small business owner. So am I. It just happens that my business was investing in other small businesses."

"I own the kind of business that Fjord Capital preyed on," I corrected her. "You were literally trying to lure me, my sisters, and Sip & Spin into your web just a few days ago."

"Think about it, Juni. A big check to do whatever you please with. Health insurance. Paid vacations. Holidays. A 401(k). All the benefits of working for someone else, but you're still your own boss."

Personally, I couldn't see why she was wasting her breath. Even if I hadn't gotten a good peek behind the curtain already, with Zack out of the picture, there was no more investment firm. "Didn't you tell me that you buy fifty-one percent so you can be the boss?"

"It's not like that. We didn't micromanage. Wait until you talk to Darlene. You'll see. It's mostly just for legal reasons. When Fjord Capital is the majority owner, then everyone under the Fjord umbrella benefits," she said.

Savannah may have thought I hadn't been paying attention, but I do remember Zack using that exact phrase. It stood out to me at the time because it sounded like nonsense then and sounded like nonsense now. "Savannah, no offense, but all you're doing is digging the hole deeper." If their other clients were anything like Frankie Hornsby, I could totally see any one of them killing Zack out of sheer desperation.

Frankie's crash-and-burn method was extreme, but it didn't nearly reach the level of murder, at least not in my eyes. I wondered if Darlene Daye was going to be any different.

Darlene's secondhand shop, Rediscovered Treasures, was on the edge of town. Out near the tiny municipal airport and train tracks was a cluster of warehouses that played host to everything from storage lockers to rental cars. My Uncle Calvin and his best friend, Samuel, used to run their gag-gift business, Prankenstein, out of one of those warehouses. I still on occasion found glitter in random places as a not-so-fond reminder.

Our local mechanic, Esméralda Martín-Brown, had a shop out this way, too. I hoped she wasn't going to be too upset when she found out that Tansy's car got towed to one of Marcus's body shops instead of her own. I should probably stop in and explain before she heard about it through the grapevine, but I had more pressing matters to attend to first.

Rediscovered Treasures would have been absolutely swarmed if it were on Main Street. The storefront was filled with intriguing pieces just beckoning shoppers to come inside and browse for an hour, during which time they could convince themselves that they did, in fact, need that 1920s settee. Or maybe that was just me.

Despite the out-of-the-way location, squeezed in between a rug wholesaler and a CrossFit box—don't ever call it a "gym" or they'll get mad and trust me, you do *not* want to upset someone who flips tractor tires for fun—Rediscovered Treasures was busy. Several cars were parked in front of the sweet little secondhand store with a lovely purple awning and enormous windows. Even the security bars were decorative, and were painted white with purple flourishes.

"Maybe you should stay in the car," I suggested.

"Don't worry, Darlene loves me," Savannah said.

"I'm sure she does, but who do you think she'll speak more freely in front of? Me or one of her predatory business partners?" Frankie had certainly opened up after she'd left. I needed honest answers, and I wasn't sure I'd get them with Savannah standing over my shoulder every time I tried to question someone.

"I don't know," she said, squirming a bit. I think she was tired of being referred to as "predatory," but if the size-six strappy sandal fit . . . "Who's she going to want to talk to? The woman who saved her business or a stranger?"

"I'll make you a deal. I'll go in there alone, and if Darlene won't talk to me, I'll come get you."

"Whatever," Savannah said. "Just leave the keys so I can roll down the windows if I get hot."

I tossed her the keys and headed inside, only to immediately get distracted by a bookshelf filled with early nineteen-hundred editions of famous books. I ran my finger along their spines, stopping at a first edition of Agatha Christie's *Murder on the Orient Express*. I picked it up and checked the price tag. It was out of my price range. Then again, these days, a bottle of water at the gas station was out of my price range. Good thing, too, because single-use bottles were horrible on the environment.

"See anything you like?" the shop's owner asked, sidling up next to me. "Oh, that's a personal favorite of mine."

"Mine too," I admitted as I carefully placed it back on the shelf. I turned to face Darlene Daye. She was a white woman somewhere between Tansy's age and my mom's. Her hair was pulled up in a neat bun and reading glasses hung around her neck on a beaded chain. She wore a green pantsuit with a floral blouse and, like most people in retail, had on sensible shoes.

"Hi!" I said. "I don't know if you remember me, but I'm Juni Jessup. Bea's daughter?"

"Of course I remember you, Juni." She leaned in and gave me a hug. "I used to come over to your parents' house all the time when you were younger, for game night. But I haven't seen you since you were in high school." She studied my face. "You're a dead ringer for your mom."

"Thanks," I said, and I meant it. Some people might

get insulted being told they look like someone thirty years their senior, but I took it as a compliment. My mom was an attractive woman back in the day. Still was, truth be told.

"Did you know that I worked at your grandparents' record shop one summer?"

"I did not." I wasn't surprised. The record shop had always been hiring teenagers, which in retrospect, was the very reason I existed. They hired my dad one summer, where he met and fell in love with Mom. The rest was history.

"Best job I ever had," Darlene said. "Except this one, of course. I hear you and your sisters resurrected the old shop."

"We did," I agreed. "Sip & Spin Records on Main."

"Well, isn't that just delightful? I keep meaning to stop in but you know how it gets. I've always got my hands full here."

"This place is pretty amazing," I said.

"Isn't it? Sorry if I sound like I'm bragging, but this shop represents my life's work."

"I could spend all day here," I told her.

"And you're welcome to, of course." Her eyes got big. "Oh, do I have just the thing for you." She took me by the hand and dragged me through a maze of aisles, each curated with perfect displays of items clamoring for my attention.

"Slow down! I want to look at everything."

"There's plenty of time for that later," she insisted. She came to a halt. "Well? What do you think?"

She slid out of the way and I found myself staring at a vintage restored upright Victrola record player. The lid was propped open and there was already a record sitting on the player. "May I?" I asked, with the excited tone of voice I usually reserved for puppies and free ice cream.

"Of course." I spun the crank a few times and was instantly transported to my grandparents' sitting room. They had a big standup Victrola just like this one from 1920 or so. It was a four-foot-high cabinet, with a record player under the lid and a horn concealed behind doors below. My grandparents rarely let me touch it, much less play records on it. "You certain?" I asked, just to be safe.

"Go for it. Records are meant to be played, aren't they?"

I eased the arm down. The needle touched the spinning record and the sweet, scratchy sounds of early New Orleans jazz filled the shop. I stood there with my eyes closed, listening to a song that was recorded a hundred years before I was born that still sounded exactly the same to this day.

"I thought you'd like that," she said when the song ended. She lifted the arm and the record stopped spinning.

"My grandparents had one just like it," I said.

Darlene laughed. "Not quite." She reached into the cabinet doors, pulled out a record, and handed it to me. On the cover was a yellowed sticker. Printed on the sticker in my grandmother's meticulous handwriting were the words "Property of Rose Voigt."

CHAPTER 13

I stared at the record in my hands. "This record belonged to my grandma."

"Honey, the whole Victrola belonged to your grandma."

"No wonder it looked so familiar," I said. I put the record back gently and closed the lid. I ran my hand over the mahogany cabinet. "I can't believe you have this."

There was a price tag hanging from the crank, but I couldn't bring myself to check it. If I still had a car, I would have gladly sold it to buy back this piece of my family's history. I wonder if Marcus would notice if I traded his cute little loaner SUV. Unable to help myself, I looked at the tag. "Ouch." I couldn't afford it. Maybe, back when I was working for a tech company and socking most of my paycheck away for a down payment on a house I never got around to buying, I could have, but not now that I'd invested my entire nest egg into Sip & Spin.

"I know, it's a little much, but it's worth that easily. Then again, it's been on the floor for ages, and you're the first person to show any real interest in it. Why don't you take it home with you?"

I shook my head sadly. "I can't."

"Sure you can. I'm sure your mom wouldn't mind."

"My mom?" I asked.

Darlene laughed. Hers was a pleasant laugh. Like the Victrola, it sounded like magic. "Bea dropped it off on consignment a few years ago. It never sold, obviously. It's been taking up valuable floor space, but I knew that the right person would come along eventually. I should have guessed it would be a Jessup. It's yours if you want it. Need some help loading it up?"

"I don't think it will fit in my car," I told her, my head spinning. Marcus's loaner SUV was too small.

"Swing by anytime, and I'll have my guys help you load it."

I was already trying to figure out where to put it. It wasn't fair to Maggie to bring it to Tansy's. It was a piece of our family history. It belonged to all of us. At Sip & Spin, we could share it with the world. Well, not the world, maybe, but Cedar River and the greater Austin area.

I caressed the lid once more. "Not a problem. Give me a day or two to get a truck, and I'll be back."

"Take your time." Darlene said. "I was about to rotate it back to the warehouse. I try to keep stock moving so nothing stays on the floor long if it isn't selling. The Victrola would have been back in storage for at least three months if you'd come in tomorrow."

"Then it's a good thing I came in today," I said.

"It is," she agreed.

"The idea of rotating your stock constantly is a good one. Tansy does that at the shop, too. Always rearranging and moving merchandise so it gets new eyes on it even if the same shopper comes in every week."

"Oh, I can't take credit for that. A while ago, business was down. Way down. I had shoppers, but just a few a day and they never stayed for long. Then I met this woman who helped me turn things around."

"Savannah Goodwin?" I asked.

"Oh, you know her? She and her partner were my

saving grace. I've always wanted to own a business but to be perfectly honest, I had no idea how to run it."

"I feel the same way," I admitted. "If it weren't for Tansy's musical know-how and Maggie's bookkeeping skills, I don't know where we'd be. But what about the drawbacks to getting outside help?"

Darlene grinned. "Are you kidding me? They gave me the money I needed to turn this place from a dark, dusty warehouse into a world-class showroom. I used to have my vintage dresses shoved onto racks. No one ever looked at them. Who can blame them? They looked like they belonged in an outlet reject pile. Now look!"

She led the way to a corner of the store that had been transformed into a boutique with antique three-way mirrors. Silk folding screens formed dressing rooms. Gorgeous hand-sewn gowns were displayed on sleek metal mannequins. "Rediscovered Treasures is the premiere destination for discriminating prom shoppers, brides-to-be, and absolutely anyone who is anyone in Travis County. Did you know that the governor shops here?"

"That's quite an improvement over the shop I remember. Don't get me wrong, Darlene. Your shop has always been a diamond. It was just a little rougher back in the day."

"You're telling me. I'll have to admit, I pushed back on some of Savannah's more radical ideas, like displaying less merchandise, raising prices, and replacing sticker prices with hand-lettered tags, but it works. I'm only open four days a week now, and I have three times as much business. Even with their cut, I'm taking home twice as much as I ever was before. It's a miracle."

"I'm glad to hear it," I told her. Darlene's testimonial was more along the lines of what Zack and Savannah promised than what Frankie Hornsby had experienced.

I wondered why one store thrived under their model and the other collapsed. Granted, Darlene had embraced their suggestions while Frankie pushed back against them, but they were still two similar businesses in the same town with completely different outcomes. I guess there was no one-size-fits-all formula for small business success. Or, Darlene got lucky and Frankie didn't.

Now came the hard part. "Speaking of Savannah, you know her partner Zack Fjord, don't you?"

"Zack? Of course I do. He isn't in here much. Mostly I deal with Savannah. But sheesh, that man is a looker, isn't he? If I was twenty years younger, I'd get myself in a heap of trouble with that one, if you know what I mean."

I blushed. One of the oddest things about moving back to Cedar River as an adult was getting to know people my parents' age, or older, as friends and contemporaries. Even women like Miss Edie, who I'd always respect as my elder, I appreciated on a deeper level now that I was a grown-up, or at least as much of a grown-up as I suspected I'd ever be. But it was one thing to connect with adults that had babysat me once upon a time; it was another thing completely to hear them talk so frankly about their private business.

"Yeah, you know what I'm talking about," Darlene said, noting my embarrassed expression.

"About Zack." I paused. I hated this part. "I'm sorry to be the one to tell you this, but he passed away recently."

"He what?" Darlene touched her own breastbone. "When? How?" She leaned against one of the displays as her eyes filled with tears.

"It was the night of the storm," I told her.

"No. That's not possible," she insisted.

"I'm sorry. I'm sure someone would have notified you earlier, but with the phones and internet being down for a few days, communication has been shoddier than normal."

"It's just unthinkable. And Savannah?"

"She's taking this about as well as anyone can expect. She's strong."

Darlene looked like she needed to sit down. "Yes, of course. She is." She pulled a lacy handkerchief out of one of the pockets of her skirt and wiped at her eyes. "I can't even imagine. You'll give her my condolences, won't you?"

I nodded. "Of course I will. But are *you* going to be okay?" I didn't know how to comfort her. At least she hadn't been downright gleeful about Zack's passing like Frankie Hornsby had been. That had been awkward.

Darlene sniffled. "I just need a minute to process."

Two women entered the boutique section. The older one kept glancing in our direction as the younger examined the dresses. Darlene dabbed at her eyes one last time before returning her handkerchief to her pocket. She straightened and took a few deep breaths. Once she looked steady, she said, "Juni, if you'll excuse me, I should see if they need help. Do come back soon."

"I will," I promised her. We both had shops that thrived on nostalgia. Maybe there was a mutual way to drive business to each other. I'd have to talk to my sisters about that.

Back in the car, I'd barely had time to buckle my seat belt when Savannah started demanding information. "Well? What did Darlene have to say?"

"She adores you. And Fjord Capital. She's horribly upset to hear about Zack's passing, and sends her love."

Savannah sniffled. "I told you. I know you see me as some evil money-grubbing leech, but unless the businesses we invest in make money, we didn't make money. It was in everyone's interest to make improvements and capitalize on the market."

"I don't get it," I admitted. "Why is Rediscovered Treasures thriving while Blow Your Own Horn is barely hanging on?"

"Think about it, Juni. If a small business is doing well, they don't need us. When we invest in a struggling business, we try to turn it around, but it doesn't always work. That's the risk we take. Look at Sip & Spin Records. You're teetering on the edge, but you and your sisters aren't desperate. Not yet."

"Oof," I said. That hurt.

"Sorry if it sounds harsh, but it's the truth. If you can't face facts, you're not going to make it."

I had to admit I was impressed. "I understand you're upset about having to start over after all the work you've put into Fjord Capital, but you're good at what you do, Savannah," I told her. After talking with Frankie, I hadn't been so sure I wanted to have anything to do with Savannah, but Darlene showed me another side of her. The details of this case—as I couldn't help thinking of it—and my feelings toward Savannah were getting more confusing by the minute. "I'm certain you'll land on your feet."

"I hope so," she said with a determined look on her face. "Where to next?"

"Lunch," I told her. "I'm starving."

There were plenty of food choices in Cedar River, as long as you were in the mood for BBQ, steak, or diner food. Anything else meant placing an order with the local delivery service, Roadrunners, making it yourself, or driving to one of the nearby towns. Roadrunners was probably busy and my cooking skills were marginal at best, so I opted to drive. Good thing I wasn't dependent on my trike today.

"What are you in the mood for?" I asked her.

Savannah gave me a half-hearted shrug. "I don't have much of an appetite."

I felt for her. Really, I did. But I couldn't remember ever being so upset that I couldn't eat something.

"What sounds good? Sushi? Fried chicken? Salad?" I prompted.

"Seriously, I don't care."

"Let me know if you change your mind," I said and headed for the highway, only to hit a literal dead end a mile later. An enormous tree lay across the road. A crew was hard at work clearing it. A man in an orange vest waved me away.

Instead of turning around and retracing our path, I choose a detour that took us along the river. It was a lovely day with clear, blue skies. After the long, hot summer, the trees lining the riverbank were full and green. The river, which was normally tame and lazy—perfect for floating along in innertubes on long summer days—roared and frothed below us. Swollen with storm water, it flowed far beyond the usual reaches of its bank, crashing around boulders and exposed tree roots.

It reminded me of the wilder parts of rural Texas, which could be beautiful and dangerous at the same time. Then again, the same could be said of downtown Austin at night.

"What's that?" Savannah asked. Her question drew me out of my reverie, and I realized I really should be paying more attention to the road, which was still a minefield of debris left over from the storm. "Another road crew?"

I slowed as we approached a bend in the road that followed the meandering path of the river. Once the road straightened out again, I could see an ambulance parked on the narrow shoulder. Its lights were on, but the siren was silent. A dozen scenarios went through my mind as I pulled up behind the ambulance and cut the engine.

"What are you doing?"

Being nosy? Being a concerned citizen? I wasn't quite sure how to answer that, so I told Savannah, "Be right back."

I walked around the ambulance. My two favorite EMTs, Kitty and Rocco, were standing near the engine, watching the churning river.

"Hey," I said.

Kitty jumped. Rocco laughed at her. "What are you doing here?" she asked.

"The road up by the airport's blocked, so I was taking a detour. What's going on?"

"Hey, Juni," Rocco said. He was a white man a few years younger than me. His hair was short and ginger with just a hint of curl. Today, he wore green scrubs. "Imagine seeing you here."

Kitty was also white, wore similar green scrubs and was about the same height, but that was where the similarities ended. It was hard to gauge with her dark blonde hair pulled back in a tight bun, but when she let it down, it was even longer than mine. Whereas Rocco was bulky, Kitty almost looked fragile—but I'd seen her sling a grown man over her shoulder and carry him up a flight of stairs, so looks could be deceiving.

"Pay up," she said to her partner, holding out her hand.

Rocco dug through his wallet and came up with a twenty. He slapped it into her palm. "Did Kitty call you?" he asked me.

Kitty pocketed the bill. "Nope."

"What's that for?" I asked, pointing at her pocket.

"We've got a pool going that you'll show up within ten minutes of anything even remotely interesting happening in Cedar River," Kitty explained. "So far, I'm up."

That was discomforting. "It's not my fault," I said.

"Maybe not, but it sure makes things more fun around here. Not to mention, I can pay my rent thanks to you. Well, you and Rocco," she said with a grin. She patted her pocket. "Lunch next week? My treat."

"Sounds great," I told her, deciding to let the betting

pool go for the moment—especially if I was getting a free meal out of it. "And don't forget family dinner tonight at Maggie's."

"If I get off work on time, I'll be there," she promised. Kitty's schedule was unpredictable. Granted, I didn't have a set schedule either and I was no stranger to working doubles when needed, but in theory I came and went as I pleased. It was the blessing, and the curse, of being a small business owner.

"What's going on?" I asked, hoping that now that the pleasantries were out of the way, one of them would give me a straight answer. I guess that was too much to wish for.

"See for yourself." Kitty gave me the "go ahead" gesture.

The banks of the river were steep. Just around the next bend was an old bridge, which was perfect for fishing from. The town was working on a project to turn it into part of a new bike path. I was very much looking forward to that.

I walked to the edge. The ground was soft from the rain and it sucked at my shoes. I was careful to not get too close. If I fell into the river when it was this angry, I'd be swept downstream by the rapids. I hoped that fate had not befallen anyone else, but as I peered over the side, my worst fears were confirmed.

Lying on the riverbank was a leg. Beyond that, an arm. A little farther still was a lump of hair. Officer Jayden Holt was bent over what looked like a human head. I shivered, turned, and almost plowed right into Beau in my haste to retreat.

He grabbed my shoulders before we could collide. "Howdy, Junebug. Fancy bumping into you here." He looked over at the ambulance, where the EMTs were laughing hysterically. I blinked at them in surprise. I knew they had a rough job and humor sometimes took the sting out of it, but it seemed callous, even for them. "Kitty called you, didn't she?"

I shook my head.

"Shucks," he said, reaching for his wallet. I don't know what was more disconcerting, that the first responders in this town were so callous, or that Beau had bet against me. He pulled out a twenty and passed it to Kitty. "You okay? You look like you've seen a ghost."

I swallowed hard. "No. I'm not okay. Not even a little bit. Why should I be?"

"Juni, you need to take a closer look."

"I really, really don't," I insisted.

"What on earth is wrong with this town?" Savannah asked, joining us. "What kind of sicko throws mannequins in the river?"

"Wait, those are mannequins?" I asked.

"Of course," Savannah said. "What did you think they were?"

I must have looked like I was about to burst into tears, because Kitty threw her arms around me. "Oh, Juni, don't cry! They're not real."

"No, it's okay," I said. "I'm fine." And I was, after the initial shock wore off. I was just a little thrown. After what I'd witnessed already this week, it wouldn't do for me to fall apart now over some plastic limbs. "Y'all remember Savannah?" I wasn't sure if she'd formally met Rocco and Kitty, but there were nods all around. She gave a cutesy finger wave to Beau.

"Mayor Lydell-Waite called in the report," Beau explained. "Apparently, she was walking her dog along the river and came across one of the mannequins. Got quite the shock."

"So it's all a sick joke?"

"Sick? Yeah. Joke? I don't think so," Beau said. "I'm

thinking someone dumped the mannequins in the river to get rid of them. They floated up with all the recent rain and when the river started to recede, they were visible along the bank. Who knows how many more limbs we'll discover downstream."

I shuddered again. Sure, I knew it wasn't real, but I couldn't help myself. "Why would anyone throw trash in the river, when the dump is right down the road?"

"Lazy. Cheap. Garbage human being. Take your pick," Kitty said.

"Hey, can I have a second?" Beau asked. I nodded, and followed him a short walk away to where the others couldn't hear us over the roar of the river. "Seriously, are you okay?"

"Yeah," I said, nodding. "Just a little shaken up."

"I'm sorry." He rested his hand on my shoulder. "Considering how many dead bodies you've found, Kitty probably thought you were immune by now. I'm sure she never would have let you see that if she thought it would upset you."

"Immune? Not hardly. If I never find another body, I'll be happy."

"You and me both," Beau agreed.

"Besides, we both know if Kitty had warned me not to look, I would have anyway," I admitted.

"True. Now here's where it gets weird," Beau started.

"Just now? This moment is when it starts to get weird?" I gestured toward the swollen river. "Cedar River is spitting out plastic body parts."

"It's been a busy week. Tempers flared during the power outage, and we've got our hands full settling disputes. Not to mention we've still got a few road closures, families displaced from the storm, and the vehicular fatality on Main. And now, this."

"Sounds like you've got your hands full."

Beau grinned at me. "That's where you come in."

I looked at him, expecting an innuendo, but none was forthcoming. "How so?"

"You hear things, Juni. You know people. Your mom might make the best pot roast in town, but she's also the biggest gossip in Travis County."

"All true," I admitted.

He took a deep breath. "How about if I ask you to keep an ear out? Don't go poking your finger into any hornet nests or anything, but if you happen to hear something about illegal dumping in the river, you'll let me know?"

"You want me to find out who dumped the mannequins in the river?" I asked. It almost sounded like Beau Russell was admitting that I was a half-decent investigator. Would wonders never cease?

He rubbed his forehead. "No. That's not what I said. Not at all. Just maybe keep your eyes open and give me a shout if you see or hear anything."

"*You* want *me* to investigate," I said gleefully. "You gonna deputize me or something? Oh, do I get a badge?"

"I knew this was a bad idea," he grumbled.

"No, no, it's a great idea," I said, clapping my hands. "Deputy Jessup. I like the sound of that."

"I'm gonna regret this, aren't I?" he asked.

I gave him a peck on the cheek. "Probably."

Jayden climbed up the bank next to us. "You talk to her?" she asked him.

He rolled his eyes skyward. "Yeah. I talked to her. And she's on board, so help us."

"I knew she would be." Jayden turned to me. "Come on, let's get a closer look."

She and Beau helped me down the slippery slope. Up close, it was obvious that the arms and legs weren't real, just as it was obvious they'd come from multiple manne-quins, unless mannequins had three arms and two left feet. I pulled out my phone and took photos of the dismembered mannequin parts. There was a lot number and a faded manufacturer's stamp on the inside of one of the arm joints, and a barely legible tag sewn into the wig.

"Can I take these with me?" I asked.

"It's evidence," Beau said. "So when we do catch the perp, we can prosecute them."

"Not even one of the arms?" I asked.

"You heard the man. Come on, Juni, I'll walk you back to your car." Jayden gave me a hand—no pun intended—to climb back up the soggy riverbank.

"Was it your idea or his?" I asked. "To ask me to help?"

"Why does it matter?"

"Because if it was his idea, I'd think that he was worried I might be looking into who killed Zack Fjord, and this was his way of distracting me," I said.

"You're not looking into who killed Zack Fjord, are you?" Jayden asked.

"Who? Me?" I tried to look innocent. I failed.

"Just focus on the mannequins," Jayden said. "And leave the serious investigations to the professionals."

"Sure thing, Officer," I said. I waved over at Kitty. "Don't forget! Family dinner tonight!"

Savannah buckled herself into the passenger seat as I got in behind the wheel. As we eased past the emergency vehicles still on the shoulder and headed back to town, I couldn't help but notice that Jayden never had answered my question about whether it had been Beau's idea or hers to ask for my help figuring out who was dumping garbage into our town water supply.

CHAPTER 14

To my surprise, Teddy was waiting in the driveway when I got home. I parked the car and waved at him as I got out. "I can't quite put my finger on it, but there's something different about your tricycle," he said, looking over the small SUV.

"It's a loaner," I explained.

Before he could respond, the passenger side of the car opened and Savannah stepped out. "Savannah Goodwin?" Teddy asked. At the same time, she said, "Teddy Garza!" She hurried around the front of the car and threw her arms around his neck. "Fancy meeting you here!"

"I was just thinking the same thing," he said, squeezing her in a bear hug.

"Y'all know each other?" I asked, my curiosity piqued. Teddy wasn't a small business owner; he was a postal employee. His family owned their farm and associated dairy business outright, and they weren't in any financial trouble, as least none that I knew about. Savannah wasn't from around here. So how had their paths crossed?

"We met on Tinder," Teddy said, and I felt a baseball-size lump form in my throat. Yes, I knew I had no right, seeing how I was dating two men at once, but I was jealous at the idea of Teddy seeing someone else. There. I admitted it. At least to myself.

It shouldn't matter that Teddy had been, or even if he still was, on a dating app. And of course, he'd attract plenty of attention. Who wouldn't want to go out with him? He was quite a catch, even if it had taken me absolute ages to realize it.

"Teddy's one of the good ones," Savannah said, entwining her arm with his.

"Yup," I agreed. I felt sorry for Savannah. She'd lost her home. Her job. Her boyfriend. She'd been witness to her partner's death and was rightfully scared. But she'd also lied to me, hid from the cops, and preyed on small businesses like mine. And now, she was getting a little too friendly with *my* Teddy. "He most certainly is," I said with forced brightness.

"What brings you to Cedar River? Work?" he asked. If Teddy sensed any tension in the air, he didn't let it show. Then he turned to me. "Savannah never takes a day off."

"Actually . . ." She swallowed hard. "It's Zack. He's dead."

"Zack, your partner? He's dead? No way. Oh hon, I'm sorry. How're you holding up?" Teddy asked.

"I've been better," she admitted.

While they talked, I wondered what would have happened if I'd asked Teddy to be my plus-one at the hockey game instead of Beau. Would the night have ended differently? Maybe Teddy and Savannah would have gone out together afterward, leaving me to grab an Uber back. Zack might have gone straight home instead of detouring through Cedar River.

I shook my head. No. It didn't do anyone any good wondering what could have been. Besides, it didn't make any sense. Savannah and Zack had been a couple. She wasn't dating Teddy anymore. She was living in Zack's penthouse. She wouldn't have gone home with Teddy. Zack would still have been too drunk to drive. She still would have been in Cedar River with Zack. Zack still would have died.

Only, why were they in Cedar River? Sure, they had investments in town, but nothing that needed their attention late at night in the middle of a torrential thunderstorm. Why were they all the way out here instead of back in Austin? And more importantly, who knew they would be here?

"What exactly were you doing in Cedar River Wednesday night?" I blurted out.

"Huh?" Savannah asked, giving me a confused look. She unwound her arm from Teddy's.

"Wednesday. After the game. Why were you and Zack on Main Street in the middle of the storm in the first place?"

Savannah shrugged. "I don't actually know. When we were leaving the game, Zack got a text. He told me we needed to swing by Cedar River."

"Back up," I said. "What text? You didn't mention a text before. Who was it from? What did it say?"

She shrugged. "I didn't see it. Zack said it would only take a minute. Cedar River was out of our way, but he was insistent, so I didn't argue. By the time we got here, Zack was asleep on the seat next to me."

"Asleep or passed out?" I asked. "Because last time you told that story, you said he was passed out." It was weird that she'd repeated the same story almost verbatim to me and then, the next morning, to Beau, but had left out the mysterious text message. Her story was changing.

"Asleep, passed out, what difference does it make?"

"Hey, I don't want to interrupt, but we're gonna be late, Juni," Teddy said.

"Late?" I asked. I felt like I was missing something.

"Family dinner? You invited me?"

"Family dinner!" I said. "That's tonight." My stomach

growled and I realized that between the investigation and the mannequins, I'd missed lunch. That wasn't like me.

"Is this a bad time?" he asked, looking from me to Savannah.

"No, of course not," she said, before I could. "I need to go get freshened up before dinner." She took Teddy's arm again. "Come on, you can keep me company. We'll catch up." She led him away toward the cottage.

I headed into the main house. Like magic, Daffy appeared out of nowhere and wound himself at my feet. "Poor Daffy. You must be hungry." I grabbed a can of cat food, opened it, and put it down on the floor for him. "You know," I confided in the cat while he ate, "whenever I have to freshen up, I hardly ever want company around."

As soon as the words were out of my mouth, I wished I could take them back. "Sorry. That was uncharitable." I didn't know who I was apologizing to. Daffy? Savannah? Teddy? Myself? I shook my head to clear my negative thoughts. I didn't have time for them, and Savannah had enough trouble on her plate without my irrational jealousy. Teddy and Savannah were old news, and I had dinner to get ready for.

A few minutes later, I was waiting by the cars when Savannah and Teddy came out of the cottage, laughing at a shared joke. "Want a lift?" Teddy asked as soon as he saw me.

I wanted nothing more than to jump in his Jeep with him and leave Savannah standing alone in the driveway, but that would be rude. "Tansy might want the car. I've been monopolizing it all day."

"No worries. I'll follow you."

I headed for the SUV and Teddy went to his Jeep. Savannah tagged along with me and buckled herself into the passenger seat. "That sure is a nice surprise, bumping into Teddy Garza," she said. "He's such a sweetheart."

"I didn't realize you knew each other," I said. I had a million questions. When had they dated? For how long? How long ago? Was it serious? Obviously, it had ended amicably. I would expect nothing less of Teddy. But did he break it off with her or was it the other way around? "So, Teddy . . . ?"

"Isn't he the best?" she asked.

"Yeah. Totally," I agreed wholeheartedly. "Except, I thought you were with Zack?" I didn't mean to pry. I was just curious. Honest.

"I met Teddy before Zack and I got together," she clarified. "I mean, we were already in business together, but we weren't *together* together, if you get my drift."

I nodded. "Yup."

"And you and Teddy?" she asked.

"Known each other since we were kids," I explained.

She nodded slowly. "But you're dating that cute cop, right? Speaking of cops, you should tell him about the text message that Zack got that made us detour to Cedar River," she said. "It might be significant." Then she tilted her head. "Wait a second, you *are* dating that Beau guy, right?"

"It's complicated," I admitted.

"I knew it!" Savannah turned toward me in her seat. "I saw the way you were looking at Teddy. You're into him, aren't you?"

"Oh look, we're at my sister's," I said, awkwardly changing the subject as I pulled into a parking spot along the curb. The driveway was full. Maggie's and J.T.'s cars were parked at the top of the driveway, blocked in by the shiny car with dealer's tags that Marcus had been driving earlier and Beau's big, familiar black truck. "Uh-oh," I murmured under my breath.

Savannah must have heard me. "Uh-oh?"

"You know, we don't have to go inside. Family dinners can be a lot," I said. I wasn't sure what was worse: the idea of spending the next hour or so watching Savannah and Teddy catch up, or spending it with Teddy and Beau competing for my attention.

"Don't be silly. I adore your sisters. I'm sure the rest of your family is great, too." Savannah got out of the car.

Teddy parked behind me and joined us as we headed up the walk. He took my hand as we reached the front door. "Looks like a full house," he remarked casually. I guess he'd noticed Beau's truck, too. Then again, the enormous truck was hard to miss.

"It's not too late to get takeout instead," I said.

"Where's the fun in that?" he asked, opening the front door. In my family, we didn't knock when we were expected.

If I hadn't lost track of time, I would have shown up early and helped Maggie put the finishing touches on dinner. She was the best cook in the family, but I was an expert at getting the sweet tea out of the fridge and carrying it over to the table. Only today, someone had beat me to it. Beau and Marcus were already setting the table when we walked in.

"We need two more chairs," I said. There was always room at the table. Family dinner was an informal affair that could range from three to twenty, depending on who was hungry. Both of my sisters were already here, along with my brother-in-law, Mom, her boyfriend, Beau, Teddy, Savannah, Uncle Calvin, and me.

As crowded as it seemed, we were missing a few familiar faces. "No date tonight, Calvin?" I asked my uncle.

He grinned mischievously at me. "If I'd known you were bringing two dates, I might have invited a friend also."

"Oh shush, you," I said, swatting at his arm.

"Don't shush me, little girl," he said, even as he carried another chair to the table.

"How was your fishing trip?" I asked.

"It was a washout, but before the storm hit, Samuel caught a whopper. Speaking of which, set a place for Samuel, too," he said. Beau shuffled plates to make room for more diners. "He said he might drop by in time for dessert."

"Just like Samuel," Tansy said, emerging from the kitchen with a bowl of salad. "He can smell pecan pie from two counties away."

"Good thing my wife makes the best pecan pie in the state," J.T. said. He was right on Tansy's heels, balancing trays laden down with food along his arm like a professional server. Then again, with the regularity that he and Maggie hosted large dinners, he might as well be one by now.

Marcus pulled a chair out for Mom. She sat. "Maggie, you've outdone yourself," he said as my sister joined us.

"Thank you," she said graciously. I wasn't sure when, or if, she was ever going to accept Marcus as part of the family, but she wasn't going to be anything less than polite to him while he was at her table. "Savannah, so glad you could join us!"

"Thanks for having me," Savannah said.

"That's our Juni, inviting everyone to dinner," Beau said. He sat and patted the chair next to him for me.

"Oh, so that's why you didn't want to come inside," Savannah said as she sat herself across the table from Beau. "Makes sense now." I blushed. I knew she was just saying what everyone was already thinking, but it was still embarrassing to be called out like that.

Teddy squeezed my hand then let go so he could pull the chair out for me before seating himself on my other side. "Funny, I don't remember inviting you tonight," I replied to Beau. I might be dating two guys at the same time, but I wasn't a monster. I was honest with both of them while trying my hardest to not throw it in their faces. I wouldn't purposefully invite them both to the same function.

Although, to be fair, I didn't remember inviting Teddy, either, but he was a regular at family dinners lately. Beau was not. Nothing against Beau, I just got tired of Tansy picking arguments with him. It was easier to keep the peace when they weren't in the same room.

"Sure you did," Beau said. He reached for a plate of warm cornbread muffins, took one, and passed them to me. "Today? At the river?"

Maggie passed a bowl. "Try it with the jalapeño jelly. Got it at the farmer's market."

I took a cornbread muffin and slathered it with jelly. "Looks great," I told her, passing the cornbread and jelly to Teddy before turning back to Beau. "For the record, that invitation was meant for Kitty. Not you. And you know it."

"Hey, any excuse to eat Maggie's home cooking," he said with a grin.

I fought the urge to roll my eyes. "Speaking of Kitty, is she coming?" I asked J.T.

"She's working late," my brother-in-law said. When his cousin moved to Cedar River, we hit it off right away. She was fun, with a mischievous edge. We didn't hang out as much as I'd like, because our schedules often clashed, but she fit right in with the family. "Don't worry, I'll save her a plate."

"This looks delicious," Savannah said. As the food circulated around the table, we all heaped huge scoops onto our plates. Savannah was more subdued, taking small portions of everything. Amateur.

Teddy leaned around me. "I hear you *caught* quite the case at the river today, pardon the pun," he said to Beau.

Beau didn't question how Teddy knew about the mannequins that the river had washed up. News traveled fast.

Instead, he put his arm around the back of my chair. "Good thing Juni offered to look into it, seeing as how my hands are already full." He wiggled his eyebrows. "Get it? Hands? As in mannequin hands?"

"Only, those mannequins didn't have hands," I said. I tried to remember what I'd seen along the riverbank.

Once I knew they were fake and the initial shock had worn off, I'd taken a closer look. The mannequins were disjointed, literally. Someone had disassembled them, probably to make them easier to carry. I'd seen heads, torsos, arms, legs, and wigs. Most of the legs still had feet attached to them, but none of the arms had hands. I wondered why that was.

"The cheap ones sometimes don't," Savannah said.

"Oh really?" Beau asked.

"Those mannequins you found at the river were bargain-basement junk. Literally." Unlike the rest of us, she politely put her fork to the side while she spoke. "You saw the mannequins at Darlene's shop. Did they have hands?"

I had to think about it. I nodded. "The ones in the boutique did."

"That's because Darlene has discriminating tastes. Put an expensive dress on a cheap mannequin, and it looks cheap. Put a cheap dress on an expensive mannequin, and it looks expensive. It's advertising one-oh-one," she explained.

"Then why would anyone buy cheap mannequins?" I asked.

"Precisely because they're cheap," Maggie said. "It's like anything else in this world. You can't always afford the top-of-the-line model, but you get what you pay for."

I recognized that argument. It was the same one she'd used when talking Tansy and me into buying one of the more expensive barista machines instead of the model that had been on sale. Good thing, too. The model I'd wanted had since been recalled after it burned someone.

"As usual, you're right," Tansy said. She must have been thinking about the barista station, too, because she nodded at our sister before turning her attention to Savannah. "How do you know so much about mannequins?"

"We've invested in a few clothing stores," she said.

"Any that feature bargain-basement, hand-less mannequins?" Beau asked.

Savannah shook her head. "Not to my knowledge. If I saw those Sears-outlet rejects on the floor of one of my stores, I'd toss them in the river myself."

"Oh, you would?" Beau asked, giving her that ridiculously handsome grin of his, the one he used to disarm poor, unsuspecting victims and charm kittens out of trees.

Savannah squirmed under his gaze. "Not that I did," she said, defensively.

Beau had his arm around the back of my chair, but he was laser-focused on the guest seated across from him.

"Can I have a minute?" I hissed at him.

He took a big bite of food and chewed slowly. He pointed at his mouth as if he was too intent on eating to be bothered to answer me.

I stood, pushing my chair back as I tugged his arm. "Y'all will have to excuse us a second." I led him away from the table. He paused in the foyer. "Not here," I told him. I grabbed his hat off the rack and headed outside. He followed. "Close the door behind you."

He did. "What's all the fuss about?" He glanced back at the house. "Or did you just need some quality alone time with me? All you ever have to do is ask."

"What I need is for you to not invite yourself to my family dinner just so you can interrogate my guest." I didn't mean that to come out as sharp as it sounded, but it was true.

"She's a material witness and potential suspect in an ongoing investigation, Junebug," he said, his drawl thickening so slightly most people wouldn't notice.

But I wasn't most people. "Nice try," I said. I pressed his hat against his chest. "You know that doesn't work on me."

"What doesn't work on you?" he asked, trying to look innocent.

"I'm immune to you, you know," I told him.

"Are not," he said, his grin widening. I swear, even his eyes sparkled. I could feel my resolve melting. It wasn't fair.

"Are too." I let go of his hat. He caught it before it could fall. "I'll make you a deal. I have some information that might interest you, and I'd be willing to give it to you. For a price."

He shook his head. "It doesn't work like that."

I smiled. "Sure it does." Spending all this time with Savannah trying to understand the ins and outs of Fjord Capital was having a bad influence on me, if I had started thinking of conversations with Beau as business transactions. Then again, he had information I wanted, and I had information he needed. Why shouldn't we trade? "Any news on Beckel?"

"Beckel?" he asked, feigning like he didn't know who I was talking about, even though I saw right through him.

"Beckel, the hockey player. Beckel who got into a fight with the biggest player on the ice at the Thunderbirds game the other night while you cheered him on. Beckel who was strong enough to hurl a brick through a window. Beckel who knew Zack was 'dating' his wife." Savannah was convinced that Zack had made up the story about sleeping with Beckel's wife, but I wasn't so sure.

"Oh, *that* Beckel."

"Yes, *that* Beckel," I parroted. I was used to Beau playing his cards close to his chest, but it was still frustrating.

"Beckel checks out. He's got an alibi. He was under observation at the county hospital all night for a possible concussion."

"See? That wasn't so hard," I said. "Beckel's just one potentially jealous person we know about. There could be dozens. So why are you so focused on Savannah?"

Beau held up one finger. "You asked your question. I answered. What do I get in return?"

"That's fair," I admitted. "The night Zack was killed, he and Savannah were heading home after the hockey game. Then, Zack got a text message from someone, asking to meet in Cedar River, so they turned around and came here instead."

The information kept going around in my head. The only person who knew Zack and Savannah would be in Cedar River after the hockey game was Zack, Savannah, and the mysterious texter. The brick thrower had to know when they would be in that exact place, or else have extraordinarily lucky timing. I needed to find out who texted Zack and exactly what it said.

"What about it?" Beau asked, but I could tell by the way he'd dropped the exaggerated country-boy charm act that he was listening.

"Whoever sent that text is the only person on the planet who knew Zack and Savannah would be in Cedar River, on Main Street, the night of the storm. You find who texted him, and you'll find your killer."

CHAPTER 15

"That's interesting, but you're assuming it wasn't a random attack," Beau said. He was playing it cool, but by the way his fingers twitched, I knew he was dying to write this new information down. I'm guessing he hadn't known about the text message, and it felt good to have a step up on him for once. "Plus, there's the obvious."

"The obvious?" I asked. From where I was standing, it was pretty obvious that the text was an excuse to lure Zack downtown.

"That Savannah's not telling us the whole truth." He glanced back at my sister's house. "You know, killers often insert themselves into investigations."

"Kinda like what I do?" I asked.

Through the front window, I could see into the dining room. My family sat around the table as they often did, enjoying a big meal together. Several of them were squinting in our direction. I was only surprised that no one was peering out the window with their hands cupped around their eyes to block out the light, or worse, with their ear pressed to a drinking glass against the window, trying to overhear every word we said. And they called me nosy.

"Don't even kid about that," Beau replied. "I trust you. I don't trust her."

"I figured," I acknowledged.

"I don't like her staying at your house."

"You already made that perfectly clear."

"I'd be much happier if she found someplace else to stay," he said.

"Yeah? And where would she go? Her car is wrecked. Sending her back to the empty apartment she shared with Zack seems unnecessarily cruel. She needs a friend right now."

"And doesn't she have any friends of her own?" Beau asked. "And what do you mean her car is wrecked? It's Zack's car in impound, not hers. Wait a second, she was living with Zack Fjord?"

I nodded. "They were."

"Romantically?"

I nodded again. "Yup. He was about to propose."

"Funny how she didn't mention that earlier."

This new cadence of give-and-take was encouraging. And since I had given him two vital pieces of information—he hadn't known about the text or the romantic relationship—it was only fair that I ask one more question. "What about his blood alcohol level?"

"What about his blood alcohol level?" Beau asked.

"I know he was drinking at the game, but Savannah claims he put away a whole twelve-pack and passed out in the car. Was he really that drunk?"

"Twelve might be an exaggeration, but not by much. Dude was wasted." Beau leaned down and gave me a kiss on the cheek. "Thanks for the tips. Save me some dessert?"

"You know me better than that," I reminded him. Even if I did manage to snag an extra piece of pecan pie for him, I'd probably eat it in the car on the way home.

"Yeah, I do." He put on his hat. "Never hurts to ask."

I watched as he got in his truck. Instead of leaving, he pulled out his phone and called someone. I hoped he was asking them to pull Zack's cell phone out of evidence so he could check the text messages, but he was just as likely phoning in a warrant to bring Savannah in for questioning. With Beau, it was hard to tell. I headed back inside. Just as I was closing the front door behind me, I heard his truck start and back out of the driveway.

It was quiet inside as everyone waited for me to return to the table. "Good job getting rid of the narc," Calvin quipped as I returned.

"He's not a narc. He's a detective," I said, swiping a cornbread muffin off his plate as I passed his seat.

"I was gonna eat that," my uncle said, reaching for it.

I held it out of his reach. I glanced at the table. The plate that had held the cornbread earlier was empty. I suppose I should have saved the last piece for Kitty, but this was more fun. I took a bite out of the muffin. "Yummy. Still warm. Got any more of that jalapeño jelly?"

Teddy reached across the table, snagged the bowl, and set it down next to my plate. "You're in luck."

"I am, aren't I?" I said as I sat back down next to him.

"Beau left? Was it something I said?" Savannah asked, glancing at his empty seat.

"Don't worry about him," Tansy said. "He's a buzzkill."

"Hear, hear," Teddy agreed.

"Juni, I noticed you pull up in that loaner," Marcus said, changing the subject. "How do you like it? She drives like a beaut, doesn't she?"

"She's, I mean it's, fine." I never could understand the need to gender inanimate objects. "We appreciate the loaner."

"We do," Tansy agreed.

"Y'all could have borrowed my car," Maggie interjected. "J.T. and I could make do with just his for a few days."

"I told you, honey, I'm meeting a client in Waco tomorrow. I'll need the car," J.T. said, patting her hand.

"Maggie, don't be rude," Mom said. "Marcus is trying to do something nice for my girls. I, for one, think it's very generous."

"Thanks, Marcus," Maggie said, but I could tell it pained her to be gracious to him.

"Like I said, it's not a problem. Use it as long as you need."

"That won't be necessary," Tansy said. "I'm sure I'll have my car back soon."

"But wouldn't the three of y'all be better off if you each had a car of your own instead of playing merry-go-round with your rides all the time?" Marcus asked.

"Maybe, but I don't want a car," I told him. I'd lost track of how many times we'd had this discussion. I was happy my mom had found someone she liked, but did he have to be a used car salesperson? Couldn't he have been a cookie merchant or something useful like that? "Even if I could afford a car payment, which I can't, there's insurance and gas to think about."

"Sure, sure. I hear you loud and clear," Marcus said. "But if you change your mind—"

"You'll be the first person I call," I said, quickly cutting him off before he could give me a sales pitch.

"Speaking of merry-go-rounds," Uncle Calvin started. "Did you know that the first merry-go-rounds weren't carnival rides? Originally, they were designed to help knights hone their jousting skills."

"Really? That's fascinating," I said with relief. Leave it to my uncle to save the day with some of the otherwise useless trivia floating around his brain.

"The first carousel was inspired by riders jousting in a circle for practice. And the brass ring you're supposed to reach for? The armored knights would try to snag it on the end of their lances to prove their accuracy."

My uncle continued, his story meandering through the way that the age of brass rings could be accurately narrowed down to date and region of origin according to the amount of copper and zinc in it, to how brass plumbing rose to popularity. I took a moment to appreciate being surrounded by friends, family, and good food. And, of course, my uncle's encyclopedic knowledge.

After dinner, I got up to help with dessert. Even though Maggie had baked fresh pecan pie, I wanted to contribute something. I poured several glasses of cold-brewed coffee and carefully stirred in cinnamon and maple extract. Then I added ice and cold half-and-half. Finally, I topped each glass with whipped cream and another dash of cinnamon. Tansy helped me carry them to the table and pass them around, along with slices of the pie. I made a plain black coffee for Teddy.

"Delicious," Calvin said, taking a long drink. "What do you call this one, Juni?"

"Shake, Rattle, and Cinnamon Roll," I told him, making sure to shake the glass so the ice would rattle around for emphasis. "It might be a little too sweet to serve with pecan pie, though."

"Don't be silly, there's no such thing as too sweet," Maggie said. "This will be a hit at Sip & Spin."

"Glad you like it." I grinned. It was fun coming up with delicious coffee combinations and punny musical names, and I was glad I could try my creations out on my family before introducing them to my customers.

Samuel did indeed drop by as we were cleaning up. He stayed long enough to snag a Shake, Rattle, and Cinnamon Roll, and a piece of pie, then took off with Calvin. Mom and Marcus headed back to Austin.

Once dinner was over, Savannah and I moved to the

kitchen and started on the mountain of dishes. Teddy offered to help us clean up, but we shooed him out of the kitchen and sent him home. "That was interesting," Savannah said. "Your uncle's a hoot."

"I think so," I agreed. Dinner was delicious. The company was fantastic. My dessert was a hit. But there were so many dishes that we might be here all night.

"Can I ask you a personal question?"

"Go for it," I told her.

"Beau and Teddy? What's the deal?" Savannah asked.

I hated that question, because I never knew how to answer it. "Why do you ask?"

"They each realize you like them both, obviously. And they're okay with it?"

I grimaced. "I don't know that either of them is truly okay with the current arrangement, but it works."

"Works for whom, exactly?" she asked. "From where I'm standing, it's not working very well for anyone involved."

"Oof." She was right, but it hurt to hear.

"I'm sorry. If you don't want to talk about it, I understand."

"Truth be told, I'd love to talk about it, but I've got no one to talk to," I admitted. It was nice to be able to talk to someone who wasn't invested. "I mean, Teddy's practically my best friend, but I can't exactly talk to him about my boy troubles when he's half of the trouble."

"What about your sisters? You three seem close."

"We are. Tansy thinks I'm a fool to even consider getting back with Beau, and Maggie thinks I'm a fool not to. And Kitty—you met her at the river today. The paramedic? She thinks I should string both of them along indefinitely, which isn't fair to anyone."

She shrugged. "Don't take this the wrong way, but have you considered that neither of them is right for you? No offense, but a cop and a mailman? Neither of them will ever be rich."

I blinked at her. Savannah and I had very different priorities in life. "That doesn't matter to me."

"Then pick one," Savannah said.

"As if it's that easy. Teddy's amazing. He's sweet and thoughtful and absolutely perfect. He would never, ever hurt me. And Beau? Just thinking about him makes my toes curl. The problem is that when I'm with Teddy, I'm one hundred percent sure he's the right one for me; but when I'm with Beau, I'm absolutely certain that *he's* the one."

"And when they're both around?" Savannah asked.

"I want to run away screaming," I admitted.

"Or kick one of them out of the house in the middle of dinner," she said.

I laughed. "I swear Beau only invited himself over because he knew I'd never run from the dinner table."

"Are you certain that's the only reason?" she asked. "You sure he wasn't there to question me?"

"Ah, so you caught onto that, too?"

"That your 'not-boyfriend'"—she put down the plate she was drying to make air quotes—"was interrogating me over your sister's delicious dinner? How could I have missed it?"

"On the plus side, I had a chance to talk to him about your text message theory. He's looking into it. I think. I doubt he'll share what he finds with us, but it doesn't matter as long as the person is caught."

"I still can't believe anyone would want to hurt Zack." She must have caught the incredulous look on my face, because she continued, "It's an awful big leap from not being someone's biggest fan to intentionally causing a car crash."

"I agree, but people will surprise you. And not always in a good way."

As if to prove my point, Tansy picked that moment to come into the kitchen. "Want a hand?" she offered.

Maggie loved to clean, but was so meticulous about it, she could take five minutes to scrub a single plate. Tansy, on the other hand, hated dish duty. When she was younger and on the beauty pageant circuit, she used that as her excuse to never get her hands anywhere near dishwater. I was the one who usually ended up washing. I didn't mind it, which was weird. I loved cleaning up after meals as long as I didn't have to cook, but I couldn't be bothered to put my own dirty clothes in the hamper.

"You?" I asked. "I wouldn't want to mar your manicure."

"What manicure?" Tansy held her hands up. Her fingernails were all cut to a uniform short length and had a single layer of clear polish on them. Her days of acrylic nails had apparently gone the way of her gallons of hairspray and hot pink lipstick, but I somehow hadn't noticed that until now.

"It's okay, we're almost done here," I said. Secretly, I thought that Tansy had timed it that way on purpose so she wouldn't have to help.

She moved to Savannah's side of the sink so she could take the dry dishes and start putting them back in the cabinets where they belonged. "Did I hear y'all talking about Beau?" she asked.

I glanced over at Savannah, hoping she would keep her mouth shut about our relationship discussion. I didn't want a lecture about him tonight, at least not from my biggest sister. "He's looking into the possibility that whoever killed Zack texted him earlier that night," I said.

"And he freely shared this information with you?" Tansy asked suspiciously.

"Actually, I shared it with him," I corrected her. "It's Savannah's theory."

Tansy nodded at Savannah. "Good theory. Do we know who it might be?"

"I'm convinced it's business related," Savannah said. "Zack would never ignore a work call, and he wasn't exactly universally loved by some of our investments."

"Maybe because you call people and their life's work 'investments,'" Tansy snapped.

Savannah slowly folded the drying rag she'd been using and laid it down on the counter. "I apologize. You're right, of course. We invested in people. For many, most, I'd dare say, we improved their businesses and their lives. For a few, we merely postponed the inevitable failure for which they now want to pin the blame on us. Which is their right."

"You bet it is," Tansy grumbled.

"I understand that you don't agree with our business model, and I respect that," Savannah said judiciously.

It was time to change the subject before Tansy lost her temper. I had a strict limit on how many deaths I could stomach in one week. As much as I had often joked that I would help either of my sisters move a dead body, I didn't want to have to put that to the test. "I think we can all agree that a business deal can get everyone's blood up, but really, can you see someone getting physical over it?"

Even as I said it aloud, I realized that yeah, I could see that. If I thought Zack was driving Sip & Spin Records out of business, I'd be upset enough to throw a brick or two at him. And if that act resulted in someone's death? I'd run and hide, too.

"I could totally see that," Tansy said, echoing my thoughts.

"Money's just one reason that people get killed over. What about love?" I asked.

"I already told you that Zack and I were together,"

Savannah said. "It was going great. I certainly wouldn't kill him."

That remained to be proven. Logistically, it was difficult, but not impossible. Savannah was in the car with him. Until I got confirmation from Beau, which he was unlikely to offer, I only had her word to go on that they were in Cedar River because Zack got a text message. What if she staged the whole thing? She couldn't have been two places at once, but there was always the possibility that she'd had help setting up the brick-throwing. But that made no sense because she could have just as easily been hurt in the crash. She was innocent in all this. I was almost certain of that.

Savannah was demonstrably worse off now than she'd been when Zack was alive. She'd lost her boyfriend, her job, and her sugar daddy all at the same time. Which, again, was based solely on what she told me. For all I knew, she was the heir of the Fjord empire now, and she was just sticking around, pretending to help me find the killer to throw us off her scent.

Personally, if I were ever in her position, I'd hire a good lawyer, like my brother-in-law, not convince a record shop owner-slash-barista to clear my name, but what did I know?

"Can you be absolutely certain Zack didn't have a side piece?" Tansy asked. "Maybe someone right here in Cedar River?"

"He didn't," Savannah said.

I'd never been cheated on, as far as I knew. But I'd had my heart broken and that was enough to make it hard to trust anyone again. Savannah didn't seem to have that problem. If anything, she trusted Zack *too* much. "How can you be so sure?" I asked. "He's cheated in the past."

"Trust me. He's changed. We lived together. We worked together. We ate meals together. We went to bars together after work. We were together practically every hour of the day. The only way Zack could have a side piece, as you call it, is if he had a clone."

Personally, I think she was protesting too much. If she didn't want to admit the possibility that Zack wasn't faithful to her, there was nothing I could do about it except try to get the conversation back on track so we could move forward with finding his killer. "Okay, but you haven't always been a couple," I pointed out. "You used to go out with Teddy. What if Zack had dated someone in Cedar River before you two got together?"

"Wait a second, she dated Teddy?" Tansy asked. "Your Teddy?"

"He's not *my* Teddy," I corrected her. "And yes. She dated Teddy."

"We went out a couple of times," Savannah said. "He's fantastic."

"You bet your shoe, he is," my sister said.

"No arguments here. It was while we were dating that I realized I was in love with someone else," she admitted.

"Zack," I supplied.

"Exactly. And Zack realized that he was in love with me," Savannah said. "And the rest is, was, history."

"How long ago was this?" Tansy asked. I leaned in to hear the answer. I was curious about that myself, but I'd been afraid that however I worded it, I would come across as me being jealous or insecure.

"Last winter sometime. Zack and I attended a corporate New Year's event together, and we've been together ever since."

I knew I was being silly, but I was relieved that all of this had played out before I moved back to Texas. But also, poor Teddy. I had no idea he'd gotten dumped on New Year's. Then again, I hadn't asked. Maybe I hadn't wanted to know.

"Ten months, give or take?" Tansy asked. Savannah nodded. "Some people might carry a torch that long. Years, even," she said. This was directed at me and how long it had taken for me to get over Beau after our breakup. Truth be told, I wasn't sure I ever did get over him, which explained an awful lot.

"If you're suggesting that there's some girl running around so in love with a guy who dumped her a year ago that she threw a brick at his car, you're barking up the wrong tree," Savannah said. "I mean, Zack's great. Don't get me wrong. But no man is worth risking jail time for."

"What if it's not someone he dated?" I asked. "What if it's just someone he flirted with who got the wrong idea?"

"Now you're just being silly. Zack would never lead a woman on, obviously."

"Obviously," Tansy and I repeated at the same time. My response was dry. Hers, sarcastic.

"She finds out that Zack's already taken, and loses her temper," I suggested.

"Or," Tansy countered, "her significant other didn't appreciate Zack coming onto their woman."

"Zack would never—"

"Spare me," I said, cutting her off. "You saw how he acted at the hockey game. He was all over me, even though you and Beau were right there. I wasn't sure what was more likely, that there would be another fight on the ice, or one in our suite."

"What happened at the game?" Tansy asked.

I shook my head. "Not important."

"Humor me," my sister said.

"Zack was a little grabby with me. Beau took exception to that," I explained.

"Uh-huh." Tansy didn't sound happy.

Savannah intervened. "He gets overly friendly when he's had a few too many, but he didn't mean anything by it. Beau, though? I thought he was gonna throw down. I mean, with a temper like that, how do we know he didn't throw the brick that killed Zack?"

"Please! Beau was a perfect gentleman, which is more than I can say for Zack," I said. I was annoyed that she kept bringing Beau up as a possible suspect when I knew he was innocent, but she didn't know him as well as I did.

I continued, "When Zack started getting rowdy, we left. End of story. If Beau wanted to fight, he would have. Besides, you saw him tonight. He sat on one side of me with Teddy on the other. Both of them know full well I'm going out with both of them. If he was gonna have a problem with someone, it wouldn't be because some drunk guy was hitting on me."

"Maybe he doesn't see Teddy as a viable threat," Tansy suggested.

"And Zack was?" I asked. I wasn't sure if I was making the case against Beau worse or better. "Not that Beau would have hurt him even if he was. Zack's not even my type."

"That's not what you thought back in college," Savannah said.

I sighed and looked over at Tansy. "Apparently Zack told Savannah that I was one of his college conquests. Which never happened."

"I can attest to that," Tansy told Savannah. "Juni was so head over heels for Beau she didn't so much as look at another guy the whole time they were together."

"Guilty as charged," I agreed.

"Does Beau know that?" Savannah asked. "You know how guys talk. Maybe Zack bragged to Beau about hooking up with you."

"He didn't." I pulled out my phone and dialed Beau on speakerphone.

He answered, "Hey Junebug. Miss me already?"

"You're on speaker."

"Hey, everyone on speaker. Miss me already?"

I got butterflies in my stomach. I couldn't help it. He had that effect on me. "Question. Did Zack tell you that we hooked up in college?"

"'We' as in you and me, him and I, or him and you?"

"Me and Zack," I clarified.

"Nope. Did you two hook up?"

"Nope," I replied. "If he had told you that we hooked up, would you have believed him?"

"I don't know. I doubt it." He paused, then asked, "But you didn't, right?"

"Not even a little bit. One more question."

"I'm all yours," he said.

I knew he didn't mean anything by it, but I grinned just the same. "Did you kill Zack Fjord?"

"Not even a little bit. You coming over later? We can watch a movie or something."

Even though we were on speakerphone and not a video call, I shook my head. "No, not tonight." I hadn't had a decent night's sleep in two days and it was wearing on me. "'Night." He said good night back before disconnecting. "Happy?"

"Oh my goodness, are y'all still doing dishes?" Maggie said, breezing into the kitchen. I wondered how long she'd been listening at the doorway before joining us. By the glances she and Tansy exchanged, I assumed she'd been eavesdropping for a few minutes at least. They'd probably flipped a coin on who'd come in and join us, and Tansy lost.

They used to do that when I was younger, taking turns spying on me when I was hanging out with friends or out on a date. They seemed to think that they were being subtle, and I wasn't about to disabuse them of that notion. "Subtle" was the one thing neither of my sisters did very well.

Maggie grabbed an apron off a hook near the sink. As she tied the waist strap, she gave us all a shooing motion. "Get out of my kitchen before you end up having to spend the night."

"That's rich, coming from someone who takes an hour to scrub one pot," Tansy said.

"Out," Maggie said. I'd wanted to follow up with Maggie to see if she learned anything interesting about Fjord Capital from reading the proposal Zack had prepared for us, but I didn't want to bring it up in front of Savannah.

"Love you, sis," Tansy replied.

"Love you too. You too, Juni. But don't you have your own house to get to?"

"Good night," I told her. "Love you."

"Shoo," she told me.

We hollered our goodbyes to J.T., piled in the loaner SUV, and went back to Tansy's house. Once there, Savannah peeled off toward the cottage.

"It's just for a few more nights," I told Tansy, although I couldn't be certain of that. Savannah had shown no sign of leaving. The power was back on. The cell phone tower was working. Most of the roads were open. She could have called an Uber or a friend in Austin at any time, but here she still was.

"I'm sure you're right," Tansy said, and headed for her room.

CHAPTER 16

Saturday morning found me, Maggie, and Savannah at Sip & Spin Records while "Rapper's Delight" played on the turntable. It was comforting to be back in our normal rhythm. It wasn't often that more than one of us was needed in the shop at a time, but weekend evenings and Saturday mornings were our busiest times, and Maggie was a welcome set of hands.

Savannah, on the other hand, seemed to be in the way every time I turned around. She must have noticed it too, because she begged to be put to work, even though she knew nothing of music and even less about how to make coffee. "Come on, Juni, you can teach me," Savannah said. "How hard can it be to foam a latte?"

"Juni's not the person to ask about that," Maggie said as she carried an armful of records to the shelves. Some were new releases. Others were classic albums that we'd managed to pick up. "We were open for months before she managed to draw anything other than a lopsided sun in the foam."

"That was a flower," I corrected her. My strengths lay in blending beans and coming up with fun flavor combinations with punny names. I could barely draw a stick figure on paper, much less on a latte.

"What's the simplest drink you can think of?" Savannah asked.

"Drip," Maggie and I said at the same time.

"I can do that," Savannah said.

I nodded my head. "Fine. Come over here." I measured out a few scoops of beans and showed her how to use the grinder. "Don't worry about blending anything. These beans are perfect on their own. They make a rich, full roast that tastes like that first sip of coffee you have on vacation."

"Juni, you do have a way with coffee," Maggie said as she organized the New Arrivals display. She pulled a remastered Queen album and set it aside to play later.

"Coffee's easy to love," I told her. Once the beans were ready, I showed Savannah how to change the filters and where to add the freshly ground beans. "Now you just push that button. This light turns green when it's ready. Here's how you choose the size. If anyone asks for something more complicated, just holler."

"Don't forget to give it a name," Maggie said as she straightened up around the cash register. "That's what separates a Sip & Spin Records signature special from a cup of joe."

I thought about it for a second. It had been a rough week. I'd spent more time running around trying to pick up clues than hanging out in the record shop with my sisters. Most of the town was still cleaning up the mess the storm left, but they'd hopefully find a few minutes to drop by for a pick-me-up today. "How about Since U Bean Gone?"

"Perfect," Maggie agreed. "What are your plans today?"

Savannah was so absorbed with trying to figure out what the different buttons on the barista machine did, I doubted she was paying attention to us.

She was wearing a Savage Garden vintage concert T-shirt—mine—and a pair of distressed denim pants, also mine. It was the outfit I'd laid out for myself this morning, but when I got out of the shower it was gone and I'd settled for a One Direction tee instead. At least she hadn't borrowed my favorite glasses, I thought, as I adjusted the rainbow pair I was wearing today. I was trying very hard to not be annoyed with our uninvited house guest who showed no signs of leaving, but she wasn't making it easy.

"We've got to do something about her," I said. Even though I doubted she could hear me over the brewing coffee, I kept my voice down.

"It's the clothes, right?" Maggie asked astutely.

"It's not just the clothes. I mean yes, the clothes are part of it. I offered to give her a lift to Walmart, and she said she was fine. But then she used up the last of my mango shampoo and hogged all the hot water. She doesn't like showering in the cottage, says it's too cramped, so I have to wait for her to get out of the bathroom and she takes all day."

Maggie nodded sympathetically. "Wow. Sounds brutal. I don't know how you're gonna survive. Just wait until she borrows your favorite nail polish without asking and uses it to decorate her science fair project."

"Point taken." They didn't remind me of it often, but Tansy and Maggie really did get the worst of it growing up. They hadn't asked for a baby sister to be dropped in their lap, but there I was anyway, taking their things without permission and spending hours in bubble baths when they needed the bathroom we shared. Having Savannah around was giving me a taste of my own medicine, and I didn't like it. "It's not just that, though. The only way she's ever going to leave Cedar River is if we find out who killed Zack, but I can't do that while she's Velcroed to my side every second of the day."

"I thought you promised Beau you'd look into who dumped the mannequins into the river instead of investigating Zack's death."

"What? Can't I do both?" To be honest, I was glad that she'd reminded me about the mannequins. I'd intended to do some research online, but I'd been busy. I truly did want to help and I knew how important it was to figure out who was polluting our river and stop them, but my priority was catching Zack's killer so Savannah could get on with her life. And get out of mine.

The front door opened and Rocco O'Brien, Kitty's EMT partner, walked inside. While most of the emergency response folks I knew ran on coffee due to their ever-changing schedules and long, difficult shifts, I couldn't remember ever seeing Rocco in Sip & Spin—unless he was here to cart away a body. Which, not counting this week, had only happened that one time.

Rocco paused at the turntable that was now playing Destiny's Child and checked out the album cover before putting it back on the display stand. He made his way up to the coffee counter. He chatted with Savannah while she fumbled around at the barista station, giving Maggie and me a chance to talk more.

"Did you learn anything more about Fjord Capital?" I asked, keeping my voice down to keep from being overheard.

"Nothing that we didn't already suspect," she said. "The model is simple and depressingly common. Low risk and high reward, for them at least. It's a short-term fix with long-term consequences for the hardworking business owners."

"Why would anyone fall for it? Why not just get a bank loan if money's tight?"

"Fjord Capital isn't a loan. It's more like a co-op. Struggling business owners get a cash influx, access to health insurance, group discounts, and a business mentor. It's an attractive offer."

"So, it's a good thing?"

Maggie frowned. "In a perfect world, it could be, but the odds are stacked in Fjord's favor. Some businesses will get lucky and thrive. Others will fold. Either way, Fjord Capital still comes out on top."

"That's what I'm seeing," I confirmed. "Rediscovered Treasures is thriving and Darlene Daye loves them. Blow Your Own Horn is collapsing, and Frankie Hornsby blames them. I'm sure there's lots of other fortunate—and unfortunate—investees out there, but I'm running out of local leads."

Maggie headed toward the back room and I followed her. "I'm sure Zack made plenty of enemies outside of our quiet little town," she said. She pulled a milk crate filled with cords and microphones off a shelf and handed it to me.

As the proprietors of a record shop, we hoarded the thick plastic milk crates like they were going out of style. Which, I guess they kind of were. Milk crates were the perfect size and shape for vinyl records, but what was once commonly used in everyday life and often discarded as junk were now rare finds. If you wanted a milk crate these days, you had to buy them at stores that specialized in organization, and they charged a small fortune for flimsy knockoff versions of the crates that were once free.

"Yes, but whoever lured Zack and Savannah to Main Street, then threw the brick that caused the car accident, got trapped here with the rest of us because the roads were blocked. Which means they live here or know someone who does."

"Good point," Maggie said. Short-term rentals were expressly prohibited within town limits to keep real estate prices reasonable, and the nearest motel was down the highway a bit. If any out-of-towner had gotten trapped in Cedar River because of the storm, they were either sleeping in their car or crashing on someone's couch.

"Need a hand with that?" I offered.

Maggie was wrestling with a big black suitcase that seemed to be snagged on the shelf. "Nah, I'm good." With a hard yank, it came free. She grunted as she lifted it. "Can't host karaoke night without this."

Tonight was our monthly karaoke. For a small cover charge, anyone in town could come out and make a complete fool of themselves on stage. The last two karaoke nights had been enormous successes and we hoped tonight would be the same. Sip & Spin's bottom line depended on it.

"You gonna sing for us tonight?" Maggie asked.

"You know better than that," I told her. I was looking forward to karaoke, but only for the money it brought in. Not for the singing. No, siree. I'd rather snuggle a jellyfish than get up in front of the whole town with a microphone in my hand.

"One of these days, you'll change your mind. I think I'm going to try something new. Think I could pull off Madonna?"

"I can't wait to hear you Express Yourself," I told her. I carried the milk crate with the cables and microphones out front while Maggie wheeled the unwieldy karaoke machine behind her. "You know, we could run the whole production on nothing more than a laptop and some wireless headsets," I suggested.

"Where's the fun in that? We sell vinyl records. If we don't lean into the nostalgia, we might as well start selling MP3s."

"True," I admitted. The old-school setup did have a certain appeal, and our customers loved it.

"What's next with your snooping plans?" Maggie asked, unwinding a cable.

"The last local I know might have a grudge is Jackson Elby. Savannah tried to steer me away from him. I don't know how to shake her long enough to have a chat with him, and I'm not even sure how to find him."

"Jackson's been staying in one of the apartments over on Armstrong ever since his wife left him. They sold their house and she moved to Texarkana," Maggie said. Unlike Tansy and our mom, Maggie wasn't much into local gossip, so if she knew all the sordid details of Jackson Elby's living situation, it must be common knowledge.

"What's the story there?" I asked.

Maggie shook her head. "You know I don't like to spread idle gossip."

"It's not idle gossip if it's for an investigation," I said.

"J.T.'s representing Jackson's wife, Sheila, in the divorce," Maggie explained. I thought again how handy it was that my sister had married one of the town's only lawyers. "So it wouldn't be right to talk about it."

It was useless to point out that she'd already shared more than she probably should have. Considering that the information was helpful, I wasn't going to complain. "Did you know that he used to run a clothing boutique in the very spot that's now Sip & Spin?" I asked.

"Juni, not everyone's been living under a rock for the past six years."

"I wasn't living under a rock," I argued. "I was in Oregon. For work."

"Yeah yeah, but you weren't *here*. Even when you came for a visit, it was never for more than a few days. You'd fly in, join us for a family dinner or two, and then dad would drive you back to the airport in Austin and we wouldn't see you for another six months."

"Uh-huh," I agreed. I'd heard this guilt trip before. I was working sixty-hour weeks. And airfare wasn't cheap. I got their logic—why should half a dozen family members fly up to Oregon to me when I could come down here and see everyone at once?—but I never got a visit from any of them.

"Hey, where's the decaf button?" Savannah asked, jolting me out of my reverie.

"There's no decaf button," Maggie replied. At the same time, I said, "Here, I'll show you how to make a pot of decaf."

As the shop filled up, Savannah had her hands full. Luckily, most of our customers were content ordering Since U Bean Gone, so she didn't need much assistance. "You good here?" I asked her.

"Sure. Why?"

"I've got to step out real quick. I'll be right back," I said.

She rang up the next customer in line. "I'll come with you," Savannah offered. "Just let me pour this cup real quick."

"No rush," I told her. Well, that had backfired. I was never going to slip out of Sip & Spin long enough to question Jackson Elby alone at this rate. Then I glanced over at my sister, who was behind the register, and a plan began to form. "Can I ask a favor?"

"Sure," Maggie said.

"Can I borrow a dress?" I asked.

My middle sister's face lit up. While my wardrobe consisted almost exclusively of retro concert T-shirts and blue jeans, Maggie had a closet full of dresses with any occasion-appropriate necklines and full skirts. Most of the prints were floral, with the exception of a black-and-yellow honeybee print and an orange-and-black skull one she only wore on Halloween.

"Of course you can! Any time! I just bought this adorable mum dress I thought would be perfect for the fall festival. It will really bring out the highlights in your hair. Want me to run home and get it now? I don't mind."

The glee on her face was palpable. As long as I could remember, she'd loved playing dress-up with me, but as soon as I was old enough, I put my foot down. "Actually, I was wondering if I could borrow *that* dress." I pointed at the one she was wearing.

"This dress?" Maggie took a step back and looked down at her outfit. It was a pink-and-white checkered dress with large purple flowers on a full skirt that ended just below her knee, with complementary smaller purple flowers on the scalloped neckline. The sleeves were three-quarter length and edged with dark pink lace. The dress was without a doubt one hundred percent Maggie. "You want to borrow *this* dress?"

She had a reason to be suspicious. The last time I'd worn that much pink at one time was because I'd lost a bet. It wasn't that I had anything against pink, it's just that I didn't own any. The closest thing I had was a P!nk concert T-shirt from an album I hadn't been allowed to listen to growing up because of the explicit lyrics. "Yup. That dress."

"Yeah. Okay." She shrugged. "I'll have it dry cleaned and drop it off at your place next week."

"Actually, I was kind of hoping to borrow it now."

Understanding dawned on her face. Maggie was a few inches shorter than me, and Tansy was taller. Both were thinner than me. Maggie's hair was medium-length and curly, and the darkest of all three of us. Mine was medium brown with occasional red highlights in the right light. I wore it long. Tansy's hair was cut super-short. I was the only one in the family who wore glasses. And yet, we might as well be triplets for all that no one outside of the immediate family seemed to be able to tell us apart.

"You don't think that old trick will work, do you?" Maggie asked.

It wouldn't fool anyone who knew us well, but if Tansy put on a pair of jeans, I donned a dress, and Maggie borrowed one of Tansy's coordinated sweater sets, it threw everyone for a loop. It was always fun for a laugh. "It only has to work for a minute," I told her.

"Fine." She looked at me. "One Direction? You couldn't have worn Korn this morning?" For all that my sister liked pretty, pink dresses, her musical tastes ran toward dark basement clubs with sticky floors and loud, live bands. What could I say? My sister was complex. "Come on."

It only took us a moment to switch clothes in the tiny bathroom, but in that time, a line had formed at the cash register. Savannah gave us a frantic wave when we returned. She looked right past me and gestured at my sister. "Juni, this woman's asking for a no-whip? What button is that?"

"Don't worry. It just means she doesn't want whipped cream on her coffee," Maggie told her.

"Oh. I can do that. Or, you know, not do that." The frazzled-looking Savannah went back to her station. "This is harder than it looks," she called back to us over her shoulder as she fumbled with a few buttons.

"Take my car," Maggie whispered as she tossed me her keys. And then, just to sell the deception, as I left, she called out, "See ya later, Maggie."

"Thanks." I hurried outside. It was probably unnecessary. Pretending to be my middle sister so I could sneak out of the shop without Savannah was a little extreme, but it bought me some badly needed alone time.

I missed my tricycle, but it wasn't cut out for ferrying a passenger around all day and I wouldn't have wanted to ride it in a dress anyway. It was a nice day, but I wasn't sure where the morning's errands would take me, so instead of walking, I drove Maggie's car to the only apartment building in town.

The same parking spot I'd used the night of the storm was open, so I pulled into it. I looked around the lot as I walked up to the front door. I didn't see Beau's truck and I had no idea what his partner Jayden drove, but there was more parking on the other side of the building and either one of them could be watching me from their window.

I glanced up at the top floor. I wasn't sure which windows belonged to Beau and which belonged to Jayden. For that matter, I wasn't certain I was even on the correct side of the building. I tried to remember what the view was like from Beau's living room and failed. It wasn't like I spent a lot of time at his place.

A list of names was printed by the front door, along with the buzzer numbers. Beau wasn't listed. Neither was Jayden, for that matter. I guess that was for the best. If I was a cop, I probably wouldn't want my name displayed outside my residence for anyone in the world to see, either.

Jackson Elby, on the other hand, was listed. His name was written in scrawling black ink, whereas the others were from a computer printout. He hadn't lived here long, the super was too lazy to print out a new list, or both.

I punched in his apartment code and waited. Nothing happened. Maybe he wasn't home. It was the middle of the morning on a Saturday. Maybe he was at the park or had gone on a walk. I didn't have his phone number, so I typed in the code again. This time, someone answered. "What do you want?"

I leaned toward the callbox speaker. "Juni Jessup here. Jackson?" There was silence on the other end. I tried again. "Is this Jackson Elby?"

"I asked what you want," came the reply.

"I think we have a mutual friend. Zack Fjord?"

"If you're a friend of his, you're no friend of mine."

I backpedaled quickly. "Not a friend. More like a former acquaintance."

"Former?"

"Haven't you heard? Zackary Fjord is dead."

"I'm in two-oh-three. Come on in, and I'll crack the champagne."

CHAPTER 17

As I climbed the stairs to the second floor, I began to question my life choices. I didn't know Jackson Elby and I wasn't in the habit of showing up at apartments of strange men, much less strange men who might have killed someone—accidentally or not—a few days ago. Maggie knew where I was, but that wouldn't be much comfort if he meant me harm.

Standing in front of his door, I hesitated. Most of the doors I'd passed had doormats in front of their units and something to personalize their space. Even Beau had a doormat. It read "Come back with a warrant." Cop humor.

The door to 203 opened. The white man on the other side of the door was several inches shorter than me and about a thousand years old. His clothes hung misshapen on his frame, as if he'd lost fifty pounds recently and hadn't bought a new wardrobe yet. His head was bald and liver spotted. His eyebrows were shockingly furry caterpillars, and he wore gold glasses with lenses so thick they put mine to shame.

"Mr. Elby?" I asked, wondering if I'd misheard his apartment number.

"That's me." He peered up at me, studying my face carefully. "Miss Jessup?"

"Call me Juni," I said. I noticed that he didn't return the courtesy. Okay then, "Mr. Elby" it was.

"Come in, come in." He stepped back and waved me inside. Whatever trepidations I'd had before were long gone. I'd suspected that Savannah had tried to talk me out of coming here because she had something to hide, but now I was convinced she'd come to the same conclusion already that I had now that I'd met him. Elby was a harmless old man.

Jackson Elby's apartment was decorated for function, not comfort. There was a single leather armchair, discolored with age. There was a single stool at the kitchen bar. It was tall, wooden, and plain. There was no television. No rug. No throw pillows. No place for guests.

The apartment had a built-in bookshelf. It was empty except for a stack of mail. I wondered if Teddy went door-to-door delivering mail to this building or if there was a row of boxes downstairs for the residents. The way Mr. Elby shuffled slowly and deliberately from the front door to the kitchen a few steps away made me think that even taking the elevator, it would take him half the day just to check his mail.

"I don't have any champagne," he said, opening the fridge. "OJ? V8?"

I shook my head. "I'm good, thank you."

"Suit yourself." He poured himself a glass of V8 and shuffled back to the leather chair. It sighed as he sat, as if it had been waiting for him. "Fjord's dead, you say?"

With no place else to sit, I pulled the stool away from the kitchen bar and sat on the stool. It was hard. "Yes, sir. Happened Wednesday night, in a car wreck."

"Did he suffer?" Mr. Elby asked.

I grimaced, and once again found myself regretting my impulse to climb into Zack's car to try to render aid. "No, sir."

"Well, that's a crying shame, that is. He sure did like to make other people suffer. It ain't right that he got off easy." He took a sip of his V8. "And Miss Goodwin? Did she suffer terribly?"

"Savannah Goodwin?" I asked. "She's adjusting."

He leaned forward in his chair, the leather squeaking in protest. "What do you mean 'adjusting'? Is she not dead as well?"

I hopped up and walked closer. "Oh no. I'm sorry if I misled you, Mr. Elby. Savannah is fine. Physically, at least." Emotionally, I wasn't sure if she would ever recover, but that was none of his business.

"Well, that is something, now isn't it?"

"Mr. Elby, how often did you see Zack?"

He shook his head. "Not often. Once every two, three months maybe. Now Savannah, she was always hovering around making changes. Buying a website without telling us first, and then admonishing us when we didn't check our email. Converting all the accounting to one of those fancy programs and then complaining when our paper receipts didn't match what was in her computer."

Mr. Elby reminded me of my uncle Calvin. We'd had to drag him, kicking and screaming, into the digital age. Even now there was no guarantee that he would take his cell phone when he left the house, and he insisted on paying his utilities by check. In person.

He continued. "She had zero sense of fashion, ordering clothing for my store that a paper doll wouldn't get caught dead in. Nothing with style like you've got. Where did you get that lovely dress?"

"Um, from my sister," I answered, fingering the skirt nervously. I wondered if he would have welcomed me inside if I'd been wearing my normal outfit. I would have been happy to answer him, but I had no idea where my sister shopped. Maybe there was a store in the mall that specialized in clothing nineteen-fifties housewives might wear to a Sunday picnic. If there was, Maggie would be its poster child.

"Tell your sister she has exquisite taste. We should have gone into business with someone like her instead of Fjord. The whole arrangement was a disaster," Mr. Elby said. "Cedar River Casuals was doing just fine before they showed up."

"Then why'd you partner with Fjord Capital?" I asked.

"The missus and I were planning on retiring once we sold the place, but couldn't find a buyer. The most valuable thing about our business, turns out, was the location, and we just leased that. Now some hipster record store opened up there. Maybe you've heard of it?"

I swallowed my initial response. I knew he was talking about Sip & Spin Records. We took over the lease after Cedar River Casuals went out of business. Mr. Elby's misfortune was our good luck. "I know the place," I replied.

"We sold good clothes. Real clothes, for real women. Not the kind of clothes they sell these days that's made out of tissue paper and falls apart the first time you wash it. 'Out of touch.' That's what Savannah called us. But we weren't. We were—what do the kids call it? When something is so old it's fashionable again?"

"Retro?" I supplied. Retro was the exact vibe we were going for at Sip & Spin Records. So far, it seemed to be working. We were slowly building our business. I just wondered what would happen when trends changed and vinyl was no longer a viable revenue stream. Would we end up defunct like Cedar River Casuals?

"Exactly. Retro. Thought with a few extra dollars, we could give the store a facelift. Then we'd find the right buyers, cash out, and walk away. Only it turns out that those Fjord folks expected me and Sheila to stay and run the place day-to-day while they siphoned off the profits."

"Sounds frustrating," I said sympathetically. I wondered what would have happened if my sisters and I had decided to take Zack's offer. Would we have ended up happy and successful like Darlene Daye, or miserable and broke like Jackson Elby and Frankie Hornsby? Why did Fjord Capitol's investments seem to have such different results? Was it luck or was there something else at play?

I also wondered what Jackson had spent his big payout check on. It certainly hadn't been on apartment furnishings.

"That's putting it lightly," he agreed.

"You said Zack wasn't around much." What was it Savannah had said to me? They were together every hour of the day? Then how was it that she was at Cedar River Casuals all the time, getting them online and updating their accounting system, but Zack was nowhere to be found? "Do you know if he was seeing anyone?"

Mr. Elby let out a barking laugh. "Seeing someone? He was seeing everyone."

"What do you mean by that?" I asked.

"I could put a skirt on a goat and Zack Fjord would have chased it off a cliff. A real ladies' man, that one."

"Oh really?" That wasn't what Savannah told me. She claimed he only flirted to keep up appearances, but was otherwise totally devoted to her. If she was wrong about that, what else was she wrong about? "Anyone in particular?"

"How should I know?" An alarm on his watch beeped. He looked down and then silenced it. "Now if you can excuse me, I've got somewhere to be."

"Sure. Of course," I said. "Thank you for taking the time. Oh, and Mr. Elby?"

"Yes?" he looked thoroughly out of patience with me now.

I had overstayed my welcome, but I had told Beau I

would look into the mannequin situation. Who better to talk to than someone who'd recently closed a woman's clothing store? "Did the mannequins at Cedar River Casuals have hands?"

He looked taken aback. "What kind of fool question is that?"

"It's just a question, Mr. Elby."

"Of course our mannequins had hands," he said, defensively. "They also had feet. And heads. And faces. And shoulders. Does that answer your question?"

"Yes, thanks. And when you closed the shop, what happened to your mannequins?"

Mr. Elby pursed his lips in disgust. "We liquidated what we could, but the market isn't what it once was. Everything we couldn't sell or fit into our storage unit, we had to pay a guy to haul to the dump. Just goes to show you can work your whole life for something, and when things go south, you end up spending your last nickel to have someone toss what's left in a hole in the ground."

That was depressing. Astute, but depressing. "Thanks again for your time. I'll let you get to your plans," I told him. As I let myself out of his apartment, I wondered if he'd always been such a miserable person, or if losing his business, and his wife, had made him that way.

I stood in the hall wondering what to do next. Nothing came to me, so I made my way outside. Beau was leaning against the driver's side door of Maggie's car, waiting for me. His face lit up as I got closer. "Is there something I need to know?" he asked, looking me up and down.

I gave an experimental twirl, letting the skirt whirl around my knees. "You like what you see?"

"Always." He glanced back at his apartment building. "Let me guess, you wanted to check to make sure your key worked?"

I blushed. "Not exactly." I should have never let him

leave that key, and all it implied, with me. It was too much pressure, and I wasn't ready for it. "You can have it back if you want."

Beau shook his head. "I don't want it back. I told you, you're welcome anytime, whether or not I'm home. Even if you just need a place to get away from your family for five minutes. If you want to snoop, go ahead. The door is literally open for you."

"I wasn't snooping," I insisted. "I was here to talk to Jackson Elby."

"Mr. Elby? Isn't he a bit old for you?" Beau teased, ruffling my hair. "I hope he appreciated that you got all dressed up for him."

"Oh, this?" I looked down at my sister's dress. "This wasn't for him. No need to get jealous." I said that last part with a grin.

He clucked his tongue. "I don't know about that. To hear him tell it, he was quite the player back in the day, before Sheila snatched him up. And now that she's come to her senses and fled the state, he's back on the market. May the best man win."

"I'm not a carnival prize to be won," I told him. "And his mannequins had hands."

"Huh?" It took Beau a minute to follow the sudden change in subject.

I clarified. "I was visiting Mr. Elby because he recently liquidated a woman's clothing store. A store which, I presume, had a mannequin or two. Apparently, he had to pay a guy to haul everything he couldn't sell off to the dump."

"Did you get this guy's name?" he asked.

"Why, do you need to haul something?"

"Just to close the loop."

I shook my head. "No, I didn't ask. Mr. Elby's mannequins had hands. They weren't the ones you found in the river."

He nodded. "Makes sense. Hey, Junebug, you don't really need to put any effort into looking for the mannequin's previous owner. You certainly don't need to be running around town asking questions. All I need from you is that if you hear anything, you'll let me know. You can do that, can't you?"

"I knew it," I joked. "You're jealous."

"You caught me," he agreed, laughing.

"You gonna be at karaoke tonight?" I asked.

"Wouldn't miss it for the world."

"See you tonight, then," I said. He watched me drive away.

I took a detour on the way back to the shop to grab lunch for everyone. Lunch was easily one of my three favorite meals of the day. Since the quickest route to Sonic took me near Blow Your Own Horn, I decided to stop in on my way to pick up our food. Frankie Hornsby nodded at me as I approached the counter. "Morning, miss. How can I help you today?"

I didn't know if he'd had so many customers that he didn't remember our visit yesterday, he didn't recognize me since I was dressed like Maggie, or he wasn't very good at faces. That was a definite disadvantage for anyone who dealt with the public. "Hi. I'm Juni Jessup? I was in here yesterday with Savannah Goodwin?"

"Ah yes. Zack Fjord's friend."

"Acquaintance," I corrected him. "The other day, I forgot to ask you something."

"Shoot."

"Did you mostly deal with Savannah or Zack?"

"Savannah. She was the people person. It was usually her that sent the emails and dropped by to check on things. Even when Zack was here, he wasn't really here, you know?"

I cocked my head to one side. "No, I'm afraid I don't know."

"Always on that phone of his, click-clacking away on the keyboard like he was writing the Great American Novel or something. Couldn't get two words in with him before his phone rang and he'd step out and take it. 'This is important,' he'd say, and walk away, jabbering into his headset. As if whatever we were talking about wasn't important."

"I imagine that would be frustrating."

"Frustrating? Insulting is more like it. How would you like it if I told you how to make the perfect cup of coffee? Or if I explained what jazz was to you?"

"I wouldn't be too pleased," I admitted.

He smacked his hand down on the counter. "Exactly. These folks come up in here and tell me how to run my business as if I didn't grow up in this store. Wanted me to use their cleaning service. Their fuel cards. Their accounting software. Their suppliers. They tried to get me to switch my toilet paper. The toilet paper!"

"Some things are cheaper if you buy in bulk," I said.

"Or they were getting kickbacks," Frankie countered.

"You mentioned they wanted you to use their accounting software. Does that mean that they had access to your accounts?"

"They were signatories on the business account, yes," he admitted.

"Did money ever go missing?"

He laughed. "Money went missing all the time, but not like you think. Sure, I was saving fifty bucks a month on fire insurance, but now I was paying a hundred a month to power wash the siding, and seventy-five a month to get the windows cleaned."

"If it makes you feel any better, your siding looks fantastic."

"Thanks, but it doesn't."

"This has been helpful," I told him, even though I wasn't sure how what I'd learned fit together. Then I took my leave.

What Frankie said matched up to what Darlene Daye and Jackson Elby had both mentioned about Zack's involvement in the day-to-day business. Zack didn't come around as often as Savannah. When she told me that they worked together, I had assumed she meant they were by each other's side all day, but that didn't seem to be the case at all. While she was hard at work, he was doing who-knows-what with who-knows-whom.

No matter how much Savannah protested otherwise, Zack could have easily conducted an affair—or affairs—right under her nose, and she would never have been the wiser.

When I finally got back to the shop, bearing lunch, Savannah glared at me from behind the barista station. "Was that supposed to be funny?" she asked me.

"What?" I sat the bag down on the cabinet. I wasn't sure what Savannah liked, so I'd gotten a hamburger, a hot-dog, and a grilled cheese sandwich from Sonic along with tater tots, onion rings, and mozzarella sticks. I'd also gotten two milkshakes and one cherry limeade. The limeade was for me. "Help yourself," I told her.

"Why are you dressed like your sister?" she asked.

I glanced over at Maggie, who was helping a customer pick out a selection of records. I wonder what she'd told Savannah when she finally realized that she'd been tricked. "What? This old thing?" I asked. And then, just because I liked the novelty of it, I twirled around and let the skirt fly around my legs.

"She called you Maggie when you left," Savannah said.

"She was joking. Because I was wearing her dress."

Savannah let out a frustrated sigh. "I'm not an idiot. I

know what you two are up to. You could have just told me to stay here."

"Would you have done it?" I asked.

She shook her head. "No. Of course not. But that doesn't give you the right to trick me. If the person you loved had just died in front of your eyes, would you be content to serve coffee all day while strangers hunted down his killer?"

"I wasn't hunting," I assured her. "I needed to ask a few questions and I was afraid you being there might unduly influence the answers."

Since Savannah had yet to pick anything for her lunch, I nabbed a mozzarella stick. I dipped it in a container of marinara sauce and popped it in my mouth. The drive from Sonic to Sip & Spin was long enough that the deep-fried cheese had cooled off from surface-of-the-sun hot to mere molten-lava hot. Hot cheese and grease burned my tongue even as I took another giant bite.

"Ooh, you brought Sonic," Maggie said, grabbing the hotdog on her way to ring up her customer. "Just don't get marinara on my dress."

"I would never . . ." I said. Then I looked down. I grabbed a napkin and dabbed at the splotch of marinara on my breastbone before it could stain the collar of her dress.

"Here, let me help you with that," Maggie offered, putting down her hotdog. She glanced over at Savannah. A line was forming in front of the coffee station, so she had her hands full. "Did you learn anything interesting?"

"I learned that Jackson Elby is older than dirt," I said.

Maggie wiped the rest of the marinara off me without getting any on her dress. "I could have told you that. He used to play cards with Grandpa."

"I also learned that Zack Fjord was quite the playboy."

Maggie clucked her tongue. "Disappointing, but not

surprising. Do we know who he was seeing? Other than Savannah, that is?"

"Not a clue. And Savannah's no help. She's in denial that Zack would ever cheat on her. But apparently, he was always glued to his phone and stepped out of the room to take a lot of 'important' calls."

"Sounds sus," Maggie said.

"Could be," I agreed. "Savannah says there's no way he was stepping out on her because they were always together, but the business owners all agree that Savannah always came around alone. Could be she was so busy working she didn't notice that he was . . ." My voice trailed off.

"Busy doing something else?" Maggie suggested. I shrugged. "Learn anything else interesting?"

"That Beau is strangely supportive of me snooping around in his apartment when he's not home."

"You broke into his apartment?" Maggie asked.

"No, I didn't break into his apartment. He gave me a key."

Maggie sucked in her lips, barely able to contain her glee about this development. This was why I didn't always tell my sisters everything. They jumped to conclusions.

"Aren't you going to ask if I was snooping?"

My sister giggled. "Nah. I know you. You'd totally snoop. I'm just surprised you haven't done it already. Can I get my dress back? I can't see how you wear jeans all day. They're so uncomfortable."

"Are you kidding? Those are my softest denim." Well, second softest. Savannah had borrowed—without asking, mind you—my softest pair. Every day Savannah stayed with me, I appreciated that my sisters never threw me in the river when we were kids.

After we swapped into our normal clothes in the back room, Maggie ate her hotdog and polished off the onion rings and one of the milkshakes. Savannah had claimed the other milkshake, the burger, and the tots, leaving me with the grilled cheese sandwich with a side of fried cheese sticks. That was a lot of cheese, even for me.

Once lunch was gone, Maggie said, "Can you handle things here? I've got some errands to run."

"No problem," I said. I turned to Savannah. "How about you? I bet you could use a break by now. I'm sure Maggie could drop you off."

"I'm good," Savannah said. "I'm actually enjoying myself. Think I'll stick around, and keep an eye on you."

That was fair. After giving her the slip this morning, she wasn't going to let me out of her sight again.

"Suit yourself. If you need anything, give me a ring. Otherwise, I'll be back for karaoke," Maggie said, and let herself out.

Customers filtered in and out all afternoon as we rotated through a variety of music on the record player. We had several small sales, but nothing of consequence. My previous annoyance at her tag-along ways aside, it was nice having Savannah to talk to between customers. Usually, I spent most of my downtime hanging out with Daffy and picking out the next record to play over the speakers. I was looking forward to having the cat in the shop again, but when he saw the carrier this morning, he disappeared. It was probably for the best. Sip & Spin would be packed for karaoke night, and he hated strangers, especially crowds of strangers.

CHAPTER 18

The afternoon passed in a blur of chatty customers and good music. While I normally reveled in creating complex drink specials, the simplicity of Since U Bean Gone was a crowd pleaser. By the time business started winding down for the night, we'd made enough sales to at least open the doors again tomorrow, and sometimes that was enough.

Savannah stifled a yawn. "How do you make one of those super-strong pick-me-ups?" she asked.

"That's easy," I told her. "How strong do you want it?"

"As strong as you can legally make it," she said.

I adjusted the grinder for espresso and added some Arabica beans. "You need a finer grind for espresso," I explained as the beans were pulverized. I loaded them into the barista machine. "There's more pressure and less water, so what comes out is practically liquified beans as opposed to a standard brew." The machine hissed as I poured two double shots, one for each of us.

"I really needed this," Savannah said as I handed her a cup. "I don't know how you stand being on your feet all day, dealing with customers."

"You get used to it," I told her. "But before you drink that, why don't you go lie down for a while? Karaoke doesn't start for a few hours, and a nap might do you more good than caffeine."

"Are you planning on taking a nap?" she asked.

"Nope." I shook my head. "But like I said, I'm used to this."

"Then I'll be just fine, too," she said. "Bottoms up." She drank the hot, thick coffee in a single gulp.

If I didn't know better, I would have been offended. Coffee was made to be enjoyed, not injected. But Savannah was exhausted. Plus, she wasn't spoiled like I was with good coffee. I sipped my espresso, taking the time to appreciate every bit of flavor and coffee goodness.

Once the shop was empty, I locked the door and turned the sign to "Closed." It was seven, and except for running out to talk to Mr. Elby, I'd been at work since we'd opened at ten. I was tired, but my day wasn't over yet.

On long days like this, my sisters and I usually split up the shifts so no one ended up working from open to close. Even though karaoke night had been my idea originally, it had become Tansy's baby. Between her love of the spotlight and her encyclopedic knowledge of music, she made the perfect karaoke DJ.

For the purposes of karaoke night, Sip & Spin was BYOB. We charged a flat fee at the door and checked IDs for anyone who planned to drink. Maggie was in charge of the door. That left me with no responsibilities other than to enjoy myself and make sure that the giant carafe of coffee never ran dry. If Tansy needed a break, Maggie would cover her so I never had to pick up the microphone. If Maggie needed a break, I took over at the door. It was a good system.

Or at least it was when I hadn't already been at the shop all day. But that was what the espresso was for.

"Seriously, if you want to go lie down or take a walk, or whatever, go ahead," I told Savannah.

"I'm good," she assured me. I guess she didn't trust me after ditching her earlier in the day. I couldn't blame her. "What can I do?"

"You can help me move some of these displays off the floor," I told her. With the exception of the shelves mounted to the walls both upstairs and down, all of the displays were movable. Tonight, we would be Tetrising them into the storage room to make more space on the floor, but first, we had to drag the small temporary platform that would be our stage out of the back room and set it up in the corner near the barista station.

As we passed the door leading to the supply closet, I made sure it was firmly closed and secured. We'd learned our lesson about leaving that door unlocked when we were expecting a crowd. Hashtag never again.

We scattered the café tables and tall stools around the room so people would have places to congregate. Next, we set up the karaoke machine. Five seconds after it was up and running, Tansy rapped on the front door.

"Talk about timing," I said as I unlocked the door and held it open for her. "We just got finished with all the hard work."

"Oh, all the hard work is done, is it?" she asked. She took a step back toward the door. "I guess I'll just go home and let you emcee all night."

I slipped between her and the door, blocking the exit. "Over my dead body." The mere thought of picking up the microphone and addressing the crowd—and by crowd, I meant a dozen or two of my closest friends and neighbors—made me break out into a cold sweat.

"I can help DJ," Savannah offered.

"I'm just kidding," Tansy said. "I like to give Juni a hard time." Then, she added, in an exaggerated whisper, "My baby sister has stage fright."

"Not all of us can hog the spotlight," I fired back, but

with a grin so she knew I didn't mean anything by it. Personally, I was happy for my sister to be the center of attention so I didn't have to be.

Maggie arrived a few minutes later, and soon after that, our first customers of the night showed up. Within the hour, we had a full house.

Jen Rachet kicked the night off with "It's Oh So Quiet," which was anything but. Pete Digby, a security guard at the Cedar River Town Hall, got everyone singing along with "Don't Stop Believin'." The mayor dragged her wife onstage for "Pretty Girls." Leanna Lydell-Waite sang the Britney Spears part. Despite her initial reluctance, her wife, Janette, hammed up Iggy Azalea's lyrics.

"Having fun?" Teddy found me in the crowd and draped an arm over my shoulders.

"As long as no one tries pulling me up on stage like that, I am," I said, leaning into him.

"Oh please, Janette loves it. She's always doing community theatre. She's just pretending to need encouragement to get attention," he said. He took a swig of the beer he was holding in his other hand.

"You working up some liquid courage to sing tonight?" I asked. "Let me guess. Did you take my suggestion? Or are you going with a classic? 'Margaritaville' maybe? Or something from *The Rocky Horror Picture Show*?"

"Tonight, it's Miley Cyrus's 'Party in the U.S.A.' or bust."

I burst out laughing. "I'll pay good money to see that." Come to think of it, Teddy came to every karaoke night, but I'd never heard him sing. This was going to be a treat.

"In that case, I need to go bribe the DJ to get me on the list," he said. He looked down at his beer. "I might need a few more of these first."

"You sure that's a good idea?" Teddy lived on the far edge of town, down a long dirt road that was difficult to navigate in the daylight, much less at night. I didn't like the idea of anyone driving anywhere after drinking.

"Don't worry, Silvie's my DD tonight."

"Silvie's here?" I felt a lot better knowing his little sister was his designated driver. Now I could relax and enjoy his performance.

"Are you kidding? Ever since you introduced Silvie to the joys of vinyl, she's been obsessed. I think she spends more time in Sip & Spin these days than I do," Teddy said. Which was saying something. Teddy always found an excuse to drop by several times a day when I was working, even if it was just to drop off mail or snag a free coffee.

I nodded. "I know. I see her in here all the time, but with her farmer's hours, I'm not used to her being out late. I didn't notice her come in tonight."

"That's because this place is packed. Any more folks stop by and I might call the fire marshal myself."

"Don't worry," I assured him. "We sell tickets in advance so we don't exceed any occupancy regs." I gestured upstairs to where the second-floor balcony formed a semicircle above the first floor. "Besides, people rotate upstairs when it's not their turn to sing, so it won't feel so crowded once people settle in."

"True," he said. He glanced over at the front counter where several people were waiting to put their names in with my sister. "Don't go far. I'll be back, but I better get in line before the playlist fills up."

"If you want, I've got an in with the emcee. I can call in a favor."

Teddy gave me a warm grin. "I knew I kept you around for a reason. Be right back."

As he headed off to sign up for his turn, Darlene Daye took the stage and belted out Pat Benatar's "We Belong." She put so much feeling into it, that I thought maybe she'd missed her calling and should have gone out on tour instead of opening a secondhand shop. She was followed by Jayden Holt and Kitty Harris doing "Tubthumping" by Chumbawamba, a perpetual crowd favorite.

Savannah drifted over to stand beside me. During a break between songs, she said, "You know, I've never been a huge fan of karaoke, but this is fun. Do you think I should get up there and sing? Will you sing with me?"

"No way, no day," I said, shaking my head vehemently.

She pouted. "Oh come on, Juni. Don't be a spoilsport. I've got the perfect song. 'No Scrubs.' What do you say?"

"You're wasting your breath," Beau said, coming over to join us. He was dressed in a dark colored cowboy hat with a gold band, a green checkered button-down shirt, and blue jeans that fit like they'd been sewn onto him. Not that I was ogling him. "You're not going to get our Junebug onstage."

"What about you?" Savannah asked, smiling up at him. "Would you sing with me, cowboy?"

"Maybe some other time." He tipped his hat at her. "You should go ask Rocco. He's always looking for a duet partner," he said, before melting into the crowd.

"Which one's Rocco?" she asked. I pointed him out. He looked like he was trying to convince Joyce Whedon, one of the tellers at the First Bank of Cedar River, into signing up with him. "Thanks," she said, and went to join them.

Next up was Joy Akers and her daughter-in-law Carole. Carole and I had gone to high school together, and she'd married her high school sweetheart, Hank, right after graduation. Now they owned a fleet of successful food trucks. Together, they had the whole shop singing along to the Spice Girls' "Wannabe." From my spot in the back, where no one was watching me, I was dancing and singing at the top of my lungs like everyone else.

After that rambunctious performance, I was surprised

to hear the familiar melodic strains of John Legend's "All of Me." Within the first few piano notes, I was transported back to the final dance of senior prom. That moment was burned into my memory as Beau and I swayed together in our formal attire under glittering garden lights in a park with the Austin skyline behind us.

That was the magic of music. Whenever a favorite song came on, I could remember exactly the way it made me feel about a time long past. In this case, I could recall every detail of that dance as if it had been yesterday. Everything had been so much easier then. I was eighteen and didn't have a care in the world beyond being in Beau's arms.

I was jerked back to the here and now when I realized that it was none other than Beau himself up on the tiny makeshift Sip & Spin stage, crooning his heart out under the glare of the spotlight.

Maggie sidled up next to me. "Am I imagining this?" she asked.

"Shh," I hissed back. "I'm trying to listen." Despite the crowded shop, it felt like Beau was singing directly to me. I remembered the first time I'd caught him singing. He was so embarrassed. He thought everyone at school would make fun of him, the big quarterback belting out George Strait when he thought no one was around.

I was flooded with all the memories and emotions I'd worked so hard to suppress over the last few years. We had something special once. Then he broke my heart. Since moving back home, he'd been doing his best to atone, even as I'd held him at arm's length. But now, in the darkened record shop my sisters and I had worked so hard to resurrect, I had a moment of almost painful clarity.

The song swelled to a crescendo, and I pushed my way through our customers so that I was standing at the edge of the stage. "All of Me" ended to thunderous applause. There was a palatable feeling in the crowd like every single woman at a wedding jockeying to catch the bouquet. Unfortunately for them, I got there first.

I grabbed Beau's hand as he stepped off the stage. He rewarded me with a grin that might have sent a weaker person into cardiac arrest. He handed the microphone off to Tansy. She glared at us as I tugged on his hand, leading him down the narrow hallway, past the "Employees Only" sign.

Behind us, the music started up again, but I wasn't paying attention to it anymore. We reached the end of the hall. I wrapped my arms around Beau's neck and kissed him.

CHAPTER 19

In the six years that Beau and I had dated, we'd kissed more times than I could count. We were young, silly teenagers in love. Then we were young, silly twenty-somethings in love. And then, we weren't.

"That's our song," Beau said once the kiss ended.

"Yeah. I remember." I took a second to catch my breath. I had realized something that, if I was being honest, I'd known for a long time but hadn't admitted to anyone, not even myself. "I love you, Beau Russell." He grinned and started to respond, but I stopped him before he could say anything. "I love you," I repeated. "I've loved you since I was sixteen years old. I'll probably still love you when I'm sixty."

Standing this close to him, I could feel him tense. "Why do you make that sound like there's a but coming?" he asked hesitantly.

The song, the kiss, it should have made me feel something for Beau. But it hadn't. "Because I'm not *in* love with you anymore," I admitted. It had taken me years, but I was finally, truly over him.

He bent his head down so his forehead was resting on mine. "You got an awful funny way of showing it, Junebug."

I unwound my arms from his neck and took a step back. "I'm not the same person I used to be."

Beau shrugged. "Neither am I."

"And that's the problem," I said. "We're not those silly kids anymore."

"Is this the part where you tell me we'd be better off as friends?" Beau asked. He'd lost his trademark playful tone.

I shook my head. It was suddenly clear. "This is the part where I tell you that there are at least a dozen women back there who would love to be with you. I'm just not one of them. Not anymore."

"I knew I should have picked a different song," he said with a wry grin.

"The song was nice," I admitted. And it had *almost* worked. I'd always been a sucker for nostalgia, and he knew it. "We had some good times together."

"We did." He leaned in and kissed me on the forehead. "Any chance I could get you to reconsider?" he asked. He wasn't the type to give up easily, but I could tell his heart wasn't in it. Which was good, because neither was mine.

"Sorry," I said. All this time, I'd convinced myself that the only reason I wasn't willing to jump back into a romantic relationship with Beau was because I didn't trust him, when in reality, I knew deep down that I didn't feel that way about him anymore.

"Okay, then." He paused to gather his thoughts. He sighed. Then he surprised me with, "Oh, and Juni, I probably shouldn't be telling you this, but there were no texts on Zack's phone."

"Huh?" I asked. Leave it to Beau to change the subject so dramatically. Then again, he always did keep me on my toes.

He continued, as if we hadn't just shared a moment. "The text message that you mentioned Zack getting the night he died? It doesn't exist. There were no incoming or outgoing texts on his phone. Not from that night, or any other time for that matter."

"That makes no sense. Who doesn't text? Besides, that text message was the only reason he had to be in Cedar River the night of the storm. Why would Savannah lie about something like that? Are you sure? He might have erased it."

"We double-checked with his provider. There was nothing. Even if he had received a text, most of his contacts were just initials, so it would have taken us a minute to track down who sent it." He turned and walked back into the shop, and I will swear on my life that I absolutely did not appreciate every single cowboy-booted step. Fine. Maybe I did notice. I might not be in love with him, but I wasn't dead.

Was Beau Russell the hottest man I'd ever met? Yes. Was he the most arrogant? Also, yes. I'd carried a torch for him almost as long as I could remember, but now that I'd admitted to myself—and to him—that Beau just wasn't my person, all I felt was closure. Even if I was still attracted to him, I couldn't be with someone who presumed he could turn my life upside down and expect me to come running back to him.

I didn't want to go back into that crowd, knowing every pair of eyes would be on me. It was the curse of growing up in a small town. Gossip traveled fast, and it wouldn't take long for the news that Beau and I were no longer an item to spread. The half of Cedar River that had been #TeamBeau would be furious at me. The half that wanted nothing more than Beau Russell to be single and back on the market would be clamoring to buy me a drink.

And my sisters . . . Oof. I didn't even want to think of Tansy's *I told you so*s or Maggie begging me to give Beau one more chance. It seemed like everyone in town had already made up their mind, and now that I'd finally figured out what *I* wanted, it was bound to disappoint a few people. Most of all, I'd disappointed Beau. But he'd get over it. I know I had when he dumped me ages ago, even if took me years to realize it.

When I returned, Tansy was at the counter, shuffling through the music selection to get ready for the next song. She looked up and studied my face. "What happened?" she asked.

"It's over with Beau," I told her.

"Are you okay?" She seemed genuinely concerned. At least she wasn't gloating. That would come later, over late-night brownies and ice cream.

"Yeah." I glanced over at the stage. Esméralda Martín-Brown and Jayden were singing "Party in the U.S.A." "I thought Teddy called dibs on this song," I said, knowing my sister would never let two different groups sing the same song in one night. If she did, we'd have to listen to three hundred different versions of "I Will Always Love You."

Tansy shrugged. "When his turn came, he was nowhere to be found."

I grimaced. "Do you think . . . ?"

"That Teddy saw you practically drag Beau off to a dark corner after he publicly serenaded you with a song that could have melted a rock, assumed the worst, and took off?" She nodded. "That would be my guess."

"Mind if I head out?"

Tansy gave me a quick hug. "Go. We've got this."

I knew it would take too long to weave my way through the crowd, so I retraced my steps to the back door. It was dark in the alleyway behind the shop. As I walked, I pulled out my phone and dialed Teddy's number. He didn't pick up.

At the end of the alley, I turned toward Main Street. I saw Teddy's familiar Jeep, the one he'd driven ever since we were in high school, flick on its lights as the engine sprang to life. I jumped off the sidewalk into the street as it pulled out of the parking spot along the curb and waved my arms. The Jeep stopped.

I walked around the front of the Jeep and rapped on the driver's side window. It rolled down and I was surprised for a moment to see Silvie staring back at me. Then I remembered that Teddy told me his sister was his DD tonight. I nodded at Silvie before leaning in so I could speak to him. "You left before your song came up," I said.

"Yup," he said.

I waited for him to say something else, anything else. When he didn't, I added, "I broke things off with Beau."

"Was this before or after you kissed him?" Silvie asked.

There really was no such thing as privacy in a town like Cedar River. I hadn't realized that we had an audience, but to be fair, I'd been so focused on Beau I hadn't noticed anyone else around. I guess that was kind of a theme with me. I addressed Teddy instead of Silvie. "After."

"Good to know," Teddy said. "I gotta admit, I won't miss seeing his face at family dinners. What changed?"

"It took me a while, but I finally realized that I was so hung up on the past, I didn't see what was right in front of me all along," I admitted.

"It's about time," Silvie muttered.

"Hush," Teddy told his sister, before returning his attention to me. Frankly, I didn't blame her for butting in, considering we had to lean over her to talk to each other because I was standing at the driver's window while he was sitting in the passenger's seat. "I mean, she's not wrong," he added.

"She's not," I agreed. It was awkward to have this conversation with Silvie between us, but there was something I needed to get off my chest. "I'm sorry it took me this long. I really like you, Teddy. If it's not too late, I'd like to give you and me a real go."

It was dark enough that I couldn't read his expression. "Yeah, I'd like that too," he said, softly.

"Can we hurry this along?" Silvie asked. Teddy playfully punched her in the shoulder. "Ow," she whined, rubbing her arm. "I'm telling Mom."

Teddy laughed. "Leave it to my baby sis to ruin a perfectly good moment."

"Little sisters are such a pain," I said. Luckily, I didn't have first-hand knowledge of that, but the short time I'd spent with Savannah made me appreciate my older sisters more than ever. Despite Tansy and Maggie once threatening to drop me in the donation bin when we were younger, not only had they not gone through with it, but we ended up actually liking each other. Who would have thought it?

"Right?" he agreed.

Silvie rolled her eyes. "As much as I want to see y'all *finally* work things out, it's late. There are two pregnant cows I need to check up on before bed, and I've got to get up before the crack of dawn. Can y'all possibly continue this conversation later?"

"Yeah. Of course." I bobbed my head. After stringing both Teddy and Beau along for months, it was fair that I might have to wait a little while to find out exactly where Teddy and I stood. "Drive safe."

"I'll swing by tomorrow," Teddy promised.

I stepped back. Silvie rolled up the window and drove away, leaving me staring at the Jeep as it retreated. Silvie was shorter and slimmer than her older brother. Unlike the gimmick Maggie and I had used to trick Savannah earlier, Silvie and Teddy couldn't just swap outfits and fool anyone for thinking they were each other, not for a second.

Even as well as I knew Teddy, I had assumed that he was in the driver's seat because I'd been expecting him to be driving his own car. I knew he'd asked his sister to chauffeur him. He'd told me as much. And yet, when I was standing in front of the Jeep, in the glare of the headlights, I never would have guessed that it was his sister behind the wheel and Teddy in the passenger seat.

It made me wonder how the brick thrower had managed to hit Zack through the windshield so accurately. Not only had he been standing in front of the blinding headlights, but the storm had been raging and visibility was zero. Plus, whoever threw that brick was strong enough to break the windshield. They either had to be very, very lucky or very, very good. Maybe both.

I don't like to think of myself as a coward, but it took every bit of my courage to walk back into Sip & Spin Records, knowing all eyes would be on me. Sometimes I wondered if the only hobby anyone in Cedar River had was gossiping. The worst part was that when I really needed the rumor mill's help, like to tell me who Zack might have been seeing on the side, or at least spread the news of his death so I didn't have to be the one telling his business partners, it was eerily silent.

When I reached Sip & Spin, Maggie opened the door. I could hear the crowd screaming along to the chorus of "Sweet Caroline." My sister grinned at me. "Ticket, please."

"I'm on the list," I told her.

"I can squeeze you in this time, but you'll have to sing. Rules are rules," she teased.

"Fine." I shrugged. "Put me down for 'I'd Do Anything for Love (But I Won't Do That).'"

Maggie cracked up. "Come on in, sis."

With the crowd chanting along with the music that it was "so good, so good, so good," I climbed the stairs up to the balcony so I could get a bird's-eye view. The music was loud, but not so loud that I couldn't hear people talking about me and Beau as I passed. Glad I could offer some entertainment value. Luckily, I could make a complete fool of myself without ever having to get up on stage and pick up the mic.

As long as people were in a talkative mood, I might as well take advantage of it. I noticed Carole Akers leaning against the rail. I joined her. "You and your mother-in-law were a real hoot earlier," I said.

"Thanks. She has a real thing for nineties pop music. It was either Spice Girls or Hansen."

"MMMBop," I replied, earning a chuckle from Carole. "When you started up your food truck business, was it terribly difficult?"

"Are you really so eager to talk about anything but Beau that you want to hear about food trucks? Or are you thinking of changing careers again so soon?" she asked.

"Me? Nah. I'd be the worst food truck owner ever. I'd eat all the profits. And I can't cook. Besides, where else but here do I get to listen to music and drink coffee all day every day?"

"True. But to answer your question, it was brutal. We got some start-up money from Hank's folks, but we were working sixteen-hour days and couldn't come close to breaking even."

"How'd you turn it around?" I asked.

"Luck." She shrugged. "We tried everything. Altering the menu constantly. Social media. Groupons. The food was great but no one was buying. Until one day I served the right meal to the right person. She turned out to be a food blogger, and the next thing I knew, we had a line around the block. We went from nothing to not being able to meet demand in a matter of days."

"Sounds like a good problem to have," I mused. Granted, that kind of popularity brought its own kind of troubles, but they were the sort of troubles I would be glad to have.

"We had to take out a small business loan to add a new truck. And then another. Before I knew it, we had a whole fleet. We're making money, but now, we're up to our eye-balls in debt." She shook her head. "Running a small business is not for the faint of heart."

"Tell me about it," I agreed. "But you made it."

"We made it," Carole said.

"And you never had to take on investors?" I asked.

"Thankfully, no. Why? You're not thinking of bringing investors into Sip & Spin, are you? Because I can tell you that if it sounds too good to be true, it probably is. There are scrupulous vultures and unscrupulous vultures. Either way, they're vultures."

"Fjord Capital was trying pretty hard to get their foot in the door," I admitted.

"I hope you told them to pound sand. I have a friend in Austin who sold them half of her bookstore, and six months later she was out of business. And you heard about the Elbys, didn't you?"

I had, of course. I felt sorry for Jackson Elby and the loss of his clothing shop, but at the same time, it sounded like it was very much out of fashion. If he refused to change with the times, there was only so much Savannah and Zack could do to save them. "What about the Elbys?" I asked.

"It was a mess. They used to own Cedar River Casuals, right here in this very storefront," she told me. I nodded along as if this was news to me. "Their clothing was straight out of the 1974 Modern Woman catalog.

My grandma shopped there, and every time I'd drive her there, the place would be empty. She'd browse and end up not buying anything."

"Why not?" I asked.

"I remember one time, she found a green silk blouse that looked great with her hair. I told her she should get it, and she told me, 'Carole, I already have three identical green silk blouses in my closet that I never wear. What do I need another one for?' We left empty-handed."

"I can see how a shop like that might go out of business," I said.

"It was inevitable, but the fallout got nasty. There were some accounting 'discrepancies.'" She said the last word with air quotes. I thought about what Mr. Elby had told me about Savannah changing his system from paper to the computer, and how he'd fought back against it. I could imagine there would be plenty of discrepancies if he wasn't entering receipts and purchases into the new accounting software.

Carole continued, "When it was all said and done, Sheila Elby packed up and left. Jackson Elby sold the house and moved into one of those sad apartments on Armstrong. If you ask me, they were probably headed that way to begin with, but those investors sure sped things along."

"Do you know Zack Fjord and Savannah Goodwin well?" I asked.

"You know Savannah a lot better than I do. Rumor has it, she's staying at your place."

"At Mom's cottage. It's temporary," I said. "But what about Zack? Did you know him?"

"Only by reputation," Carole said. "He, um, had a way with the ladies if you know what I mean, but I wasn't having anything of it."

"Any ladies in particular?" I asked.

She shook her head. "From what I hear, he wasn't very particular." The song on stage was winding down. "You'll have to excuse me. I promised Joy we'd do one more number before calling it a night." She hurried down the stairs and made her way to the stage for "Karma Chameleon."

The crowd was starting to thin. I watched Carole and Joy from my spot on the balcony. Part of me envied the way they were so comfortable hamming it up on stage. The rest of me wanted to pass out just thinking about going up there. I was much more comfortable here in the shadows where I could sing along with the music without anyone paying attention to me.

Not that I was completely anonymous. I could feel eyes on me even if I couldn't hear the whispers in between Boy George's choruses. I'm sure the good folks of Cedar River would find something else to gossip about sooner or later, and they'd forget all about me. Hopefully.

Savannah sidled up next to me.

"Ready to go?" I asked.

"Actually, I am. I appreciate everything you've done for me, but the roads are open now and I think it's time I head home."

"What?" I asked, trying to not sound relieved. Not having to share my bathroom and my clothes with Savannah any longer? Yes, please! "I thought you wanted to stick around until the police found Zack's killer." I didn't add that if she left town now, it might not look so good for her, as far as the police were concerned.

"I'm not going far," she said. "The last few days have been overwhelming, and I might feel better after a good night's sleep in my own bed. Besides, there's a killer running around Cedar River. Until he's caught, the safest place for me is back in Austin."

Downstairs, Tansy announced the last song of the night. "Kitty and Mickey, get up here. This one's a throwback for my baby sis." I didn't know if J.T.'s cousin Kitty, and Mickey, who worked at the car rental place out by the airport, knew each other or if they'd both requested the same song so Tansy combined them, but they looked like they were having a blast even before the ultra-catchy "Baby Shark" tune started. I found myself doo-doo-dooing along with the crowd to the hook.

Beside me, Savannah's phone beeped. She looked down at her screen. "That's my ride. I'll check in often, and I'll be back in a few days to pick up my stuff." She hesitated a second before giving me a hug. "Thanks for everything, Juni. And thank your sisters, too. I couldn't have made it through the last few days without y'all."

She waved and trotted down the stairs. I had a feeling that was the last I would ever see of my Savage Garden T-shirt.

CHAPTER 20

Today was my day off. We were all out late yesterday for karaoke night, but I'd spent most of the day in the shop and Sunday was always a slow day. I'd probably stop by and check on my sisters at some point to make sure that they were okay, but until then, I got to sleep in.

I'd already tested and named the coffee special of the day. Yesterday, we'd gone simple with drip coffee, so today would be "Jagged Latte Pill." It started out with a double shot of our darkest espresso, twice as much steamed milk as espresso, a thin swirl of foam, and a dash of colorful sprinkles. As it cooled, the sprinkles dissolved into a foamy rainbow of colors. It was strong and sweet at the same time, just like my sisters.

When I finally rolled out of bed, I dressed in a No Doubt T-shirt and made a cup of coffee in the kitchen. It was oddly quiet with Savannah gone. I needed to figure out a way to get the Victrola from Rediscovered Treasures to Sip & Spin.

The problem was, the player was almost four feet tall and probably weighed at least a hundred pounds. If it wasn't going to fit in the loaner SUV Maggie was driving, it certainly wouldn't fit in the market basket mounted to the back of my tricycle.

One of the good things about living in Texas was that

everyone knew someone with a truck. I was no exception. I just so happened to have broken up with the guy with a pickup *and* muscles last night. Luckily, Beau wasn't the only man with a truck in Cedar River.

After I got dressed, I pedaled my trike over to my uncle's house. Calvin only lived a few blocks away, and it was nice to be back on my tricycle again. Don't get me wrong, cars were convenient, great for long-distance trips, and best of all, were air conditioned. But my trike was low maintenance, cheap, and a great way to get a little exercise.

I pulled up to Uncle Calvin's house. Before knocking on his door, I made sure to turn and wave in the direction of Miss Edie's house across the street. She might not be watching out her window, but chances were good that she was. A more uncharitable person might call Edie nosy. I called her vigilant. Who needed a neighborhood watch when you had Miss Edie?

"Good morning, Juni," Uncle Calvin said as he answered the door. If he'd been expecting me, I would have let myself in, but it was rude to come over unannounced and then walk in without knocking. "How's my favorite niece this morning?"

I grinned at him. "I could have sworn that Maggie was your favorite," I said. He liked to play favorites, but I knew he loved us all more or less equally.

"She is. So are you. And so is Tansy," he admitted. "Come on in. Can I get you something?"

"I'm good. I was wondering if I could borrow your—" He cut me off. "No."

Just as I knew he'd claim we were all his favorite, I knew he would never loan me his pride and joy, a 1986 Ford Bronco. It was mostly blue, with a tan stripe running around the bottom and a single red door. Depending on who you asked, the original door had not survived a collision with a deer, had been stolen during a crime wave, or had been used to save a family of kittens. Personally, I think that Calvin's best friend, Samuel, had taken it as a prank and then forgot to give it back.

Calvin loved his family, the racetrack, and his Bronco. Not necessarily in that order. If my uncle had his way, the only way I'd ever get behind the wheel of his truck again was if I pried the keys from his cold, dead hands. And, considering I had a suspicion he'd made arrangements to be buried with his truck, maybe not even then.

"Fine. Then I guess you're driving," I said, making sure to sound extra chipper to let him know that was my plan all along. "No reason for me to try to drive that beast if I can get you to chauffeur me around town. Besides, your brakes need work."

"My brakes do not need work," he said gruffly. He took great pride in doing the maintenance and repairs on the old Bronco himself. Which, come to think of it, was probably the real reason why the doors didn't match. "Where are we going?"

"The secondhand store down by the airport."

"Darlene Daye's shop?" he asked. "What are we shopping for?"

"You'll see."

When we got to Rediscovered Treasures, it was already busy. Darlene came over to greet us. Her hair was in a bun like it had been the other day, but today, her pantsuit was lilac. "Juni, nice to see you again so soon. And Calvin Voigt! It's been too long."

"It has been," he agreed.

"Follow me. I had the Victrola moved to the warehouse. One of my guys will help you load it up," she said.

"I'll bring the truck around back," Calvin offered.

As we walked past one of the clothing displays, I asked Darlene, "How long have you had those mannequins?"

"They're nice, aren't they? They were one of my first purchases as soon as the check from Fjord Capital cleared." Frankie had used his payout to pay for his dad's medical expenses. Darlene had reinvested hers back into the business. No wonder she'd had more success than he had.

"Very nice," I said. "Classy." I thought that was what Savannah had called them. To me, they just looked like mannequins. "What did you have before? I can't remember."

"We didn't. I thought racks were the way to go. Give people more choices. Turns out, customers don't always want endless choices. They want someone to tell them what's best. Notice anything different today?" she asked, waving her hand at the fancy dress section.

"Not really?" I said, hesitantly.

"Every single dress that was on display last time you were here has gone home with someone." She snapped her fingers. "Just like that."

"You must have made some good sales." I wish the inventory at Sip & Spin turned over that quick. "Speaking of sales, did you ever notice any inconsistencies with your books?"

"With *my* books? No way. Why? What did you hear?" Darlene asked.

"Nothing, it's just that Jackson Elby said his bookkeeping got all messed up after Savannah and Zack came in."

"That old fool? For the record, his wife took care of the books. I wouldn't be surprised if Sheila helped herself to a little something extra before she left. She was entitled to it, if you ask me, putting up with him all those years. It's enough to make me glad I'm still single at my age. But what's your excuse?"

"Excuse me?" I asked.

"You're young. Pretty. Boys are falling all over you. So why are you still single?"

Darlene was somewhere between Tansy's age and my mother's, so I'd put her in her forties. She was smart, owned her own business, was active, and was involved in the community. There was no legitimate reason she should be single if she didn't want to be. Me, on the other hand? Well, that remained to be seen. "Um, just lucky, I guess."

She let out a bitter laugh. "Some of us aren't meant to be lucky in love. But you, Juni, it's not too late for you."

"Thanks?" I was profoundly uncomfortable with the turn our conversation had taken, and was relieved when she introduced me to one of her employees who could help me with the Victrola.

He strapped the record cabinet to a dolly and wheeled it down the back ramp to where Calvin was waiting with the Bronco. He even loaned us some packing blankets to cushion it for the ride home. It ended up taking two guys to load the unwieldy Victrola into the back of the Bronco. I was questioning our ability to unload it once we got it back to the shop. Then again, both of my sisters were working this morning and together, we could do anything.

"You know, Mom and Dad used to have one just like that," my uncle said, as the employee tucked blankets on either side of it so it wouldn't slide around.

"Same one, actually," I told him.

"Well, what are the odds?" he asked.

"In a town this small? Pretty good. Apparently, when my mom sold the house, she brought Grandma's Victrola here on consignment. Lucky for me, it never sold."

"I was wondering where it had disappeared to," Calvin said. "It must be worth an arm and a leg by now. What do you plan on doing with it?"

"I don't plan on selling it and giving you the money to take to the racetrack, if that's what you're wondering," I told him. I loved my uncle, but he'd never met a pony or a pyramid scheme he didn't like.

"If your grandma could hear you talking to me like that . . ." he muttered.

"If Grandma could hear you thinking about selling her Victrola for poker money . . ." I countered.

"Fine. Where to?" He passed a bill to each of the employees who had helped us load. Knowing my uncle, it could have been a five or a fifty, depending on what he happened to have in his wallet. It was another reason he was always broke. When he did have money, he was generous to a fault, which wasn't necessarily a bad thing.

"Sip & Spin," I told him.

Calvin had driven around the back of Rediscovered Treasures to load the unwieldy Victrola. It was mostly warehouses back here along with a few storefronts, like the one that used to hold my uncle's prank shop. There was a line of cars in various states of disrepair parked along the edge of the lot. I assumed they were the cars that Esméralda fixed up at her auto shop when she was between customers. Beyond that was the town's only self-storage with rows after rows of buildings partitioned into individual lockers.

"What was it that Jackson Elby said?" I mused aloud.

"Huh?" Calvin asked. "And how are you involved with that old coot?"

"He mentioned that when Cedar River Casuals went out of business, he liquidated as much stock as possible, but what he couldn't fit into his locker, he paid someone to haul off to the dump," I said.

"So?"

"So, do you know of any other storage lockers in town?"

"No."

"Let's go take a look," I said. It was a long shot, but he had gotten awful squirrely when I mentioned the mannequins. Then again, maybe I was reading too much into things. Elby had alternated between grumpy and defensive during our entire conversation.

We pulled up to the gate. "I don't suppose you have a code?" Calvin asked, looking at the keypad.

Then the gates swung open. "Guess we don't need one. Drop me off at the manager's office, will you?" Calvin pulled into a parking spot out front. "I'll be right back."

Inside the manager's office was a Black teenager I didn't recognize. He was tall, skinny, and couldn't have been much more than sixteen. "Can I help you?" he asked. He reached under the counter and pulled out a glossy piece of paper that listed the prices of different sizes and types of lockers. "We've got a special going on right now. If you pay upfront for a year, you'll get the first three months free. Will you be needing an air-conditioned or non-air-conditioned unit?"

He wouldn't have been a bad salesperson if not for his monotone voice. He was clearly bored and eager for me to go away so he could get back to his phone or whatever he did to entertain himself all shift long. I didn't blame him one bit. I'd done a stint in retail in high school, and it had been mind-numbingly dull. It wasn't until I owned my own shop that I found any joy or pride in my job.

"Actually, Mr. Elby sent me to pick up a few things out of his unit," I said. I didn't know the teen, and wasn't sure what I was going to do if he questioned my story, but he didn't seem to care.

"Yeah, okay, go ahead." He waved at the door.

So much for security. Not that I needed a storage locker but if I did, I hoped it would be a place that checked IDs. "See, the problem is, I can't remember the locker number he gave me. Was it 1682 or 1826?" I shrugged and tried to look forgetful.

"Elby, you said?" he asked, typing into his computer.

"Jackson Elby," I replied. "E-L-B-Y."

"He's in one-twenty A."

"Wow, I was way off," I said with what I thought was a vapid-sounding giggle. "Thanks."

"Sure."

I hurried out of the office and got in the passenger side of Calvin's Bronco. "Unit one-twenty A."

"You'll have to read the numbers to me," Calvin said as he drove down the first row. "I left my glasses at home."

"Do you really think you should be driving if you can't see well enough to read?" I asked him.

He made a derisive sound in the back of his throat. "Oh please, what am I gonna need to read? Street signs? I know this town like the back of my hand."

"Stop," I said. Calvin pumped the breaks. Nothing happened. He pumped the brakes again, and we rolled to a halt. "I told you, those breaks need work."

"They just need a minute to warm up," he said.

"That's not a thing, Uncle Calvin," I told him.

"Shush, kiddo. Do you want my help or not?" We both got out of the car and looked at 120 A. There was a padlock on the door. "Well? What did you expect?"

I stood on my tiptoes so I could reach above the doorjamb. There was no key conveniently hidden just out of sight. "I was hoping to catch a break."

Calvin rattled the lock. "Maybe you did. Be right back." He went back to the Bronco and rummaged around the glovebox, coming back with something that looked like a narrow leather wallet. He flipped it open to reveal several skinny metal tools.

"Uncle Calvin, that's not a lock picking kit," I said in surprise.

"Like nothing, it's not." He lifted the lock, looked at the keyhole, and selected two picks. "Ever since Samuel and I were just boys, we've been honing our skills."

"You mean, you've both been trying to best each other with one-up pranks," I interpreted.

"Something like that. One time, I came home and he'd wrapped my refrigerator in about a mile of heavy-duty chain and padlocked it a dozen times. Took me nearly an hour to get into it. Halfway through, I got thirsty so I took the door off the hinges to grab a beer but I didn't give up until . . ." There was a metallic click as the padlock opened. "Still got it."

"Look at you!" I said, appreciatively. There were times when my uncle's less-than-legal hobbies were a source of embarrassment for the family, but they were certainly coming in handy now.

Calvin pocketed the lock and rolled up the garage-style door, revealing a locker packed to the ceiling. "What are we looking for?" He loosened a box that was wedged between several others and opened the top. He pulled out a long prairie dress. "You going shopping?"

"Not my style," I told him. When I was talking with Elby, I got the impression that his clothes were so old-fashioned as to not be saleable, but I'd seen similar clothes gaining popularity lately. If Cedar River Casuals had been able to hang on for another six months, they might have been relevant again. Then again, if they hadn't folded, Sip & Spin might not exist.

"Keep your eyes out for receipts, notebooks, anything with numbers." There was a narrow, winding aisle through the junk. I picked my way carefully. "Mr. Elby is convinced that someone was skimming. I don't know if he's being paranoid because he didn't trust the computerized accounting system or if money really was missing, but if we find something, I'll see if Maggie can make heads or tails of it."

I pulled a box off a stack at random. It was labeled "Fragile." It was filled with wire coat hangers. "I swear he's a worse packer than I am," I muttered. The last time I'd packed, it had been a rush job. As a result, I was still finding favorite books buried in boxes that contained bras, spare shoelaces, and a toaster. "We're never going to find anything in here," I said.

The next box, helpfully labeled "Keep" was wedged in tightly. "Can you give me a hand?" I called out to my uncle. Together, we were able to Jenga it out without toppling the rest. "I'll bet it's pantyhose," I said, peeling up the tape holding it closed.

"Ten dollars it's silk scarves," he countered.

I opened the box and stared down at a dozen dismembered human hands.

CHAPTER 21

———

"Juniper," Uncle Calvin said slowly, backing away from the box. "I think we ought to get out of here."

Fixated, I stared at the box of hands. "Just another minute."

I hated it when Beau was right. What had he said? Something about I should have asked Jackson Elby who he hired to haul his old mannequins to the dump? And I'd said it didn't matter, because his mannequins had hands. Now, I was going to have to eat crow.

In a perfect world, I could avoid Beau for a little while. Long enough to take the sting out of our breakup last night, at least. Sure, this time I had been the breaker instead of the breakee, but that didn't mean I wanted to spend the rest of the day with him as he cataloged the contents of the locker. Last time we'd broken up, we'd successfully avoided each other for six whole years. Was it too much to ask for at least a full day this time around? It wasn't fair. It wasn't even noon yet.

But I was an adult, and I didn't conveniently have a job waiting for me on the other side of the country. I pulled out my phone and dialed. It went to voicemail. "Huh," I chuckled to myself. Beau had never failed to answer my calls before. Maybe I wasn't the only one who could use some space.

"The way I see it, we've got two choices," I told Calvin. "One, we leave everything here, tell the cops what we found, and hope they show up before Mr. Elby decides to dump the rest of his locker in the river."

"And two?" he asked, grumpily. I think he was still salty about not winning our bet, not that he would ever pay up. Uncle Calvin wasn't always the most reliable person when it came to, well, anything, but especially when it came to money.

"We take it with us and drop it off at the station."

"There's always the third option. We put everything back where we found it and pretend this never happened."

"That's a lousy option," I told him. "This is proof that Mr. Elby is responsible for polluting our river."

"Or, it's proof that he's got a thing for mannequin hands. I don't judge," Calvin said. "Did I ever tell you that the word 'mannequin' comes from a Dutch word that means 'little man'? Which is ironic, because most of the mannequins used in the United States these days are women."

"Fascinating," I told him. I guess he didn't get my sarcasm, because he kept talking, regaling me with the origins and evolution of mannequins from the headless wicker forms of the eighteenth century to the full-body ones in use today. I tuned him out.

It was a bright day, but the storage locker was packed and little light reached the back. I shifted a few more boxes around to try to see if there were any more boxes full of hands, and found the mother lode. Two full-sized mannequins, hands still attached, were crammed in the back corner.

I used the camera on my phone to get a picture of the lot number in each of the mannequin's armpits, then scrolled back through my pictures. They matched the worn numbers on the mannequins that had washed up on the riverbanks. I stepped back and took a few more pictures of the mannequins, the box of hands, and the storage locker as a whole. I texted them to Beau. He might not be picking up the phone for me, but once he saw those pictures, he would want to talk.

"Oof," I said, trying to lift one of the mannequins. It was heavier than it looked. "A little help here?"

Uncle Calvin gingerly stepped around and over boxes and other discarded remnants of Cedar River Casuals. "What do you want her for?" he asked. "She's creepy."

"She's evidence," I said. "We'll take one with us, and leave the other."

"And the hands?"

"The hands stay here." I couldn't explain why the dismembered hands were so much more disturbing than the complete mannequins, but they were. I had a picture of the box of hands and one of the mannequins. That would have to be enough.

Now that I had an assembled model in front of me, I could see how the limbs came together. The hands had long screws in them that would fit into the end of the arms, so it would have been easy to assume that these particular mannequins had never had hands. I had no idea why Elby had tossed most of his mannequins but had saved the hands. I wasn't sure I wanted to know.

Together, Calvin and I manipulated one of the mannequins out of the crowded storage locker and into the sun. He reached into a box, pulled out the prairie dress he'd teased me about earlier, and tugged it in place over the unclothed mannequin. "There. That's better." We lifted the mannequin and slid it into the back of the Bronco, next to the Victrola. "At least this way if I get stopped for driving around with a dead body in the back of my truck, she won't be naked."

"Good thinking," I agreed. I grabbed a wig out of an open box on impulse before rolling the locker door back down. I hooked the padlock onto the door but didn't close the shank.

Uncle Calvin got in the driver's side and I buckled myself into the passenger seat. "Where to? The police station?"

"Can you imagine the ridicule we'd get if we walked that thing right into the Cedar River police station?" I shook my head. "We'd never live that down."

"Sounds like a good time to me," he said. Then again, my uncle and I had very different ideas of what constituted humor. He leaned toward snakes-in-a-can. I preferred puns.

"Take me back to your house," I suggested.

"You're not leaving that thing at my house. It's creepy."

"Then take me to Tansy's."

"Your sister will have your hide if she comes home and finds that thing in her living room."

"Then I'll put it in the cottage," I told him, running out of options. "No one's using it right now." With Savannah back in her own apartment and Mom staying with Marcus most of the time, the cottage was the best place for it. "It won't be for long."

I checked my phone. Still no response from Beau. Even if he was avoiding me, he wouldn't be able to ignore those pictures. He was probably busy. He'd call me back any minute now, maybe even before we got back to the house.

Once again, he proved me wrong as we pulled into Tansy's driveway without a peep from Beau. My uncle and I wrestled the mannequin into the cottage. He wanted to shove her into the closet, but she was heavy and awkward to carry. I was content to stand her up in the corner and lock the door behind us.

"Where to now?"

"Sip & Spin, if you don't mind," I told him.

"You know, I'd be happy to keep the Victrola at my place," Calvin offered.

"Golly, that's awful generous of you. You'd have it listed on eBay within the hour."

"That's my parents' Victrola you're talking about," he said.

"And my grandparents'," I pointed out. "If you want to come visit it, it will be at the record shop."

"I can't believe you don't trust me. My own niece." He turned in his seat to get a good look at the large cabinet. "Just out of curiosity, how much do you think I could get for it?"

"Just drive," I told him.

"Sure thing."

We found a parking spot relatively near the shop. "I'll be right back," I told him. Despite his earlier comments, I knew he'd be there when I got back with my sisters. Calvin wasn't so hard up for cash that he'd sell his own mom's antique record player. At least, I didn't think he would.

Once I got in the shop, I realized the flaw in my plan. It would take all three of us to unload the Victrola and walk it inside, but we had customers milling around. I should have thought this through better. "Hey, Maggie, how long do you think it would take J.T. to get down here if you called him?"

"Not long," she said. "He's out back loading up the generator to return it to the Garza farm. What's up?"

"It's a surprise. You're gonna love it," I told her, and hurried out through the back door where my brother-in-law was grunting as he tried to maneuver the heavy generator into the trunk of his car. "Need a hand?" I asked him.

"Please," he said.

With both of us working together, it was easy. He closed the trunk. "You've got great timing," he told me.

"So do you. Can I ask one more thing of you?"

He wiped his hands on his pant legs. "Of course."

We stopped to get the dolly out of the stockroom and then he followed me out to Calvin's Bronco. Despite my earlier reassurances to myself, I was a little surprised that he was still there. "I see you decided not to pawn it," I said with a grin so he'd know I was teasing.

"It's too heavy to pawn," Calvin said as the three of us struggled to get it out of the back of the truck without damaging it or us.

"You're telling me," J.T. grunted. "What is this, anyway? A dresser?"

"It's a Victrola," I told him. "An old record player. It belonged to my grandparents."

"Where does it plug in?" he asked, walking around the wooden cabinet.

"That's what the crank's for," I told him. I opened the little doors on the front. "The sound comes out here."

"It's weird," J.T. said.

"It's retro," I corrected him.

"It's heavy," he countered. He strapped it to the dolly and we all headed into Sip & Spin.

After much fawning from my sisters, we set the Victrola up in the corner in front of the checkout counter. I propped open the lid so that the record player was visible. "I'm afraid if we leave it closed, someone will put their coffee down on it," I said.

"Good idea," Maggie said.

"I'm gonna get going," J.T. said. "See ya at home, Mags." Maggie gave her husband a goodbye kiss. There was a time when I was much younger and they'd first started dating when I thought their displays of affection was gross, but now, I thought it was sweet.

"Tell the Garzas thanks for the genny," I said. I had to admit I was a little disappointed that Teddy hadn't come to pick it up himself. I still hadn't seen him since karaoke. I was looking forward to our conversation, which would be much better to have in person than over the phone.

"Will do." J.T. went out the back.

"What's the special of the day?" Calvin asked, gravitating toward the coffee station.

"Jagged Latte Pill," I told him.

"Yes please, I'll take one of those," he said. I mixed a drink for my uncle.

"Thanks again for all your help today."

"Always more than happy to help my favorite niece move a body," he said.

"Wait a second, I thought I was your favorite," Tansy protested. At the same time, Maggie said, "Body? What body?"

"It's been fun, but I've got to go," Calvin said, starting trouble like always. He lifted his coffee cup in salute as he departed.

"Juni?" Tansy asked in a warning tone.

"It wasn't a *real* body," I told her. "It was a mannequin, like the ones found in the river. Only this one was in a storage unit."

"I still get the willies thinking about them. I heard that Hank Akers was fishing down by the river, and caught what he thought was a bunch of body parts, but they turned out to be chopped-up mannequins," Maggie said.

"Well, I heard that those mannequins were part of some weird ritual," Tansy said.

"How on earth do these rumors get started?" I shook my head. "It was Mayor Lydell-Waite who found them, not Hank. There was no ritual, just plain laziness. And they weren't chopped up. They were just disassembled to make them easier to carry because, I don't know if you know this, but mannequins are heavy."

"I knew that," Tansy said. "Maggie, did you know that?"

"Of course I knew that," my middle sister said. "But you still haven't explained what you and Uncle Calvin were doing with a mannequin."

"We found a couple of matching mannequins in Jackson Elby's storage unit, along with a box of the missing hands. He claims he hired someone to take them to the dump when Cedar River Casuals folded, but I'd like to hear him explain how they ended up in the bottom of the river instead. If it weren't for the storm, we'd never have known they were down there. The police are looking for leads, and I was afraid that if he found out we were poking around his locker, he'd get rid of the evidence, so we took one with us."

"So there's a naked mannequin rolling around in the back of Calvin's Bronco?" Tansy asked.

"Not exactly," I said. I didn't think that Tansy would be upset at me for leaving it in the cottage at her house, but I couldn't be sure she wouldn't be, either.

"You complain about the rumor mill, but just imagine how fast tongues would wag if he got pulled over with a naked mannequin in his truck," Maggie said.

"Wait a second," I said, holding up a finger to get my sisters to be quiet for a second. Not that it was ever completely silent in Sip & Spin. Right now, PJ Harvey was playing on the record player. Steam was hissing from the barista station. Customers were milling around, chatting with each other as they examined the record covers.

"That's it!" I turned to my sisters. "We use the gossip to our advantage."

My sisters exchanged glances.

"What's she talking about?" Maggie asked.

"Beats me," Tansy replied.

"Y'all, I'm right here," I said. "What do we know? Wednesday night, someone texted Zack to come to Cedar River in the middle of the night." Technically, I still had no proof that such a text ever existed, but I was willing to take Savannah's word for it, for now. "Maybe they knew the storm was coming. Maybe they didn't. Either way, they couldn't have known that Zack was going to tie one on at the hockey game and Savannah would be driving his car."

I paced as I talked, letting the pieces fall into place. "Whoever threw the brick was standing in front of the car. At night. With the headlights in their eyes." I thought back to last night when I'd jumped out in front of Teddy's Jeep. Even as familiar as I was with him, and knowing that his sister was his designated driver, I couldn't tell that it wasn't Teddy behind the wheel until after the window rolled down and I saw that Silvie was driving.

"They threw the brick at the passenger's side, where Savannah normally sat."

Tansy nodded. "There's no way they could have known that the brick would break the windshield, that the car would crash, or that anyone would be seriously hurt."

"Maybe not," I agreed, "but they knew they were going to scare the living daylights out of them even if they weren't trying to cause any permanent damage. We've been looking at this wrong all along. They weren't aiming at Zack."

"Which means that someone in Cedar River had it out for Savannah. Even if they didn't intend to kill her, they wanted to frighten her."

"And she was terrified," Tansy said. "She said as much. She was cowering in the shop when we found her. If all they wanted to do was scare her, they succeeded."

"What if that's not all they wanted?" Maggie asked. "Then they have unfinished business."

"Exactly," I said.

I lowered my voice. "Right now, we're the only people who know that Savannah left Cedar River." My sisters nodded. "We spread the word that she's still staying with us in the cottage, and that she has remembered something about the person who threw the brick, something that might identify them. Something that can send them to prison for manslaughter."

Tansy waved her hand. "You can stop that thought right there," she said. "I'm not letting my baby sister dangle herself out as bait."

I grinned. "That's where it gets good." I leaned in, making sure we couldn't be overheard. "I don't have to do anything. The mannequin's gonna do all the hard work for us."

CHAPTER 22

No matter what anyone said, stakeouts were boring.

My sisters had the fun jobs. Tansy went around town spreading rumors as fast as she could run her mouth. She really should have listed that as her special talent back in her pageant days, instead of tap dancing. She didn't like to admit it, but Tansy already had quite the reputation in Cedar River for being one of the authorities on information, so no one thought it was weird that she was handing out gossip like it was Halloween candy.

Maggie held down the fort at Sip & Spin, pouring coffee and serving up the dish to any customer who walked through the door. On top of our popular Jagged Latte Pill, I'd blended two of my favorite roasts before I left and christened it My Brew Heaven. My sisters and I dragged the sidewalk sign out of storage and offered a free small drip coffee to all customers, knowing that would drive in foot traffic. With any luck, everyone in town would be buzzing with news—and My Brew Heaven—before evening.

As the sun set, there were no lights on in the main house, except the yellow porch light we always left on and the screen of my laptop. In contrast, every light was on in the cottage and the television was tuned to a mystery marathon, which I thought was appropriate. Anyone passing Tansy's house would presume that the big house was empty but the cottage was occupied, which was exactly what we were hoping for.

My trike was still parked in Calvin's driveway, so everyone would assume I was over there. My phone was set to silent. I had a bag of donuts and an insulated mug of cold brew coffee. I was ready to settle in and watch patiently.

The problem was, I wasn't a very patient person.

At first, I watched the doorbell camera footage on my laptop closely, while still keeping an eye out the kitchen window for anything the camera might miss. J.T. had been kind enough to swing by the hardware store, buy the camera, and install it for us. We told him it was a surprise gift for Mom. He knew better than to believe us, but he also knew better than to argue when the Jessup sisters were on a mission.

As the night wore on, I grew increasingly bored until a familiar Jeep pulled up in front of the house. Teddy got out and headed to the front door. I opened the door before he could knock, grabbed his arm, and pulled him inside. I kicked the door shut behind him.

"Happy to see you, too," he said, sounding confused.

"Shh," I told him, pressing my eye against the peephole and watching for a sign that anyone had seen him.

"Sorry I didn't come by sooner. It's been a busy day at the farm." He looked around. "Why's it so dark in here?"

"I, um, well . . ."

"Is this a bad time?"

"No!" I said quickly. "I've been wanting to talk to you all day. It's just that . . ." My voice trailed off. It wasn't right, hiding anything from Teddy. "Okay, don't get mad."

"I'm confused," he admitted. "Not mad."

"My sisters and I figured out that Zack was never the intended target, so we spread a rumor that Savannah would be alone in Mom's cabin tonight, hoping that the killer would reveal themself."

Teddy ran a hand through his hair. "I see." I don't think this was the conversation he'd been expecting we would have tonight.

"You're upset, aren't you?" I asked, bracing myself for his answer. Beau would have been furious.

"That you thought luring a killer over to your house in the middle of the night would be a good idea? Nah. Why would that upset me?" He was taking this in stride. "Got any coffee?"

"In the kitchen," I said, a little bewildered. Teddy always did have a good sense of humor and didn't get his feathers ruffled easily, but I had to admit that this nonreaction was unexpected.

I led the way into the dark kitchen, stopping to peer out the window before getting down an extra glass and pouring a serving of iced coffee for Teddy.

He took a sip. "It's cold."

"It's iced," I explained.

"It's not bad."

I wanted to cheer. Teddy had tried something new, and he liked it! I'd make a fancy coffee drinker out of him before he knew it.

We sat side by side in the dark as he drank some more coffee and we studied the laptop screen. Minutes ticked by while nothing happened. The doorbell camera would go into sleep mode, only flickering to life when it sensed motion. A neighbor walking his dog paused to study Teddy's Jeep, then glanced toward the house.

We both ducked. I don't think the glow of the laptop screen was enough to illuminate us, since I had it turned way down and facing away from the window, but I didn't want to draw any attention to us.

"Maybe I should move my car," Teddy whispered, even though the dog walker had already moved on.

"Too late," I said. "You could be seen and scare someone away."

"Or, they see my Jeep and assume you've got company."

"In a dark house?" I asked.

He laughed at me. It was a good thing it was too dark for him to see me blush.

Before I could reply, a car I didn't recognize drove slowly down the street. We turned our attention to the kitchen window. The car slowed in front of our mailbox before resuming its path forward. "Drat," I muttered. I should have known better than to get my hopes up. Then, a few minutes later, the same car returned. This time, it stopped on the far side of the street. It idled for a minute. Then the engine died. The driver's door opened, turning on the interior light.

I caught a glimpse of a person wearing a hat. Despite the mild night, they were wearing a bulky sweater. They got out of the car carrying something clutched to their chest. They closed the car door behind them softly enough that I couldn't hear it through the open kitchen window. They checked both ways for cars coming down the street before crossing toward the house.

Our driveway cut across the sidewalk just past the mailbox and ran toward to the main house. From there, there was a concrete walkway leading to Tansy's front porch on one side and a smaller walkway splitting off to the cottage on the other.

Our mysterious nighttime visitor walked slowly up the drive, glancing at the darkened house before choosing the cottage path. We watched the laptop screen closely. I hoped that once they reached the edge of the porch light,

I would be able to make out their face in the doorbell cam footage. I wasn't disappointed.

Jackson Elby's wrinkled features made him easy to recognize as he stepped onto the porch. He hesitated, then rang the doorbell. When there was no immediate response, he shifted over a few steps to peek into the window next to the door. We had deliberately left the heavy curtains open with only the lacy sheers providing any kind of privacy, so anyone peeking in the windows would see someone inside without being able to make out any details.

He rang the doorbell again, longer this time. When he didn't get an answer the second time, he bent over and propped the package he'd been carrying close to his chest against the door. My angle from the kitchen window was all wrong to see what he'd dropped. Elby checked the window again, and seeing no movement other than the television, shuffled back to his car.

I gave him a moment to drive off before hurrying over to the front door.

"Where are you going?" Teddy asked.

"I want to see what he dropped off. Besides, I can't just leave a package out on the porch like that. It will look like there's nobody home, and then all this is for nothing." Without waiting for his response, I dashed outside, ran across the lawn, and hurried up the porch steps. Propped up against the door was a cheap bouquet of flowers.

I hesitated for a second. What was Jackson Elby doing bringing flowers? I thought he hated Savannah. Over the sound of the television playing inside the cottage, I could hear a faint car engine. Not knowing if it was a block over or heading this way, I snatched the flowers and hurried back toward the house. When I opened the door, there was a flash of orange fur as Daffy dashed out of the house into the night. "Daffy!" I called after him, but he ignored me, instead making a beeline for the crawlspace under the cottage.

Cats. Go figure. You can feed them and love them and they're still just going to do what they want to do, ignoring everyone around them until it's convenient for them. He might be more comfortable back at Sip & Spin, but any time I got near his travel carrier so I could take him back, Daffy disappeared. Maybe he was a house cat now.

I stepped inside and locked the door behind me. Teddy took the note out of the flowers and read it aloud. "'Sorry for your loss.' Sweet. Should I put these in water or something?"

"Yeah, I guess so?" I wasn't sure what to do with them. They were technically Savannah's but I didn't know when I would see her again. "Why would he bring her flowers?"

"It's polite?" Teddy asked.

"You never bring me flowers," I pointed out. Granted, Savannah's business partner had just died so the situation was different, but who didn't like flowers?

"I guess I'll have to remedy that," he said.

The next hour crawled by. Teddy and I were shoulder to shoulder in the dark kitchen. There was plenty we needed to talk about, but we sat in companionable silence instead, sipping coffee and staring out the window. That was one of the things I'd always appreciated about Teddy. We enjoyed each other's company even when we weren't doing anything interesting.

We polished off the donuts and now I was having muffin cravings. It was too late to call Miss Edie, or I would have begged her to make another batch. I might be a menace in the kitchen, but I made a mean pot of coffee. Once the cold brew was gone, I switched to drip. I put French vanilla cream and sugar in mine. To absolutely no one's surprise, Teddy took his black.

The doorbell camera alert flashed on my laptop. I strained to see anything out the window. No one was in sight. I checked the camera feed and saw an entire family of armadillos parade past the porch. Following behind them was Daffy, a silent stalker.

"Be right back," I announced. Abandoning my post, I raced out into the yard and scooped up the cat before he could do any harm to the local wildlife. I doubted he knew what to do if he managed to catch an armadillo. They were slower than a cat, but when scared, they rolled up into an impenetrable armored ball and waited patiently until the threat went away.

Maybe if I'd had the patience of an armadillo, I would have been in the kitchen instead of running barefoot across the lawn carrying a loudly protesting cat when another car approached. I almost didn't see it at first. Its lights were off and it coasted silently up the street, partially hidden by Teddy's Jeep, but some sixth sense made me turn at the last minute. The yard was dark. I flattened myself against the side of the cottage to avoid being seen.

The car rolled to a stop just past the house. From my position, I couldn't see anything, but I heard the distinctive sound of a car door opening and closing. Daffy yowled a complaint, and rather than let him advertise my presence, I let him go. He dashed off toward the backyard, his orange and white fur disappearing into the shadows.

I heard squelching footsteps coming my way as someone bypassed the walkway and cut across the grass instead. Last Wednesday's storm had caused such a soaking that the lawn had yet to completely dry. At least we didn't live closer to the river. Some of the lower-lying houses still had standing water in their yards.

There was only one small window on this side of the cottage. It was the same window in the kitchenette that I'd gotten caught peeking into the night I thought there was an intruder. I was afraid that the light from the window would give me away. The back of the cottage had no place to hide. There were motion sensor lights on both the cottage and the main house that would trigger if I snuck around back.

That only left one option. I flattened myself to the ground and wiggled into the crawlspace under the house. The mud made for slow going, but I pushed myself as deep under the house as I dared, trying not to imagine what other critters might be sharing this space with me. Spiders, scorpions, and snakes, oh my.

I held my breath as dirty shoes walked past where I'd been crouched only a minute before, and reminded myself that Teddy was right next door and he'd surely come to my rescue if I stirred up any snakes. Then again, they weren't my biggest problem right now.

From my vantage point, I saw the shoes pause. They lifted up on their tiptoes to see into the kitchenette window. I wasn't quite tall enough to reach that window, even on my toes, so assuming they were able to see inside, whoever was casing the cabin was taller than me. I was average height. Most of the guys in Cedar River were taller than me, and a few of the women, including my sister Tansy, so that didn't narrow it down much.

Miss Edie was shorter than me. So was Maggie, Joyce from the bank, and Mickey at the car rental place. I couldn't remember if Darlene Daye was shorter than me, but Jackson Elby was.

Beau was a good deal taller than me. So was Teddy. Esméralda the mechanic, Janette the mayor's wife, and Kennedy the local conspiracy theorist were all tall as well. Kitty, Silvie, Jayden, and Carole were around my height, but Rocco, Hank, and Pete Digby could have all peeked into the window easily.

Trying to sort everyone in town by their height successfully kept my mind off the snakes, but it wasn't helping me figure out who the nighttime creeper might be. I wondered if Teddy could see them from the kitchen. I could come out and confront them, but all I had on them so far was one count of being sneaky. For all I knew, it could be Jen Rachet trying to gather intel for her circle of gossip mongers. As hard as I thought about it, I couldn't remember if Jen was taller than me or shorter. She had big, fluffy hair and usually wore heels, so it was hard to gauge her actual height.

The owner of the muddy shoes moved on, walking stealthily until they triggered the motion sensor on the back, at which time they scrambled out of the light. The side of the cottage farthest from the house didn't have any windows. It faced a few bushy trees that separated us from the neighbors. It was always dark on that side of the house, so I had trouble following the shoes until Daffy let out an annoyed yowl and dashed under the cottage to get away from the stranger. Some guard cat he was turning out to be.

Daffy looked surprised to see me hiding under the guest house, and let out a tentative meow. "Shh," I told him, putting a finger to my lips. Even though the cat couldn't have possibly understood what I meant, he looked at me quizzically then fell silent.

I felt moderately better now that Daffy was in the crawlspace with me, knowing he could watch my back. Not that he would warn me if a spider started crawling up my pants leg, but he'd give me fair notice if a can of cat food tried to sneak up on us.

I lost track of the shoes, but then heard footsteps and realized that they were climbing the steps to the front porch. I held my breath, expecting to hear the sound of breaking glass but instead, there was a knock on the door, followed by someone punching the doorbell several times in quick succession. Then I heard footsteps hurrying away, followed by the slam of a car door and the growl of a car's engine springing to life.

As I crawled out from under the cottage, I felt the squelching mud soak into my T-shirt. I tried to tell myself that this was what it must feel like to have a spa day. That didn't make the experience any more pleasant. I emerged from under the cottage and scrambled to my feet. I dashed to the curb. It was too late to see any details of the car speeding down the street away from the house. At this point, I could only hope that the doorbell cam had done its job.

I turned to glance at where I knew the camera was mounted, and noticed a flash of light as the welcome mat on the front porch caught fire.

CHAPTER 23

The doormat went up in flames.

I heard my front door open and Teddy's footsteps running toward me. He scurried up the porch stairs, grabbed the doormat by the edge, and hurled it into the yard. In mid-August after a long, dry summer, this might have caught the whole neighborhood on fire, but the soggy lawn kept the sparks from spreading.

It was an old straw doormat that Mom had owned for who knows how long. It had been on the front porch of the house she raised us in before Dad died and she moved into the cottage. The welcome mat had weathered countless dirty shoes over the years and was probably long overdue to be chucked in the recycle bin.

As it burned, I realized that it wasn't the only thing on fire. It wasn't until Teddy Frisbeed the mat that I noticed a paper bag sitting on top of it. It tumbled to the damp ground and burnt itself out, leaving behind a stinky lump that I didn't want to think too hard about.

"You okay?" Teddy asked.

I nodded.

"I was worried about you for a minute," he admitted.

"Me too. Thanks for not rushing in too soon and scaring them off. Did you see who did this?"

He shook his head. "Once you disappeared under the

cottage and I lost sight of you, I was trying to get a better vantage point, and I missed all the action." He turned and pointed toward Tansy's bedroom window, which overlooked the side yard and thus the mother-in-law cabin. As he did, I noticed someone else striding up the driveway.

"Ahh, the old flaming-bag-of-poo trick," Beau said as he approached. "Haven't seen that one in ages."

"It's a classic," I agreed.

"Teddy," he said with a curt nod.

Teddy returned the greeting. "Beau."

Careful to avoid the stinky surprise that had been left for us in the paper bag, Beau and Teddy stomped out the remaining embers on the lawn. Then Beau turned to me and looked me up and down. "You're a sight."

I looked down at myself. I was covered in mud. "What else is new?" I asked. "And where'd you come from, anyway?"

He jerked his thumb over his shoulder. A car I didn't recognize was parked across the street and two houses down. "Jayden caught wind of the rumors your sisters were spreading and told me something hinky was going down in the Jessup household." I started to say something, but he held up a finger to stop me. "Just a hint, if you don't want the local cops hanging around, don't advertise free coffee. It will backfire every time."

"Noted." I had figured that the gossip would eventually get around to Jayden and Beau, but I'd hoped that it would take a little longer.

"Did you know he was watching the house?" I asked Teddy.

"I didn't notice him," he said.

I was annoyed that I hadn't noticed Beau, either. I guess I wasn't as observant as I thought. "How long have you been staking out my house?" I asked.

"Long enough. I would have been here sooner, but it

took most of the day to empty out Jackson Elby's storage shed." If Beau was upset, he wasn't letting it show, which was more worrisome than any lecture he could give me.

"Elby came by earlier. If you got my text and found the mannequin hands, I'm surprised you didn't arrest him," I said.

"We wrote him a ticket for illegal dumping. It's up to the judge to figure out what to do with him."

"Did he explain why he only kept the hands?" A dozen theories had been floating around my head, ranging from creative to downright creepy. Maybe he was going to open an Etsy shop and needed hand models to display his creations. Mr. Elby could have an artsy side I hadn't seen yet, and had plans to repurpose the hands much like we repurposed old, scratched junk records during our Arts & Crafts nights. Or maybe he had some kind of weird fetish I didn't want to know about.

"He claims he hired a company to clean out Cedar River Casuals and put what they could fit in his storage unit. I reckon they started disassembling the mannequins, then either got lazy or ran out of room, and dumped the rest." Beau glanced back at the cottage's porch. "Were those flowers I saw him drop off?"

I don't know what was weirder, that Beau had been parked across the street for the past few hours watching us and neither Teddy nor I had noticed him, or that he'd seen Jackson Elby and our mysterious arsonist both pay us a nighttime visit, and hadn't done anything to stop either of them. Not that Jackson leaving flowers was a crime, but he couldn't have known that was his intention.

"They were condolences," I said.

"Is it too much to hope that you recognized the person who tried to burn down the cottage?"

I shook my head. "Sorry, I was in the crawlspace at the time."

Beau nodded. "I know. I saw the whole thing. Good thing you were only trapped under the cottage before it caught on fire or I might be worried about you."

Even in the dark, I could see his jaw clench and unclench. He wasn't mad. He was furious. And, if I let myself see things from his point of view, I could almost understand why. Breaking up with him didn't mean he couldn't still worry about me, and I'd given him plenty to worry about tonight.

"Good thing I had backup," I said, glancing over at Teddy. "Neither of us saw his face, but there's a doorbell camera." I pointed to the cottage's front door.

Beau nodded. "Let's go take a look."

I led the way across the lawn, with Beau and Teddy behind me. I stopped to wipe my feet on Tansy's welcome mat. This one was also made of straw. I cringed, knowing now how quickly it could catch fire. I walked into the kitchen and flicked on the lights. "Come on in." I tapped on the laptop's keyboard and the screen sprang to life, already queued up to the live camera feed.

"Go get cleaned up. I'll take care of this," Teddy offered. "If the camera caught anything interesting, I'll let you know."

Normally, curiosity would have overwhelmed my common sense, but getting the mud out of my hair took priority. As I headed toward the shower—trying to not make any more of a mess than I had to—Beau positioned himself in front of the laptop.

While the shower heated up, I wadded up my dirty clothes and tossed them in the sink. It was strange, knowing that Beau was on the other side of the door but for once he hadn't said anything even remotely flirtatious. He hadn't called me by his own private nickname. Sure, Teddy was right here the whole time, but that had never stopped him before. He'd even waited to be invited inside. This new phase in our relationship was going to take some getting used to.

I showered as quickly as I could, but getting mud out of long hair was no easy feat. When I was as clean as I could get without going through a carwash, I pulled my hair back into a ponytail and dressed in sleep shorts and an Erasure T-shirt from the Cowboy tour, the one with the cow-print bucking bronco on the front and the tour dates on the back. I was too young to remember that tour, but that album was an old favorite.

"Beau's gone," Teddy said as I entered the kitchen. "Does it make me a bad person to be happy about that?"

"He was just keeping an eye on the cottage, same as we were," I said. Just because I wasn't seeing Beau anymore didn't mean I wasn't going to see him at all. It was a small town. Our paths were bound to cross now and then, especially if I insisted on trying to solve every murder in Cedar River.

"Uh-huh. Oh, he left you a note." He handed me a sticky note that read "Gotta go see a man about arson." It wasn't signed with an X like every other note he'd ever left me. I crumpled up the paper and tossed it in the trash.

"So? Who was our mystery visitor?" I asked.

"Why don't you see for yourself? It's cued up."

I hit play on my laptop. "I'm surprised Beau didn't erase it," I muttered.

"He tried to take the laptop for evidence but I wouldn't let him. Instead, he sent himself a link to the feed."

"Thanks," I said. I probably would have handed over the laptop if Beau had asked, but I was glad Teddy hadn't.

The camera didn't catch much more than I did. A shadowy figure walked around the cottage, just beyond the porch light's reach. There was no movement for long enough that the camera stopped recording.

Then the screen flickered back to life as Frankie

Hornsby, owner and proprietor of Blow Your Own Horn, hurried up the steps. He removed a small cigarette lighter from his pocket, lit it, and held the flame up to a brown paper bag. As soon as the bag caught fire, he dropped it on the mat. Then he banged on the door, rang the doorbell a few times, and sprinted down the steps, away from the cottage.

Frankie ran out of frame. For a few seconds, I watched the bag burn. Sparks drifted up before settling down onto the apparently highly flammable doormat. It caught fire, but Teddy's quick thinking saved the day as he flung the doormat onto the wet lawn.

Now I appeared in the camera's lens, looking like a cross between a swamp monster and the mannequins that had been spit out by the river. I paused the feed. I didn't need to see any more. I closed my laptop lid. "I guess all's well that ends well," I said. "I'm glad you were here."

"I'm glad I was, too. Are you going to be okay being alone tonight? I promised my sister I'd be home hours ago to help out with calf watch." Strictly speaking, cows gave birth just fine by themselves all the time, but it was good to have someone nearby to help if the need arose.

"Want me to come with you?" I volunteered. "I don't know how much help I would be, but I could keep you company."

"No need. It won't be half as exciting as being on a stakeout with you. Besides, you look like you could use some sleep."

"You're not kidding," I said, stifling a yawn. "Hold on, let me make you a cup of coffee to go."

"Juni, the last thing I need is more coffee," Teddy said with a laugh.

"Text me pictures of the baby calves when they come," I said.

"Will do."

As I locked the door behind Teddy, I took a moment to reflect. Frankie had almost gotten away with murder. If he hadn't come back to try to silence Savannah tonight, the police might never have connected him to Zack's death. What would have happened if she had been inside instead of a mannequin? I think maybe I was better off not knowing. It was bad enough that he almost burned down my mom's cottage. He'd be under arrest soon. That wouldn't bring Zack back, but at least now Savannah might find some peace.

I texted my sisters an update and took my laptop back to bed. Tansy had plans to spend the night in Maggie's guest bedroom. In case the killer took his time revealing himself, she didn't want to scare him off by coming home in the middle of my stakeout. Which meant I had the house all to myself.

Half an hour later, Beau texted me that Frankie Hornsby was in custody. When I texted back to ask if he'd confessed to throwing a brick at Zack's car, I didn't get a reply. That was rude, considering I had solved the case before the Cedar River P.D. *and* delivered the killer tied up in a neat bow.

I'd also uncovered who'd been illegally dumping garbage in the river. Did I get a thanks for that? An atta girl? Nope. Nothing.

I started to text Savannah an update, and then realized I still didn't have her contact info. I had Zack's number, but his phone was in an evidence box somewhere. The whole time Savannah had been here, we'd either been without cell phone service or she had been glued to my hip. I googled Fjord Capital, but, to no one's surprise, the only number listed was Zack's personal cell.

There was a loud thump. I got out of bed and opened the door. "Hey, Tansy, you're home?" I called out, thinking she'd changed her mind about staying the night at Maggie's.

There was no response. That was weird. Tansy had an odd schedule. Sometimes she got up at the crack of dawn, or earlier, to go for a run. For fun. She was the only person I knew who went to the gym early and then stayed out late at the clubs, looking for new bands. Ever since I moved in, she'd gotten good at slipping in or out of the house without waking me up, but when she knew I was home and awake, she always said hi.

"Tansy?" I called again.

The lights were off in the hall, but small LED night-lights glowed from the outlets. I checked her bedroom first. It was empty and the bed unruffled. Tansy was the kind of person who made her bed every morning. I was the kind of person who knew making the bed was just a waste of time. I was going to unmake it to sleep in it that night, wasn't I?

Her bathroom door was open, and the bathroom was dark. There was no one in the living room, the spare bed-room, the kitchen, or the dining room. The back door was locked and the motion sensor indicator was blinking, but the back porch was dark. The front door was locked as well. I jiggled the handle just to make sure, and it didn't budge.

I peeked out the kitchen curtain. The loaner Tansy was driving while her wrecked car was in the shop wasn't in the driveway. There were no strange cars parked in the street. I couldn't see where Beau had parked earlier from the kitchen window. I think that was by design. He didn't want me knowing he was there, watching me.

The curtain fell back into place, but I couldn't get over the feeling that I wasn't alone. It was doubtful that Beau would come back, but I couldn't be certain. The noise I'd heard may have been a car door, or may not have been. If

I knew he was still out there, watching over me, I could at least try to get some sleep, knowing no one else would bother me tonight.

I walked to the back door and flicked the switch. The motion sensor activator light went dark. I removed the bar from the track of the sliding glass door, thumbed open the lock, and slid the door open as quietly as I could. Outside, it was colder than I'd expected. I guess the long, hot summer was finally behind us.

We didn't have a fence around our yard, but the neighbor behind us did. Like Tansy's house, theirs was a one-story ranch. I could see their roofline, but not their windows. I didn't hear or see anything suspicious. I stayed close to the house as I circled it, keeping my eyes open for anything out of the ordinary.

As I slunk around the house, my heart beat loudly in my chest. I didn't know if it was the excess coffee I'd had today or the earlier scare at the cottage, but I was starting to think that all this excitement was bad for my health. I saw movement and froze, remembering what Kennedy had warned me about earlier. "Watch out for the shadows," they'd said. "That's where they like to hide." I waited, but the movement didn't come again. I reminded myself that I was the one hiding in the shadows now, and that gave me the courage to continue.

When I reached the front corner of the house on the side opposite the cottage, I peered out into the street. I checked out each car parked along the curb carefully. There was the sedan that belonged to Mrs. Norris, and the van that belonged to George's youngest grandson. I recognized an oversized pickup truck that Marv drove to the public works department every day, the sporty little convertible that Sue Gross bought after her divorce, and the classic VW Bug Edward had lovingly restored. All was normal.

I didn't see Beau, or the car he'd been using earlier to surveil my house, anywhere. Why did that feel like a letdown instead of a relief?

As I continued my rounds, I kept an ear out for anything that could have made that noise earlier. Maybe it had been the wind, although it was a calm night. It was more likely Daffy, returned from his night's adventures and looking for a way back inside. He had some kind of secret entrance that let him slip into and out of the record shop, but I didn't think he'd found one into the house yet. Or who knows? Maybe the sound was the armadillo family burrowing under the foundation and hitting a rock or something.

I was shivering as I stepped onto the front porch. It wasn't actually cold, maybe in the mid-fifties, but I was barefoot, wearing only a T-shirt and sleep shorts, and my hair was still wet. It would be nice to get back inside. Maybe I'd treat myself to a nice warm cup of cocoa before bed. For a moment, I even considered a hot cup of coffee, but I'd already had more than enough. I reached for the front doorknob before remembering that it was locked.

"Juni, you're losing it," I told myself. I hadn't slept nearly enough the past few days. I'd even missed a meal or two—an unprecedented occurrence for me. Combined with the stress of having an uninvited house guest, finding yet another dead body, and finally ending things with Beau, I'd had about as much as I could take. As soon as I got back inside, where I'd left my phone, I was going to text my sisters asking if one of them could cover the morning shift for me so I could sleep in until Tuesday.

I continued my circle of the house, headed for the back door. I was eager to get inside and put on some fuzzy socks—if I could find them in the jumble of boxes I still hadn't finished unpacking. Then I'd burrow under the covers and finally get a good night's sleep.

Only, something was wrong. I couldn't figure out what it was, but something felt off. I stopped and looked around the dark yard. There were no shadowy figures hiding in the shrubbery. There were no lights on where there should be no lights. In fact, there were no lights at all coming from Mom's house. The heavy drapes that I'd deliberately left open to tempt Zack's killer into coming back for a chance to finish off Savannah were now closed.

Someone was in the guest cottage.

CHAPTER 24

It was late. I had no idea how late without my cell phone, but Teddy had left after midnight. "I should call nine-one-one," a little voice in the back of my head said as I crept across the side yard to the cottage. "No, I shouldn't," I whispered aloud to reassure myself. There were a million innocent reasons, maybe more, why someone, maybe even my mom, would be in the cottage at the wee hours of the morning.

Instead of walking up the front steps, I approached the tiny porch from the side. I tried to look in the window next to the door, but like the one in the kitchenette, the drapes were pulled closed. There was a char mark by the front door. Where the welcome mat had been earlier in the night, there was now only the faint smell of campfire and the unmistakable outline of a shoe print in the ashes.

The front door was slightly ajar, not enough to let me see inside but enough for light and sound to leak out. And it sounded like someone was waging a war. I reminded myself I'd left the television on, turned to the mystery channel. It could be playing louder shows this time of night, maybe even an old war movie like the kind my uncle liked to watch. Then someone yelled, and it didn't sound like it was coming from the T.V.

I pushed on the door. It opened to reveal a woman

swinging a softball bat at the mannequin I'd arranged on the couch. The mannequin's head was missing. The blonde wig she'd been wearing had been tossed across the room. The assailant took another swing at the torso. It connected with a loud crack.

"What on earth are you doing?" I cried out, unable to help myself.

Darlene Daye straightened. Her hair had escaped her normally neat bun, giving her the look of a woman caught in a wind tunnel. Her face was red with exertion and her hands gripped the bat so hard that her knuckles were white. "Where is she?" she asked, between gasps for breath.

"Where is who?" I asked. I wasn't trying to provoke someone who was clearly in the middle of a crisis, but I legitimately had no idea what she was talking about. If Frankie Hornsby killed Zack, what was Darlene doing here? "My mom? Are you looking for Bea?"

"I'm not looking for Bea, you stupid girl." Darlene swung the bat again. It hit one of the lamps next to the couch. Glass shattered.

I covered my face. Even though I was on the other side of the room, it was a very small room and I didn't want to get hit by flying glass. "Then who *are* you looking for?" I asked. My voice was high and squeaky and I felt panic surge through my body akin to stage fright times a thousand.

"That thieving homewrecker, Savannah!" Darlene shouted. She swung the bat again. This time, she missed the mannequin and hit the love seat. Couch stuffing exploded.

"She's not here," I said, trying to calm my own breathing. I'd never be able to take control of the situation until I could control myself.

"I know she's not here." She stepped around the love

seat and pointed the fat end of the bat at me like it was a sword. "If she was here, I wouldn't have to ask you where she was, now would I?" she asked, getting louder with each word. She punctuated the sentence by poking the bat at me. "Did you know that she was sleeping with my boyfriend?"

I took a step back and almost tripped over the café table that doubled as a desk, a dining room table, and a hat rack in a pinch. "I thought you didn't have a boyfriend," I told her. I tried to recall our earlier conversation. Hadn't she referred to herself as single?

"That's because we were trying to keep it quiet. People wouldn't understand."

"Why wouldn't they understand?" I asked. Texas, especially small-town Texas, had a reputation for being less than open-minded about a lot of things. I liked to think that Cedar River was an exception.

"So what if he was younger than me? Or richer? Or more attractive? We were in love. Doesn't that count for anything anymore?"

Younger? Richer? More attractive? It all clicked into place. "You were in love with Zack Fjord."

Darlene bobbed her head. "*We* were in love. We were going to get married. But that meddling brat couldn't let us be."

I held out one hand toward her, hoping to calm her down with the truth. "Darlene, I don't know how to break it to you, but that was Zack's MO. He was dating Savannah. They were living together. He told her they had to keep it a secret because his family wouldn't approve. He probably told you the same thing."

"You're wrong. Zack wouldn't do something like that," she insisted.

"He would," I said, calmly but firmly. As long as she was talking to me, she wasn't destroying the cottage. "I've known him for a long, *long* time and this isn't the first time he's done it. He cheated on one of my friends in college, and eventually it came out that he was cheating on the person he was cheating on my friend with. Do you know that he told Savannah that we used to date? At the time, I thought it was some weird flex, but the more I think about it, I'm starting to think that he'd been with so many women, he couldn't keep track of them all anymore."

"You. Take. That. Back," Darlene said, shaking the bat at the end of each word.

I held both hands out now. "Think about it. When you called Zack, did he always have to rush out of a room before he could talk? Did he come over in the middle of the day with some excuse as to why he couldn't take you out on a normal date at night? Did he save your name in his phone under some innocuous nickname like your initials?"

She scowled at me. "He called me DeeDee, so of course that's how he had me in his phone. And I never called him at work. I knew better than to interrupt him. If I needed to talk to him, I'd text him and he'd call me back as soon as he could."

"Wait a second," I said. "Zack didn't have any incoming or outgoing texts on his phone." If Darlene had sent him any texts, the cops should have seen those messages by now.

She shrugged. "I don't know what to tell you. I texted him all the time."

"Frankie Hornsby told me that Zack would get calls constantly, and he'd always take them in private. And most of his contacts were saved under initials instead of names, not just yours." I cocked my head to the side. I couldn't tell if I was getting through to her or not. "Don't you get it? You weren't the only woman he was cheating on Savannah with."

"Nonsense."

I shook my head. "I wish it was. I think he had a lot of people fooled, Darlene."

"I'm no fool!" she roared, and charged.

I spun and threw myself out the front door. Darlene slammed into my back. I landed face-first onto the porch. I couldn't shake her, so I did the only thing I could think of. I covered the back of my neck and head with my arms and braced myself for the blow from her bat.

Just when I thought I was a goner, the night lit up and a woman yelled, "Darlene Daye, you drop that bat right now, or I drop you."

I lifted my head off the porch and found myself staring into several bright flashlights. "Jayden?" I rasped out. When Darlene had caught me in a flying tackle, it had knocked the wind out of me.

"I swear, Juniper Jessup, you are more trouble than anyone I know," Jayden replied, without ever taking her attention off Darlene.

"You've got that right," Beau muttered from next to her. He clicked off his flashlight and reached for his handcuffs. He hauled Darlene off me. I scrambled off the porch as he snapped the cuffs around her wrists and recited her Miranda rights. Then he handed her off to Jayden, who escorted her to the squad car. "I'm right behind you," he told his partner.

Once they were gone, he sat down on the porch stairs. He patted the spot next to him. I sagged against him and rested my head on his shoulder. "You're a mess," he said.

"I know. I don't know why these things happen to me. It's not like I go out of my way to—"

He cut me off with a finger to my lips. "No. I mean, you're covered in ash." He picked a piece of glass out of my hair and flicked it onto the lawn.

"Oh," I said.

"And also"—he put his arm around me—"you're a mess."

"I am," I agreed. I didn't think either of us was referring to my current appearance anymore. It was true. My life was off the rails. Tonight was proof of that.

"Where's Teddy?" he asked.

"We figured once you had Frankie in your sights, all the excitement was over, so I sent him home," I said.

"Frankie Hornsby didn't kill Zack Fjord," he told me. "But I guess you've figured that out by now."

"I came to that conclusion when Darlene tried to take my head off with a baseball bat, yes."

"Softball bat," Beau corrected me. Then he added, "By the way, Hornsby wasn't in Cedar River the night of the storm."

"He wasn't?" I asked, straightening up and turning sideways so I could look Beau in the eyes. After all the clues I was trying to collect and puzzle together, I'd never once thought to ask such an important question.

"He was out of town, visiting with his mom. Got home late. The roads were already closed. Turned around and got a motel room down the highway. He's got a receipt, and the clerk remembers him."

"He's innocent."

"Not entirely," Beau corrected me. "He almost lit your cottage on fire. He's going to have to answer for that. He swears that he looked inside and saw Savannah sitting on the couch, watching TV. Which is odd, because Savannah's home in Austin."

"Yeah," I said. I tried to dust the ash off my shirt, but just succeeded in smearing it around more. "That was probably the mannequin he saw. You see, when Calvin and I were in Jackson Elby's storage unit . . ." I started.

"*Broke into* Jackson Elby's storage unit," he corrected me.

"Do I need my brother-in-law?" I asked. J.T. was getting used to me calling at all hours of the day and night, needing his legal expertise.

"No need to drag a lawyer into this. You're not in any trouble. This time. Elby was so distraught over the idea that his mannequins ended up in the river that he gave up the name of the junk removal company without any argument. And said he wasn't going to press charges against you or your uncle for 'doing a community service.' His words, not mine."

I grinned. I was glad I'd been wrong about Mr. Elby. "Anyway, I was worried that he might decide to clean out his storage unit before you had a chance to check it out, so we kept one of the mannequins for evidence."

"And that mannequin that you took somehow ended up sitting on your couch in a blonde wig, watching television in your guest cottage. Which just so happened to coincide with a rumor that's floating around Cedar River that Savannah Goodwin, a blonde woman who was staying in said cottage, had information that would put Zack Fjord's killer behind bars. Is that about right?"

I shrugged. "You tell me."

Beau rolled his eyes skyward. "Which is how come when Hornsby dropped by to leave a flaming bag of dog poo on the porch, he thought Savannah was home. He assumed she'd open the door, stomp on the fire, and get a mess all over her shoe and he'd get a good laugh. He hadn't considered that he might start an actual fire. All he cared about was getting revenge on Savannah because he blamed her for his money problems."

"Zack and Savannah were vultures," I said, "but Blow Your Own Horn was already having money problems, or he never would have signed up with Fjord Capital."

Beau nodded. "That's the way I see it, too. Judge might be sympathetic. Then again, they might not."

I thought about it. Frankie hadn't been trying to burn the cottage down. No actual damage was done. But if anyone had been in the cabin, someone could have been hurt. "Do you think it will help if I talk to the judge?" I asked.

"Depends. Are you going to try to lessen his sentence or get the book thrown at him?"

I shook my head. "I haven't made up my mind yet."

"That's my Juni," Beau said with a chuckle. For once, I didn't mind him calling me his. It was comforting to know that not everything had to change between us just because we were no longer dating. "Decisive to a fault."

"Darlene Daye was secretly dating Zack," I told him, getting back on topic. "She thought Savannah was a home-wrecker, not the other way around. Oh, and she's on my sister's softball team."

"That explains the softball bat," Beau said. He looked over his shoulder to where the bat lay on the porch behind him.

"And the brick through the window. Most folks wouldn't be able to throw a brick hard enough or with enough accuracy to do more than bounce off a windshield."

"Yeah, but why throw it at Zack if she blamed Savannah for his infidelity?" Beau asked. "I'll never understand the fury of a woman scorned."

I shook my head. "She didn't know that Zack was drunk and Savannah was driving his car. Darlene was in front of the car. It was dark. With the headlights in her eyes, there's no way she could have seen that Zack was in the passenger seat."

Beau tapped the middle of my forehead. "Smart. I hadn't figured that part out yet."

"You're welcome," I said.

"Thank you," he said.

Beau stood and offered me an arm up. "Are you okay or do I need to take you to the ER?"

"I'm okay. Nothing another shower won't fix."

"Wait out here." He walked into the cottage. I could hear him snapping pictures with his cell phone. He turned off the television, turned off the lights, thumbed the lock, and closed the door. "Do me a favor and keep everyone out of here until I say otherwise, just in case we need to get back in there for evidence or whatnot."

"Okay," I agreed. Cleared or not, I wasn't planning on going back into the cottage anytime soon. "How did you know Darlene Daye was here?"

He wiggled his phone at me. "I meant to send myself the link to the saved footage of Hornsby almost catching the cottage on fire, but accidentally emailed the live feed instead." He chuffed. "Good thing I did, too."

"Yeah," I admitted. Beau might be an enormous pain in my neck on occasion, but he was always there when it mattered.

"I logged in to download the footage and caught our friend Darlene breaking in. Jayden and I raced over, and got here just in time for the fun part."

"I'm glad you did." If I hadn't kept Darlene talking, Beau wouldn't have made it in time. The thought made me shiver.

"Cold? I'll walk you home," he offered, gesturing at Tansy's house.

"I really don't want to be alone tonight," I admitted.

"How about I give you a lift to Maggie's?" he suggested.

"Perfect."

He waited while I let myself in the back door and locked the slider behind me. I gathered my cell phone, laptop, a clean T-shirt, and a toothbrush and tossed them in a reusable shopping tote bag. I grabbed my keys on the way out.

Beau met me at the front door with Daffy in his arms. "Forgetting someone?" he asked.

"There you are," I said, taking the cat from him. "Let's go."

"Are you sure you don't want to put him in a carrier or something?"

"No!" I said quickly. "I think tonight has been traumatic enough already, don't you?"

Beau took my bag and carried it to his truck. He opened the passenger door for me. Once Daffy and I were settled into the seat, he put my bag at my feet.

He drove to my sister's. I hopped out with Daffy before Beau could get out of the truck, and leaned back in. "Thanks."

"Anytime. I mean it, Juni. I'm always gonna be here for you, no matter what."

"I know," I told him.

"Just do me a favor? Stop finding dead bodies," he said.

I shrugged, which was quite the feat while holding a cat in one arm and a bag in the other. "I'll try, but no guarantees. Good night."

"'Night, Junebug."

CHAPTER 25

Two weeks later, I carried the last moving box into my new home. The curtains were open, letting in the sunlight. A record player was set up on the only part of the counter not covered in boxes. The new Taylor Swift album was playing.

"Here, let me have that," Teddy said. He took the box from me and set it down on top of the existing pile of boxes. "That's the last of it?" he asked. We'd finally gotten around to having that talk, and now we were a bona fide couple. His first official act as my boyfriend was helping me move. Was he great, or what?

"It is," I confirmed. I looked around the tiny cottage that was now all mine.

Mom announced that she was moving out after the incident with Darlene Daye and the softball bat. I didn't blame her one bit. I'd been nervous about coming back over here, too.

Once we got the all-clear from the police that we could clean up, Maggie had sprung into action. She brought over her favorite vacuum and got straight to work. I felt bad leaving the mess for my sister to sort out, so I'd joined her. By the time all traces of that night had been erased and the broken furniture removed, I realized that no lingering bad memories could scare me off.

Daffy jumped up on top of the pile of boxes and me-owed plaintively.

"He looks hungry," Teddy said. "When's the last time you fed him?"

"Five minutes ago," Maggie said. We'd closed Sip & Spin for the day so everyone could help me move. She was sorting through my boxes. "Seriously, Juni, who taught you to pack?" She reached into a box and pulled out a curling iron, a box of macaroni and cheese, and a Beanie Baby dragon.

"That's where Scorch went," I said, snatching him away from her. I put him on the bookshelf we'd just picked up from the Rediscovered Treasures going-out-of-business sale. Between Zack's family executing the nuclear option Savannah had told me about, and the owner being in jail, the secondhand shop's days were numbered.

Darlene Daye confessed to throwing the brick that caused the car accident and led to Zack's death, and was now awaiting trial. She'd hoped to get off with criminal mischief, but it wasn't looking too good for her.

Beau finally located the text message that lured Zack and Savannah to Cedar River that night. Zack had been using a privacy app on his phone to send and receive texts. It was apparently a handy app for serial cheaters, and other people who didn't want their text histories on full display. It might have kept him out of trouble with his girlfriend, but it also helped cover his killer's tracks. Once the police discovered the app, they were able to trace the text back to Darlene.

She had indeed lured Zack and Savannah to Cedar River that night, which proved that the brick incident was premeditated. Even so, the DA might have gone with a lesser charge if Darlene hadn't attacked me a few days later. Now she was facing manslaughter charges for

Zack's death, along with separate charges for the assault on me. And unlike with Frankie Hornsby, I had no intention of dropping those charges.

I should probably feel guilty about taking advantage of her misfortune to buy a really nice bookshelf at fire-sale prices, but considering that Darlene was the one who'd wrecked the cottage in the first place, it only seemed fair. Once we had new cushions on the love seat and I'd swapped my soft mattress for the bed made of concrete that Mom had been so fond of, the cottage was complete.

Even Beau helped with the move. He'd come bearing a housewarming present. It was a blue fire-resistant doormat. He got a matching one for Tansy, too, only hers was yellow. He also brought pizza and beer, which my family eagerly devoured in between trips from the main house to the little cottage in the side yard.

While I was packing up my bedroom, I found the key to his apartment he'd given me. I tried to return it to him, but he wouldn't take it back. Instead, he took the loose key and added it to my key ring. "In case of emergencies," he told me. "Besides, I feel better knowing someone I trust has a spare in case I ever lock myself out."

"Doesn't your partner live across the hall?" Tansy asked as she reached over me to grab a handful of T-shirts from a box to put away in the closet, next to my new Austin Thunderbirds hockey jersey. Today I was wearing one of Teddy's plain gray T-shirts. I'd spent enough time lately trying to get mud and ash out of my favorite vintage shirts and didn't want to ruin another one in the move.

"Yeah, but Jayden's hardly ever home," Beau said. He hung my key ring, now with an extra key on it, on the hook next to the door. "I always know where to find Juni."

"And don't we know it?" Teddy muttered as he shouldered his way between us. "Juni, I mean this in the nicest possible way, but do you think that you might have a problem?"

I peered into the box he was carrying. If was full of my collection of colorful glasses, each in a coordinating case. My prescription hadn't changed in years, and every time I got a new pair it was funkier than the last one. Today's pair was red rectangles, and I looked fantastic in them. "As long as I'm wearing glasses, I might as well have some fun with it," I said. "Go ahead and put that box in the bathroom. I'll sort through them later."

As Teddy walked away, Beau said, "Unless you need anything else, I gotta get to work."

"Thanks for your help," I told him.

As nice as it was for him to come by and lend a hand, I admit I was relieved when Beau left. The cottage was tiny even when it wasn't filled to the brim with boxes. With most of my family, Teddy, and Beau all inside, it was starting to feel a little crowded.

"Those are my dishes," Mom said, taking a stack of plates out of the cabinet right after Tansy put them on the shelf.

"No, they're not," I said, taking them back from her. "You gave them to me when I left for Oregon, remember?"

She reached for them. "No, I most certainly do not remember that. These were my very favorite dishes, and I've been wondering where they got off to."

"Bea, we'll buy all new dishes after we move into our new house," Marcus said, steering her away from the kitchenette so I could put *my* plates back in the cabinet.

Marcus had sold his house in North Dallas and his condo in Austin, and he and Mom were moving into a house in Cedar River, right across the street from Maggie. As much as I loved my mother, it had been a lot, living in such close quarters with her for the last six months. I hoped that Maggie was up for the challenge. If she wasn't, Tansy had two open guest rooms now.

"When do you close on the house?" Teddy asked.

"Monday," Marcus said. "Got a moving crew coming later in the afternoon. No offense, y'all, but I'm too old to move my own stuff."

"I know what you mean," I said. I'd lost track of how many boxes I'd carried today. At least it was a short trip. It was nice to finally have some independence and yet still be only steps away from my biggest sister anytime I wanted to see her. "Has anyone seen painkillers in any of these boxes?"

"Wimp," Teddy said.

I swatted at his arm. It was as solid as my new book-shelf. "Not everyone can spend all day walking for miles and then go home and throw hay bales around for fun."

"Actually," Tansy said, holding up one finger, "I can." I'd never understand my sister's passion for exercise. Sometimes I wondered if we were even related.

"And I don't throw hay bales for fun. If the cows don't eat, they don't produce milk, and then what are you going to blend in your cappuccinos and frappés and all the other fancy-schmancy coffees you serve at Sip & Spin?" Teddy asked. Despite the progress we'd made the night of the stakeout, I still hadn't managed to make him into a coffee drink connoisseur. I was determined to convert him some-how, and looked forward to many, many days of trying.

"Oat milk," Maggie said.

"Soy milk," Tansy added.

"Coconut milk. Non-dairy creamer. Almond milk," I said.

"We haven't tried hemp milk yet," Maggie said.

"And I heard there are a few more nut milks being tested as we speak," I said.

I was relieved that we would be in business at least long enough to test those new nut milks. Sales at Sip & Spin Records had taken a hit with the power outage, but thanks to Teddy loaning us a generator and the success of karaoke night, it wasn't as bad as it could have been. We wouldn't make the Forbes 500 anytime soon, but business was slowly growing. My sisters and I would be turning a profit in record time.

"Fine, fine. I get your point," Teddy said. "You don't need Garza Farm's milk."

"We didn't say that," Maggie corrected him. "We just like having options."

"Like tonight, I have the option of sleeping in my own house without having to listen to my baby sister snoring right down the hallway," my oldest sister said.

"I do not snore," I said.

"Oh, you snore!" Maggie and Tansy said at the same time.

I tossed a dish towel at Maggie because she was closest. The box I was currently unpacking held an assortment of cozy mysteries, a dead potted plant that I could have sworn I'd left behind in Oregon, and a bunch of dish towels that had once belonged to my grandmother. By some miracle, no dirt had gotten on the books.

"Would you look at the time?" Maggie declared. "I've got to go pick up J.T."

J.T. had been in court or he would have helped with the heavy lifting. With money still being tight at the shop, Maggie and J.T. had decided to turn in one of their leased cars and share the other. It would be an adjustment for them, but right now every dollar counted if we didn't want to end up at the mercy of predatory investors like Fjord Capital.

"Don't worry. We've got this," Tansy said, flattening a box and adding it to the growing pile of empty ones. I'd moved home six months ago, but this was the first time I'd made a concerted effort to unpack. It felt good. "Calvin's coming by later to help take these to the recycling center."

Funny how when there was manual labor to be done, Calvin was nowhere to be found. But at least he was willing to help us haul away the boxes, so I couldn't complain.

"Speaking of recycling, did you hear the news?" I asked. Without waiting for an answer, I continued. "Turns out the company Jackson Elby hired to haul his trash to the dump settled with the town to avoid fines and possible jail time. The money's going to a fund to clean up Cedar River. No more mannequins in our water supply."

"Good," Tansy said. "And Elby?"

"He reconciled with his wife. He's moving to Texarkana to be with her."

"That's sweet," Tansy said. "Speaking of sweet, I talked to Savannah today."

"Oh?" I asked.

"Yeah. Apparently, she landed on her feet. The Fjords are starting a foundation in Zack's name, and they tapped her to help run it. She asked if Sip & Spin wanted to buy advertising space on their website."

I chuckled. Each of us had our specialties at the shop. Maggie kept the books. Tansy curated the collection. I ran the website and handled promotion. "I'm surprised she didn't ask me," I said.

"And what would you have said if she had?" Teddy asked.

"I would have told her to pound sand. Look, she's a nice person and all, but her moral compass is just a piece of paper with the word 'North' written on it."

"True," Tansy said. She looked around at the cottage. With everyone working together, we'd made short work of the move. "You sure you're gonna be okay in here?" she asked.

I nodded vigorously. "One hundred percent. It's perfect." I tossed a fuzzy blue throw pillow onto my bed. Living in a studio had its advantages. If I got tired while doing dishes, I could lay down and take a nap.

On the downside, in such a compact space like the cottage, I'd have to make my bed every day and I was going to have to start using the dirty laundry hampers for dirty laundry instead of throwing clothes wherever. Come to think of it, maybe that wasn't such a bad thing. I kept complaining that my family didn't see me as a grown-up, and maybe this was my chance to prove that I could adult with the best of them.

Daffy the cat had apparently decided he was moving into the cottage with me. Now that things had settled down, I could take the time to get him acclimated to his cat carrier so he didn't freak out when it was time to take him back to Sip & Spin. In the meantime, I enjoyed his company.

Outside, a horn honked. "That would be Calvin," Tansy said.

Each of us grabbed a stack of empty, flattened boxes and loaded them in the back of Uncle Calvin's Bronco. He waved and took off, headed for the recycling center. Tansy went back to her own house. As much as she loved her family, she needed her space. I was forever grateful that she'd put up with me as long as she had, and was now willing to let me make the cottage into my own.

I walked back inside and took a look around my new home. It felt good to have my own place again. It wasn't exactly the cottage by the ocean I'd been saving up for before moving back to Texas and investing my nest egg into Sip & Spin Records instead, but it was cozy. And best of all, it was close to family and friends.

"What else do you need?" Teddy asked. He stood

behind me with his arms around my waist and his chin resting on my shoulder.

"Nothing," I told him. "I already have everything I could possibly want right here."

ACKNOWLEDGMENTS

Let me start by stating the obvious. I took a couple of creative licenses in this book. Technically, the Kansas song is "Carry On Wayward Son" (waves in SPN fandom), but when I hear the coffee pun in my head, it's "Cherry On *My* Wayward Son," so I ran with it. Special thanks to Lexi for backing me up there (miss you, girl!). Also, baseball has "jerseys." Hockey has "sweaters." Before any hockey fans (y'all know who you are!) come at me, just because *I* know this doesn't mean *Juni* knows it. Besides, this time she figured out the real killer before I did, so it all evens out in the end.

Speaking of figuring things out, I've got some of the coolest readers in the world. I'm looking at you! I want to give credit to everyone who participated in the "Name That Brew" contest for helping name Sip & Spin drinks in this book. I got so many fantastic, punny entries and want to give special shout-outs to: Liz Ashe for "Chai Can't We Be Friends"; Provocateur Secateurs for "Smashing Pumpkins Spice Latte"; Diana D. for inspiring small, medium, or Ariana Grande; Rebecca Worley for "Never Gonna Give Brew Up"; Tara Kat for "Bohemian Frapsody"; Kate Lansing for "Jagged Latte Pill"; and Hector DeJean for "My Brew Heaven." "Shake, Rattle, and Cinnamon Roll" was inspired by Tiffany Gullion-Krieg, Ovi's goal song, and the great Beachbum Bookworm audience. Seriously, y'all are hilarious.

On the serious side (wait, I have one of those?), I gotta thank Dare for all the hours we ~~wasted~~ spent at our favorite used record store and garage sales, hunting for new and interesting music. I don't think there's a single song on my favorites playlist that doesn't remind me of you. We'll always argue over music (she was singing to me, gorramit!), but at the end of the day, you are and always will be my bestie and my biggest cheerleader.

Also, I have the best agent in the world. Not only does BookEnds Literary's James McGowan know how to talk me off ledges *and* found the perfect home for this series with St. Martin's Paperbacks, but his dedication to puns is second to none. "The Rhythm Is Gonna Get You" was all his idea and not only is it permanently stuck in my brain, now it's permanently stuck in yours, too! (You're welcome!)

While we're on the topic of St. Martin's Paperbacks, I was lucky enough to have TWO fabulous editors working to get *Rhythm and Clues* out in the world. Nettie Finn, you always believed in Juni and her sisters (and me!). I don't know anyone else who loves a good em dash or a bad pun as much as I do, and I feel so lucky to know you. I thank you from the bottom of my heart and will so selfishly miss you! Who else can ever figure out the proper past perfect tense of words that were never meant to be verbs or help me Tetris an accidental cow into a scene? And Lisa Bonvissuto, working with you is a fantastic new adventure! I love your enthusiasm and your fresh point of view.

To Sara Beth Haring and Sara LaCotti (my wonderful brunch pal!), who love chocolate almost as much as I do, thanks for all of your dedication and cheer. The whole team at SMP is the best in the biz! Special thanks to Olya Kirilyuk, Katie Minerva, Mary Ann Lasher, John Rounds, Jeremy Haiting, and John Simko for all of your hard work and for making Juni come to life. ♥♥♥

Many, many thanks to all the early readers, reviewers, bloggers, blurbers, and to everyone who enjoys reading about Juni and her sisters as much as I enjoy writing about them!

I'd also like to thank Potassium for supporting me through Sarcasm School (or *did* he?) and to Baileycakes for demanding that I close my laptop on occasion to play with her. Thanks to the Little Screaming Eels for keeping me from going completely feral; the Berkletes for helping navigate this strange, nonsensical ride; and Killer Caseload for continuing to write fantastic mysteries. As always, much appreciation goes to the immensely talented Ellen, Danica, and Michelle for keeping me company through the all-too-short hockey season. A special shout-out goes to #43 Tom Wilson for inspiring the hockey brawl that kicked off this book.

And finally, La, I've waited *thirty freaking years* to say this. ". . . and a brick flies by."